Praise for Will Lavender and
DOMINANCE

"If you like puzzles you will enjoy this book. If you are a fan of twists you will like this book. If you like both puzzles AND twists then you will probably flip over this book. It will have you guessing until the final page."

—*Seattle Post-Intelligencer*

"A twisting, tilting, hall-of-mirrors funhouse of a book . . . [The plot] unfolds like origami with razor-sharp edges . . . *Dominance* reveals its secret stealthily, maintaining the mystery and suspense of the present while divulging the secrets of the past. That is a tricky tightrope, and it is marvelously executed."

—*The Louisville Courier-Journal*

"The self-reflective process of literary criticism known as 'deconstructing the text' becomes a diabolical game of murder in *Dominance,* an academic mystery by Will Lavender that gleefully illustrates the dangers of losing yourself in a book . . . Lavender has the devious skills to write a twisted puzzle mystery."

—*The New York Times Book Review*

"*Silence of the Lambs,* Agatha Christie, and maybe Pynchon are prerequisites for this thriller set in small-town academia."

—*San Antonio Express-News*

"If anyone out there is looking for a good summer book, maybe a beach read, instead of reading something frivolous and light, why not try something that will actually make you think? Will Lavender writes puzzle books: half mystery, half thriller, with a literary twist thrown in for good measure. His newest book, *Dominance,* will make you think. A lot."

—*Fort Worth Fiction*

"If you enjoy puzzling twists and turns, and suspense that doesn't let up even on the last page, you should delve into *Dominance.*"

—*Bowling Green (KY) Daily News*

"[A] taut second standalone . . . Full-bodied characters, an effective gothic atmosphere, and a deliciously creepy, unpredictable finale."

—*Publishers Weekly*

"Lavender's exciting second literary thriller (after *Obedience*) pulls readers right into the hunt. Aldiss reminds us of a sexy Hannibal Lecter, and the mystery of the reclusive author Paul Fallows and his connection to the class is riveting. Well-drawn characters, excellent plot, good use of flashbacks, and many red herrings will keep the pages turning to the very end."

—*Library Journal*

"Lavender takes on another puzzle-within-a-thriller . . . Twisty and turny, with all kinds of side roads . . . [He] manages to maintain the novel's taut, sinister atmosphere from the first page to the last . . . Readers who loved Lavender's first book will doubtless delight in this one."

—*Kirkus Reviews*

"With nods to Christie, Poe and Lovecraft, Lavender crafts a deadly game of obsession, full of riddles, subterfuge, grim revelation and red herrings galore."

—*Winnipeg (MB) Free Press*

"A brilliant concept, brilliantly executed. *Dominance* soars to the top of the thriller genre by infusing its rapid-fire plot with the mysteries of literature and authorship and offering cutting-edge (so to speak) psychological insights into minds both noble and horrifically demented. You'll never look at professors, authors or, well, books the same again. Oh, and that last page . . ."

—Jeffery Deaver, #1 international bestselling author of *Carte Blanche* and *The Burning Wire*

"Will Lavender constructs plots with the expertise of a Parisian baker, masterfully layering mystery on top of mystery until, just when you think the whole thing might topple over, he sets it all together into a dangerously delectable mille-feuille of storytelling. Do save room for seconds."

—Graham Moore, *New York Times* bestselling author of *The Sherlockian*

"*Dominance* is a twisting, intriguing and compelling psychological thriller of the first order. Will Lavender has created a clever maze of a plot, fraught with dark corridors and deadly ends. With this novel in your hands, you'll be voraciously turning the pages late into the night, maybe thinking you're a step ahead, until you realize you've always been a step behind—right up until the stunning final scene."

—Lisa Unger, *New York Times* bestselling author of *Fragile*

"Will Lavender has laid out a rich feast for fans of psychological thrillers— at the heart of it all is a weird, addictive game that's far more dangerous than anyone realizes. This intricately layered story of murders past and present generates plenty of chilling twists and turns, right up to the final sentence."

—John Verdon, bestselling author of *Think of a Number* and *Shut Your Eyes Tight*

Praise for Will Lavender's debut puzzle thriller, *Obedience*

"It's a genuine, if slightly perverse, kick to follow every Byzantine clue in this bizarre game . . . If you solve this one without peeking at the last chapter, it's an automatic A."

—*The New York Times Book Review*

"Evidence that crime fiction is hardly a played-out genre . . . A mystery as ambitious as one could imagine."

—*The Wall Street Journal*

"Taut, twisty, and highly original: the pages turned themselves."

—Peter Abrahams

"A thriller that will strike some as a mix of John Fowles' *The Magus* and Stephen King's *The Shining* . . . The conspiracy becomes so all-encompassing, so elaborate."

—*Publishers Weekly*

"*Obedience* draws you in and never lets go—and what a ride!"

—David Baldacci

"Quite a twisty tale . . . Haunting . . . Irresistible."

—*New York Daily News*

"*Obedience* is a full course-load of sinister fun."

—Salon.com

"A taut and timely thriller that explores the dark side of academia, where classrooms are dangerous and paranoia abounds."

—Karin Slaughter

"A devilishly inventive debut that reads like a house of mirrors. Nothing is what it seems, right up to the devastating finale."

—Brian Freeman

"With superb confidence, Lavender constructs a brilliant fictional web of lies, inventively warping the psychological thriller to fit the confines of a scholarly investigation. An inspired thriller."

—*Kirkus Reviews*

"Terrific debut . . . A wonderful book with an emotional punch at the end."

—*St. Petersburg Times*

"Tautly strung debut . . . Lavender tears a page of out Milgram's notebooks and sets into motion a chain of events that escalates far beyond its intended intellectual exercise. . . . Mystery fans will be satisfied to hang on around the story's hairpin turns as the list of suspects swells and narrows with the unearthing of each clue, but Lavender . . . is aiming at a broader target and posing deeper questions."

—*BookPage*

"Chilling, unpredictable . . . a delicious mystery."

—*Sacramento News & Review*

"Lavender's first novel suggests he has a bright future. *Obedience* builds to a swirling conclusion."

—*The Tampa Tribune*

"Will Lavender stuns with this compelling thriller . . . A new master of the genre."

—*The Louisville Courier-Journal*

"Infuriating, brilliant puzzle . . . [An] intriguing and addicting psychological thriller from a talented new writer worthy of our undivided attention."

—Bookreporter.com

ALSO BY WILL LAVENDER

Obedience

DOMINANCE

A Puzzle Thriller

Will Lavender

Simon & Schuster Paperbacks

New York London Toronto Sydney New Delhi

Simon & Schuster Paperbacks
A Division of Simon & Schuster, Inc.
1230 Avenue of the Americas
New York, NY 10020

First Simon & Schuster trade paperback edition September 2012

SIMON & SCHUSTER PAPERBACKS and colophon are registered trademarks
of Simon & Schuster, Inc.

For information about special discounts for bulk purchases,
please contact Simon & Schuster Special Sales at
1-866-506-1949 or business@simonandschuster.com.

The Simon & Schuster Speakers Bureau can bring authors
to your live event. For more information or to book an event,
contact the Simon & Schuster Speakers Bureau at
1-866-248-3049 or visit our website at www.simonspeakers.com.

Designed by Jill Putorti

Manufactured in the United States of America

10 9 8 7 6 5 4 3 2 1

The Library of Congress has cataloged the hardcover edition as follows:
Lavender, Will, date.
Dominance / Will Lavender.—1st Simon & Schuster hardcover ed.
p. cm.
1. College teachers—Fiction. 2. Murderers—Fiction. 3. College
students—Fiction. 4. Serial murder investigation—Fiction. I. Title.
PS3612.A94424D65 2011
813'.6—dc22   2010046118

ISBN 978-1-4516-1729-0
ISBN 978-1-4516-1730-6 (pbk)
ISBN 978-1-4516-1731-3 (ebook)

"The heart of the matter is that in this gentleman's article all people are divisible into 'ordinary' and 'extraordinary.' The ordinary must live obediently and have no right to transgress the law—because, you see, they're ordinary. The extraordinary, on the other hand, have the right to commit all kinds of crimes and to transgress the law in all kinds of ways, for the simple reason that they are extraordinary. That would seem to have been your argument, if I am not mistaken."

Raskolnikov smiled again.

—Dostoyevsky, *Crime and Punishment*

Oh, what we once thought we had, we didn't
And what we have now will never be that way again
So we call upon the author to explain

—Nick Cave and the Bad Seeds, "We Call Upon the Author"

1

Just after dark they rolled in the television where the murderer would appear. It was placed at the front of the lecture hall, slightly off center so the students in back could see. Two men wearing maintenance uniforms checked the satellite feed and the microphones, then disappeared as silently as they had come. It was now five minutes before the class was to begin, and everything was ready.

This was the first class of its kind, and its novelty—or perhaps its mystery—made it the most talked-about ever offered at tiny Jasper College. As mandated by the school president, there were nine students in the classroom. They were the best of the best in the undergrad literature program at Jasper. Now, on the first night of the semester, they waited anxiously for their professor to emerge on the screen.

The class was LIT 424: Unraveling a Literary Mystery. It had been offered at night because this was the only viable time, the only hour when the warden would allow the murderer free to teach. He would teach, if you believed the rumors, from a padded cell. Others said he would be in front of a greenscreen, with special effects to replicate a lectern before him—an illusion of a classroom. The rest claimed he would simply be shackled to his chair in an orange jumpsuit because state law prohibited anything else. They had to remember what this man had done, these people said. They had to remember who he was.

The room was warm with the closeness of bodies. The chalkboard seemed to glisten, even though the Vermont night outside was bitterly cold. The quads were mostly silent, save for the protesters who stood the stipulated two hundred yards from Culver Hall, where the night class would be held. The class met in the basement of Culver for this reason: the powers-that-be at Jasper did not want the protesters to be able to see what was happening on that TV screen.

The few students who were out at that cold hour witnessed the nervous candlelight of the protest vigil from a distance, through the copse of beech and oak that dotted the woodsy campus. A light snow fell, flakes rushing upward in the January wind like motes of dust. Not far away, Lake Champlain purred in the wind. It was as if, one freshman said as he looked down at the scene from a high dormitory window, someone were about to be executed.

Just beyond the protesters, in a building that was dark save for a few bottom-floor lights, a pair of state policemen sat in a room the size of a broom closet, drinking coffee and watching their own blank feed on a tiny screen.

Unraveling a Literary Mystery—this too had been contested. The president of the college chose the title because it sounded to him fitting for what the professor had in mind. But in fact the president did not know exactly what the class would entail. He *could not* know; the murderer had only hinted at a "literary game" his students would play in the class. About his syllabus he had spoken to no one.

It was this inability to even guess at what was about to happen that silenced the classroom now. In the weeks before the semester had begun, when they went home to their families on Christmas break, the students who had registered for LIT 424 had time to think. To weigh their decision to take this strange course. They wondered if something could go wrong in that lecture hall, if their professor could somehow . . . it sounded crazy, yes. Most of them did not say it aloud, or if they did, they spoke only to their roommates or their closest friends. Slight whispers, torn away by the wind, carried off into nothingness.

If he could somehow get out.

This was what they were thinking in those final seconds. Some of them talked about their other classes that semester, flipped through textbooks and highlighted paragraphs in trembling arcs of yellow. But mostly they sat, saying nothing. They stared at the dead television screen. They wondered, and they waited.

Finally the television went to a deeper black, and everyone sat up straight. Then the box began to hum, an electrical, nodish oohing, a kind of flatline that moved left to right across the room. Their professor—the MacArthur-winning genius, once a shining star at nearby Dumant University and the closest thing to celebrity a professor of literature could possibly be, the same man who had viciously murdered two graduate students twelve years before—was ready to appear.

Then the blackness dissolved and the noise died away and the professor's face came to them on the screen. They had seen pictures of him, many of them preserved in yellowed newsprint. There were images of the man in a dark suit (at his trial), or with his wrists shackled and smiling wolfishly (moments after the verdict), or with his hair swept back, wearing a tweed jacket and a bow tie (his faculty photograph at Dumant in 1980).

Those photographs did not prepare the students for the man on the screen. This man's face was harder, its lines deeper. He was in fact wearing a simple orange jumpsuit, the number that identified him barely hidden beneath the bottom edge of the screen. The V of his collar dipped low to reveal the curved edge of a faded tattoo just over his heart. Although the students did not yet know this, the tattoo was of the thumb-shaped edge of a jigsaw puzzle piece.

The professor's eyes seemed to pulse. Sharp, flinty eyes that betrayed a kind of dangerous intelligence. The second the students saw him there was a feeling not of surprise, not of cold shock, but rather of *This, then. This is who he is.* One girl sitting toward the back whispered, "God, I didn't know he was so . . ." And then another girl, a friend sitting close by, finished, "Sexy." The two students laughed, but quietly. Quietly.

Now the professor sat forward. In the background the students could see his two prison guards, could make out everything but their faces—the legs of their dark slacks, the flash of their belt buckles, and the leathery batons they carried in holsters. One of them stood with legs spread wide and the other was more rigid, but otherwise they mirrored each other. The professor himself was not behind a pane of glass; the camera that was trained on him was not shielded in any way. He simply sat at a small table, his uncuffed hands before him, his breathing slow and natural. His face bore the slightest hint of a smile.

"Hello," he said softly. "My name is Richard Aldiss, and I will be your professor for Unraveling a Literary Mystery. Speak so I can hear you."

"Hello, Professor," someone said.

"We're here," said another.

Aldiss leaned toward a microphone that must have been just out of the camera's view. He nodded and said, "Very good. I can hear you and you can hear me. I can see you and you can see me. Now, let us begin."

Alex

Present Day

2

Dr. Alex Shipley got out of her rental car and walked to the front door of the silent house. She'd worn heels, goddamn it, maybe on the notion that the people at Jasper College would be more impressed with someone who showed up to a crime scene dressed unlike the academic she was. Now she was ashamed of the choice. Ashamed because the professor would surely notice, and this would give him an advantage in the mind game they were about to play.

Above her a flock of winter wrens exploded from a tree, and she flinched. It was then that Alex realized how terrified she was to be back here, to be near him again. She urged herself to focus. The professor was one of the most brilliant men in the world, but he was also deceitful. He would have fun with this—if she let him.

She must not let him.

"They lie. All birds are death birds."

Alex looked up. He leaned against the open screen door, staring at her with dead eyes. His mouth was frozen in a cruel smile. The stroke had taken his features, polished his face into a mask. One side was completely lifeless, the pasty skin stippled with reaching blue vessels, the lip curled upward into a tortured grin. The other side, the living side, had learned how to do the same—he had trained himself in a bathroom mirror. Now he always smiled, *always,* even when there was nothing to smile about. Even when he felt pain or sadness or rage.

"Alexandra," he said. Not *Professor,* not *Dr. Shipley.* (She, too, noticed these things.) He did not invite her in. In true fashion, he would make her stand there on the cold front porch, suffering a bit. Always a challenge, always a test. Alex would not give him the pleasure of seeing her put her arms around herself for warmth.

"Good morning, Professor," she said.

"I was told about what happened to our mutual friend. How . . . tragic." The smile touched his eyes. "I knew they would send you to me in due time."

"No one sent me," she said.

He was amused by the lie. "No?"

"I came here on my own accord."

"To see me, then. Like old friends. Or perhaps old lovers."

Something caught in her throat. She stared at the destroyed face, the wind slicing against her exposed neck. *Damn him.*

"Would you like to come inside, Alexandra?"

"Please."

Inside the small house there were books everywhere. Piles of them, mountains of them leaning in the dark. No artificial light in the tiny, not-quite-square rooms, just the natural dishwater seep of the morning sun. Through a window she could see the dark fingerprint of a half-frozen lake behind the house.

He led her to a back room and sat in a frayed armchair, facing that window. More books here, studies on dead writers, an Underwood on a small desk buried beneath a landslide of ink-crowded paper. Above that a poster depicting a man's face, one solitary word scrawled across his eyes, nose, mouth. The word was *Who?,* a pencil dusting barely visible in the weak light. The face was that of the mysterious novelist Paul Fallows. Below, in a fierce red font, the poster's caption read:

WHO IS FALLOWS?

He did not offer her a chair. She stood in the center of the room, watching the great professor breathe. Even there, with his back turned to her, he emitted a kind of ferocity. It was worse now. Worse, she figured, because he knew they needed him. She needed him.

"Tell me," he said.

"The reason I've come to you this morning is because . . ." But she could not say it. She felt him watching her even as he faced away, seeing her not as a tenured professor of comparative literature but as the dithering student she had once been. A child.

"You haven't accepted it yet," he said. "The fact that it has happened again."

"You're wrong." But it was weak, hollow.

The professor caught her eyes in the reflection in the window, held them. "Michael is dead. He's dead and there's nothing you can do about that now."

The words, the finality of them, stunned her. She looked away.

"Do you remember him?" she asked.

A beat, then, "Not especially."

But of course he did. Dr. Michael Tanner, Jasper College resident modernist, was teaching at his alma mater. Michael had been with her in the night class fifteen years ago. She even remembered his seat: right in front, not very far from that television screen.

"The murder," he said. "Like the others, I presume."

"Yes—but different."

He looked up, his interest piqued. "How so?"

"This murder was more cautious than the first two. More controlled."

"Are there suspects?"

"None," she said, then added, "But there has been some talk on campus. Gossip."

"Go on."

"There are some who believe it could have been his wife," she said, meaning Sally Tanner, née Mitchell—another student from the night class. Alex had never imagined her with Michael, never thought they would end up married and both teaching at Jasper fifteen years later. But of course there had been so many things she had missed. "Sally discovered the body. Also the timeline she's given to the police—there are inconsistencies."

A moment passed, then he mused, "And so the authorities contacted you."

"They did."

"Why?"

"I think you know why."

The professor's eyes dragged slowly toward her. "It is not because you are brilliant with the subtleties of literature. I can think of so many other professors who might be better equipped to interpret the symbolism of this crime—and of course there will be literary symbolism, or else you would not have called on me this morning. We both know that."

"Professor," she sighed. "Let's not do this. If you can't help me, fine. But if you can, then I—"

"Us."

"Excuse me?"

"If you can't help *us*, Alexandra. You have masters at Jasper now that they have called on you to play the sleuth again, do you not? And I'm sure at the university where you are currently teaching as well. I've forgotten, where is it again?"

Alex was silent. He knew she taught at Harvard.

"You have men who are above you there."

"And women."

"But mostly men. I've seen them. Cocksure oafs who walk into a room and each believes he is the most brilliant one there, every time. I went up to Cambridge once, before my smile was perfected. It was an awards gala in my honor, but no one seemed to want to look at me. They were intimidated. Perhaps they were afraid."

She said nothing.

"Are they intimidated by you, Alexandra?"

Still nothing.

"You and your fuck-me shoes?"

"That's it."

She turned around, picked up her purse, and went out the door. The house was too dark now, the sun having swung behind a cloud outside. She couldn't remember her bearings. All she could see were books and shadow-books, stacks of them leaning and toppling and forcing themselves out from the walls. The rooms like a chambered Nautilus, spiraling outward and on top of one another. She began to move through the labyrinth, cursing herself for coming here, for believing the professor could give her any answers. *Damn it, Alex, why do you want to believe he's changed? Why—*

"Dostoyevsky."

That stopped her. She stood there, listening to the seams of the old house scream in the wind, waiting.

"Dr. Tanner," the professor said from behind her. "I know that he was murdered by an axe. And the two others, the ones from before—they were killed in the same way. 'He pulled the axe quite out, swung it with both arms, scarcely conscious of himself, and almost without effort, almost mechanically, brought the blunt side down on her head. He seemed not to use his own strength in this.'"

"Crime and Punishment."

"Yes. Not one of my favorites in the canon, but there is the answer for you, Alexandra. The connection. This is nothing but a pale copycat, a mimic on the loose. Your killer—he is a stupid man with no original ideas of his own."

"I don't think so," she said. "As I said before, there was something different about this crime."

"Different how?"

Alex measured her words now. She needed to be clear at least on this, needed to say to the professor what the two men from the college had told her to say. *It has to be perfect,* they'd warned her.

"On the surface Michael's murder looks just like the ones you—just like the Dumant murders from the eighties," she said. "But if you look closely, there is something else. Something new."

He waited for her to go on.

And so she gave him the phrase the men had supplied to her, *the bait:* "This murder . . . it's like a puzzle."

This made him stiffen. Just those few words, the challenge Alex Shipley had put before him—she felt the tension rise in the tiny room. She had him.

"I live just a few miles from that dreadful place," he said then, almost to himself. "I hear the things they say. I know how they can be."

"Is that your agreement to help, Professor?"

He gazed at her. "Do they think I had anything to do with what happened?"

She said nothing. She wanted the silence to answer for her.

"Very well. Perhaps it is good to be believed in again. To be feared."

"Will you help, Professor?"

"Because I owe you?"

"Because whoever did this is still out there. Because we both have a history with Michael Tanner. And yes, because you owe me." *You owe me fucking big-time.*

"It's more than that, Alexandra."

"I don't—"

"You worry that this unfortunate twist in the plot will shine a light on everyone who took the night class. Especially you."

"This has nothing to do with the class."

"Is that what you told yourself on the flight back to Vermont? The thought that screamed through your mind as the businessman from Amherst was oh-so-subtly hitting on you? *It's not about the night class. It's not about the night class. IT'S NOT ABOUT THE NIGHT CLASS.*" The professor's voice rose, then was swallowed by the house. Then he laughed—a cruel, nasty bark.

"Michael," she said softly. "He was part of it. He loved books, just as we do. He lived for literature. Whoever did this to him had a plan, had been perfecting that plan for a long time. What you said before—there is some truth there. The police believe this killer is a copycat, that he is re-creating what happened twenty-seven years ago at Dumant University. The victim is a literary scholar, there is blood on the wall in the Rorschach pattern, the books have been arranged around Michael's library—the killer studied those old crime scene photographs, Professor. He learned them."

She fell silent, watching him. She could feel his mind moving, somehow, the electric churn of his thoughts. He was the most brilliant and the most aggressive man she had ever known. In the strangest hours she would find herself thinking about him, remembering the class, the search for the identity of a mysterious writer and all the secrets she would uncover about the professor's own crimes.

"Please," Alex said. "I need an answer."

"Just one question."

Alex waited. She recalled the faces of the men that morning. Two faces, a college dean's and a police detective's, broken by what they had seen in Michael Tanner's cluttered home library across campus. She knew; she carried those same scars.

"Anything," she said.

Dr. Richard Aldiss leaned closer. "Tell me again how you discovered that I was innocent."

3

Twenty-four hours earlier Alex Shipley strode into her lecture hall and the room fell silent. There were stares, as always. The electronic chatter on campus about Shipley was immense. She was tall, lean, beautiful—but she was also brilliant and extremely demanding of her students. Her classes were some of the most popular at the university, and it was not uncommon to walk into a Shipley lecture and see students lining the walls, like a queue at a rock concert. This course in particular was a hit: it was called The Forger's Pen: Literary Hoaxes of the 20th Century, and teaching it was what had made her name as a young professor at Harvard.

She wore a pencil skirt because the weather was getting warmer, a thin knit jacket her mother had sent from Vermont. She never carried a bag, because at her age a bag made her look even more like a student. The comparative lit department chair, Dr. Thomas Headley, needed no more reason to treat her like someone who should be sitting at the children's table.

She carried only a few sheaves of transparency paper and a single text. One leather-bound volume, the threads on the spine catching the stark light of the classroom and glinting. The book was Paul Fallows's masterpiece, *The Coil*.

"What are you doing tonight, Dr. Shipley?"

Alex looked up, found the student who had posed the question. Anthony Neil III. He sat in a middle row, a frat-boy smirk on his face. His friends flanked him, hiding behind their Norton Anthologies.

"I'm working on my Camus translation," she said flatly. "Do you read French, Mr. Neil?"

"Tu as un corps parfait," the boy said.

"Funny, I don't remember that line in *The Stranger.*"

"Try the abridged edition."

Alex kept her eyes straight on the boy and said, "That must have been the version of the text you read before our last exam."

Then she turned away and began to make notes on the whiteboard as the class howled.

"What is literature?" she asked when everyone was quiet. It was the question she always asked, without hyperbole, to begin this particular lecture.

"Literature is emotion," said a dark-haired girl from a back row.

"Literature is a writer's secret life recorded in symbols."

Alex nodded. "Great books are both of those things," she said. "The emotion in *Anna Karenina* is fierce. The symbolism in books such as *Ulysses* and *Beneath the Wheel* and *Through the Looking-Glass, and What Alice Found There,* is still being fought over in lit programs across the world." She paused for effect, drawing them in. Forty faces, all of them belonging to upperclass English majors on their way to bigger and better things, were held by her words. "But what if literature were more than that. What if it were *a game?*"

"A game?" a gaunt boy toward the front asked. "How do you mean?"

"I mean," she said, "what if you could read a book and treat it as a competition between you and its author? Like a contest."

"In any contest there has to be a winner," another student said. "How do you win against a book?"

"Point duly noted," Alex said. "But a brilliant professor once told me that you win *when you know you have won.*"

"Richard Aldiss said that?"

Alex froze. Even the professor's name did that to her. Her blood raced. It was the student from before—Neil. One of her tricksters. They always sought her out, gravitated to her because of her past.

"Paul Fallows," Alex went on, picking up the loose thread of her lecture. "Of course you've heard of him."

At first there was nothing, only the tight, nervous silence of the hall. They knew of her history with the writer.

Finally a boy just behind Neil said, "The reclusive writer. The madman."

"Some say he was both. Others say he was neither."

"What do you mean, Dr. Shipley?"

Alex steeled herself. It was still difficult to talk about Fallows, more difficult now because there had been no closure. Things had ended so suddenly that she could never truly understand how the nightmare of Aldiss's night class had gone as far as it went. Fallows, the famous recluse, was the very reason Alex was in this lecture hall right now.

She answered the student's question with movement. She approached the document camera and switched it on. The lights in the lecture hall were synched to the machine, and they automatically dimmed.

She laid the first sheet of transparency on the platform.

"What I am about to show you," she said, "has been seen only by a select few."

Alex stepped to the side, letting her students see what was projected on the screen behind her.

It was a page from a manuscript. The columns were rigid, the font blocky and thick. There were scratch-outs in the margins, done in a manic and careless hand. On the bottom of the page were strange glyphs—the images looked, when you studied them closely, like the legend of a bizarre map.

"What is it?" someone asked.

"It's a page from an unpublished novel by Paul Fallows," Alex said, and the class buzzed.

"But where did you get it?" another student asked. "Fallows is dead. You found him and then you—"

"Killed the Fallows myth," finished Neil, and when Alex looked back at the boy he smiled impishly. *Your play, Prof.*

Alex shivered. There were ways to evade this topic. It had taken her years to even think of Fallows again, and when her therapist suggested teaching this class—well, at first she told him to go to hell. But as the years passed she realized she would have to confront what she had done during the night class. Tackle it head-on. Thus this class, this lecture, these questions.

"Four years ago I received a package in the campus mail," Alex explained now. "The warden of an asylum for pathologically violent offenders in upstate Vermont sent it to me. There was a short note attached to the manuscript. It read in part, *Could this be it?* The warden took the night class with me at Jasper College. His name is Lewis Prine. Lewis had heard of the existence of another, unpublished Fallows novel and he wanted me to read the page and see if this could be part of that lost manuscript."

"And is it?"

Alex sighed and stepped to the document camera, ran her palm across the veined paper. "I have rigorously studied the document. Five hundred words inside one unbroken paragraph, with bizarre notes in the margins. Sort of reminds me of the essays I receive from some of you."

Laughter, and then one of them asked, "Is there more?"

"No. This single page was all Warden Prine had been given. We believe that the rest of the manuscript is in the possession of Dr. Stanley Fisk, my old friend and one of the last great Fallows scholars . . ." She trailed off, thinking of what else Lewis had said in his note to her: that Fisk had slipped in his old age and allowed someone to steal a single page from his treasure. This could mean only one thing: the manuscript was real. *Can you imagine, Alex,* he'd written, *what it would be like to finally discover the third Fallows? Daniel would have loved this.*

"Is it legit?" someone asked, bringing her back to the North Yard classroom. "Is there any doubt that Fallows wrote that page?"

"There is absolutely no doubt in my mind."

The class chattered in astonishment. They knew how major the find was, how important the image burning on the projector screen would be to scholars worldwide if Professor Shipley could ever really prove its authenticity. They wondered what was stopping her—the monetary worth of one page alone would be staggering.

But Alex did not share in her students' excitement. For years she had felt, each time she touched the page, a sense of absolute fear.

*   *   *

That night Alex went out with her boyfriend, Dr. Peter Mueller. He was a few years older, but so what? He was a psych professor who was good-looking in an older-prof way. Interesting in bed. A shock of dark hair fell over his left eye. He took her dancing. Alex could have done worse at Harvard. Much worse.

They ate at a new place in Boston called the Well. A throng of students gathered there, the room churning and loose—just as she liked it. Peter didn't. He was a whisperer, enjoyed leaning close to her ear and telling her what he might do to her later. But Alex liked the noise, the sounds of college life. It reminded her of Jasper.

She took a bite of her bacon cheeseburger and followed it with a swig of cheap beer. Vampire Weekend trilled out of the old-school jukebox.

"Faculty reviews coming up soon," Peter said. It was not a conversation she wanted to get into, not tonight. She looked away, swept her eyes over the room. One of her old students was in the corner with a rugged townie, the girl too sweet for her own good. Alex was always falling for them, the students with pensive smiles and fiery minds, who knew the answer to every question but rarely spoke it aloud for fear of being wrong. *Girls like you, Alex. Girls just like you before you took the night class. Before Aldiss.*

"Alexandra, are you listening to me?" She looked at Peter, at that dangling hair, those liquid blue eyes. She hated it when he used her full name.

"I'm listening," she said. "Loud and clear."

"Are you going to apply to Oxford again?"

This was, what, the fourth or fifth time he'd brought it up? The summer in London. The grant money, the semester to finish her book. It wasn't a book yet, really, just a seed. A true-crime thing. A book on the night class, about what happened to them in that classroom. What happened to her.

"I don't think so," she said.

"Why not? Alex, we could both apply. Get away, spend a semester in Europe together working, teaching, learning. Learning each other . . ." He squeezed her hand under the table. Despite herself, she pulled away.

Peter made a face, poked absently at his steak.

"You should've gotten the position last time," he said.

Alex shrugged.

"I know it. Everyone knows it. To hell with Tom Headley. You're one of the best this university has to offer, Alex. If only you could play by the rules a bit more, humor Headley and the rest of them."

It was then that her cell phone chirped, saving her.

"Excuse me," she said, and slipped out of the restaurant.

A cool night, April just coming on, traffic crawling down Tremont Street. Sometimes she imagined them, the passengers in those cars. Imagined where they were going, who they really were. To be anywhere but here—the thought enticed her, but then she swept it back with indignation. Hadn't there been a time when she would have done almost anything to get a chance to teach at Harvard University?

She checked the face of her cell, saw a Vermont number. She dialed it.

"Hello?" a man answered.

"With whom am I speaking?"

"This is Dr. Anthony Rice, interim dean of Jasper College."

Alex recognized the name from a research conference somewhere in the Midwest. Rice hadn't been at Jasper when she was a student there.

"What is this about, Dr. Rice? I was in the middle of dinner."

"I won't keep you long. We've had . . . something happen at Jasper. A tragedy."

Oh God. Oh no. Not again, please.

"Dr. Shipley?"

"Yes," Alex said, composing herself. She saw Peter staring out at her from their table and turned her back to the front window of the restaurant. "Go on."

"Michael Tanner was murdered last night."

Everything fluttered. She focused on the dean's words, watched their heat bloom outward in her mind as if they were a spreading stain. The streetlights along Tremont seemed to blink once, hard, off and on. Alex was leaning now against the stone building, her forehead scraping the uneven cut of the jagged brick, the pain reminding her that she was there. (A memory: Michael at a frat party one night doing a perfect impersonation of Aldiss. His eyes became sharper and his voice dropped to an eerie, pitchless calm and everything about him *changed*. Laughter around her, but all Alex felt was a cold dread. *Please stop, Michael,* she wanted to say. *He'll find out about you.*)

"Are you okay?" the dean was saying.

"Sally," Alex managed. "Is she . . ."

The dean did not respond, and in his evasion Alex knew the answer to her question.

"Let me explain to you what we know," Rice went on.

He gave her the known details: Michael Tanner's ransacked house, the book-strewn library, the staged signs of struggle, the young professor's blood type on the wall painted in a kind of Rorschach pattern, his books carefully arranged on the floor, Sally Tanner coming home to find her husband's body. It was all, of course, achingly familiar. *Dumant University,* Alex thought. *Whoever did this was copying the murders at Dumant. Christ.*

"Jasper police have just begun their investigation," Rice said. "Right now there are few leads. And the crime scene—they think it was staged. There was no sign of forced entry, so their theory is that Dr. Tanner must have known his attacker." Alex could almost hear the man wince.

"What does it all mean?"

"It could mean nothing. The professor might have upset a disturbed student, or maybe someone knew of his history as an undergrad at this college. But given what happened to the victims at Dumant twenty-seven years ago . . . we are taking everything into consideration, of course."

Everything. The word jarred her. What he meant was *everyone.*

"We are a small school, Dr. Shipley. You know this as well as anyone. We are not Harvard. Our size has always defined us. We call ourselves *quaint* in the brochures, and we use that word without irony. We believe in our insularity. Nothing like this has ever happened at Jasper. Everyone is in a state of shock."

"Have you spoken to Richard Aldiss?" she asked.

Another pause. She knew exactly what it meant.

"This is the reason I called you tonight," Rice said. "We thought that maybe you could do that for us."

Later she and Peter lay in bed.

"You don't have to go back," Peter said.

"I do."

"We don't have to do anything we don't want to do, Alex."

She didn't answer him. She knew how untrue it was.

He burrowed into her hair, breathed hotly in her ear. Normally it turned her on, but tonight it only annoyed her. The Chemical Brothers played on the stereo. Theirs was a students' existence, and Peter wouldn't have it any other way. But lately Alex had begun to want something different. Something deeper. She knew it would not be with him. Perhaps she had always known.

"How come," Peter said now, "you never talk about your past?"

"What is there to talk about?"

"Scars."

"I don't have any."

"I can see them all over you, Alex." He ran a hand up her abdomen, traced a circle around her navel. Sometimes he would write words there, ancient verse for her to identify. "I can feel them."

"We all have scars."

"Some of us more than others."

"I'm all Vermont. Grew up in Vermont, went to undergrad there. You know all this, Peter."

"I know about the class, Alex. I know you were a hero. But it always seems so . . ." She looked at him. "I don't know. It's like you've never told me the whole story."

She rolled away. "Not tonight."

"Is it Aldiss?" Peter asked. "Is he in trouble again?"

She tensed, hoped he didn't notice it. She rarely spoke of Aldiss and the night class to him, and usually Peter had to press her for information.

"Did he do it?"

"No," she said hotly, defensively. "Of course not."

"But they think—"

"To hell with what they think. They don't know Dr. Aldiss like I do."

A moment of silence passed. The CD ended, shuffled back to the first track.

"So is that why you're going back there? To save him again?"

"No."

"Then why?"

"Because they need me."

That was all. The room fell still. She felt him draw even closer. His leg went up and over her, pulling her tight, trapping her. She thought she heard him whisper, thought she heard two muffled words on his lips—*Don't go*—but Alex could not be sure.

Then Peter's breathing became even, and she carefully maneuvered herself out from under him and went into the library down the hall. There was a window on the far side of the room blocked by a dust-heavy fold of venetian blinds. Alex picked the blinds up and removed what was on the sill. The pack was cold from touching the glass. She checked the doorway for Peter and then lifted the window a sliver with her fingertips. For a moment she listened to the breathing of far-off traffic, and then she took one of the cigarettes from the pack and lit it. Sucked in with her eyes closed, listening. Thinking.

She did not turn on a light. She simply smoked in the clinging darkness, waiting. Waiting for what? Waiting for a sign, a truth, some notion that she was doing the right thing by going back to Jasper.

She remembered Michael Tanner. Dead now, dead and quiet. She remembered Michael's face when they were in the class. In her memory the classroom was always semidark, hazy—everything stretched and elastic. The students were framed in static darkness, as if the night had forced its way inside.

Do you like this class? he'd asked one night.

No, she said. *Not at all.*

Neither do I. None of us do.

Right then, standing in the little library that could have been a closet, surrounded by books, nothing happened and everything happened. The world outside roared along. All those strangers continued on to wherever they were going and Alex was stuck here with all her unanswered questions about a dead professor.

But no. That wasn't quite right. A big question had been answered tonight.

It had very much been answered. Alex was sure of that.

The game had begun again.

4

Richard Aldiss's eyes remained open, that permanent smile etched on his face. He appeared to be waiting for something. An answer, perhaps. A solution to the puzzles of the dead. Alex's hands, meanwhile, fluttered to her jacket pocket. The nicotine gum was there, and she had to fight the urge to slip it out, press a square from the package and chew like mad.

Instead she merely watched the professor. Watched and said nothing and thought, *Please tell me you had nothing to do with this.*

"There is a type of very rare puzzle," Aldiss said finally. "It is called a *cyndrot*. Its pieces are found in the world. A sharp stick, perhaps, the page of a book. The rules are moving and unfixed, as in any good game. Chaotic. You will receive a clue, a sheet with the number two written on it, and then you will begin your search. Two sticks, two pages, two socks. The best players, however, go outside the game. They do not collect objects in exact pairs, they collect objects that *reciprocate* each other. A stick and a seed. A seed grew the tree that formed the branch that created the stick. A book and a pen. The pen wrote the page that made up the book. Everything is genesis, evolution."

"What does this have to do with Michael Tanner?"

Aldiss waited. His breathing was soft, plaintive.

"Perhaps nothing, Alexandra. Or perhaps it is heavy with meaning." He stood up, whirled out of the dark toward her. His hands were out. Instinctively Alex leaned back, away from him. "Please," he said. "Let me show you what I mean."

He took her wrist. It was a simple gesture, a lover's gesture. She felt a brief shock when he touched her. The professor's thin, feminine hands circling the delicate bones of her wrist and pulling her toward him. She had always been amazed at his strength. The first time she had touched him—she had brushed against him on a visit here four years ago, when she had stolen off from Dean Fisk's house on the day of Daniel Hayden's funeral; his body, so tight and muscular before the stroke, dripped gray water from the lake and as her arm touched his, Alex felt something coiled in him, something rock-hard—she found herself amazed at the strength of even this accidental touch. It was a brutish power, consistent with the way his mind moved.

"Stand here," he said now, pulling her to the center of the room. "And I will stand behind you. I am the killer."

He was in the doorway. It was just after nine o'clock, the morning light gashing the balled carpet into light-dark slats. The professor with his jagged smile stood half in and half out of darkness, looking at her.

"I come inside as a friend," Aldiss said. "Because as you and your slave masters believe, Alexandra, Michael knew the one who did this. So, slowly, I approach." He moved into the room, shadows throbbing around him. "Perhaps I sit. Or maybe I do not. Maybe I want to be ready, prepared for what I have to do." He was close now, close enough to smell. The smell of books, of old paper, clung to him. "Here we have two friends, two acquaintances, together in a room."

"Do you think the murderer is a student of Michael's?"

Aldiss scowled. "You are jumping to conclusions again, Alexandra. We have spoken about this. Here." He pulled her to the armchair. She sat. "The man is sitting. It is his own library, after all. His comfort zone. His killer moves about him. Their conversation becomes more intense. They speak of great literature, because this is what two friends do when they meet at night."

Now Alex saw him only in shadow. Aldiss was moving behind her, flitting this way and that, playacting the crime. She wanted to see exactly what he was doing, but she was taken in by the lake outside the window. Enraptured by it. There was something about the way the ice drifted, the weak April ice, the way it dissolved and fell to loose, gauzy shreds . . .

The professor touched her again. Ran his fingers through her hair.

"This crime," he whispered. "You said before that it is different from the ones I was accused of. What did you mean?"

Alex closed her eyes and said, "There were mistakes. The crime scene—it isn't as clean as the two at Dumant. He was more nervous, perhaps . . . weaker than that man. But there was something else."

"What?"

"The struggle seemed to be staged. Manipulated to mirror the Dumant scenes."

"The police told you this?"

"Yes."

Aldiss scoffed. "Do not listen to them. They are men of a false science. They do not know what we know."

"And what do we know, Professor?"

"We know . . ."

She let him touch her. Let him move his fingers in and out of her hair, play against her neck. She tried not to imagine his face. She closed her eyes.

"Is it the game?" she breathed. "Has the Procedure begun again?"

No answer. Aldiss's shadow twisted on the wall.

"What kind of person do I tell them to look for?" she pressed.

Again: nothing. He only kept moving his hands about her hair, his fingers so sure and powerful as they began to massage her scalp.

"Who killed Michael Tanner?"

"In the *cyndrot*," he said finally, hands clasping her skull, "you look for what mirrors the original object. Its twin opposite, the illusion of sameness it creates. In this case we are looking for someone who knows the Dumant murders so intimately that he or she can replicate those crimes perfectly. To do this one must have secret knowledge of the events. This person must have studied that brutal history so carefully that nothing—no detail, no gesture—could be left unused. The killer has created a *cyndrot*. For this reason I believe the person we are now searching for is . . ."

"Who?" she pleaded. "Tell me."

"Someone who was part of the night class."

Alex inhaled deeply, kept her hands perfectly still on her lap.

"The killer was there with you in that lecture hall. It is someone you know, Alexandra. There are things about Dumant University that I have shared, both during the class and afterward, with only the nine of you. If I am correct, as I fear I am, then a few of these details will have been used in the murder of Michael Tanner. This oversight might be the killer's first mistake."

"But how do I know who it is?" she asked.

"There are two ways to find your killer," Aldiss said. "First, you must get into Michael's home. See how the killer arranged the books, which ones he chose to highlight. You have to make them let you see what the killer saw that night."

"I don't know if they will—"

"You must."

She looked down at her hands, at the pyramid of books at her feet. "And the second way?"

"You must bring the students from the class back together," the professor said softly. His voice, the way he said the words, suggested a kind of pity; it spoke to Alex of a keen apprehension that she had never heard out of Aldiss. "You are the only one who truly understands these people and their motivation, the only one who knows what they desire. And when you have done this, when they are back on the Jasper campus, then you will observe them. That is how you will find the one who committed this murder."

"But how do you know?" she asked, desperation in her voice. "How can you be sure one of us did this?"

Aldiss pulled away. He removed his hands but left something behind, an indentation, a phantom pressure on her scalp.

"It is someone who was there," he said again, and then: "I know it in my blood." Alex thought about what this meant, the path it would take her down. She thought about the others—*There are seven of us now,* she reminded herself—and imagined them all there, back again on campus for the first time since Daniel Hayden's funeral. But this time it would be different. This time one of them could possibly be watching her, watching and—

"Richard?"

A voice at the door. The trance was broken, and both Alex and the professor turned. Alex thought she saw a blush, a flash of purple deep beneath the mask of the professor's face.

"Richard, who is she?"

The girl was young. A college student. She was model pretty, with full lips and green, intelligent eyes. She wore a Jasper College sweatshirt and torn blue jeans. She had clearly just awakened.

"Daphne," the professor said, "this is Alexandra Shipley, one of my former students."

The girl said nothing, only stared at Alex. There was the flare of a challenge in her eyes. Alex got up, dusted down the wrinkles in her trench, and forced a smile. *The girl is fifteen years younger than you, Alex, and you're intimidated by her? Christ.*

"I was just going," she said weakly. "Professor. Daphne." Alex nodded awkwardly and went to the doorway. The girl hesitated there in the threshold, then she moved to the side and Alex inched past her to navigate the corridor of books.

She found the front door and pushed into it, hard, reaching for the air.

But Aldiss was behind her again, pulling her back by the shoulder. Alex stopped on the porch, almost out. Almost free of him.

"She's just a child," she spat into the wind.

"A toy," the professor said. "Nothing but a plaything."

Alex jerked away.

"We could continue our session, you know," he said, his lips close to her ear now. Alex looked out at the small rental car, at the steep drive that would take her back to Route 2 and toward the college. "Fair Daphne wouldn't have to know."

Alex yanked free of him. She heard him laugh behind her as she went for the car, opened the door, and began to get in.

"Alexandra, wait."

She paused, hunched inside the car, one foot still planted on Aldiss's drive.

"If I am right," Aldiss said, "and it is one of them, then you will be putting yourself in grave danger. When the students from the night class have returned and you have begun your observation, be careful, Alexandra, because one of them will also be observing you . . ." He trailed off, ran his eyes beyond her as if he were searching the woods behind his small house. "I would die if anything happened to you. First I would kill the person who did it, and then I would take the axe to myself. I promise you that."

Before she pulled away she looked back at the house. She saw him there in a front window. He watched her descent.

Later, when she returned to Jasper, Alex paid a visit to a trusted old friend.

And then she began to call them, one by one, until all those who remained had agreed to return and honor the life of Michael Tanner.

The Class

1994

5

"Now, let us begin."

The image of Dr. Richard Aldiss on the television screen seemed to wobble a bit and then right itself. Nine faces stared at him, waiting for the professor to begin his lecture. They wondered if he would tell them about what he had done twelve years ago. The two murders (an axe, it was believed, but the murder weapon was never found), the grisly scenes on the Dumant University campus . . . no one knew if it would be a point of discussion. He wasn't supposed to speak of the crimes, but Aldiss didn't seem like a man who would play by the rules.

"What is literature?" the professor asked now.

No one in the class spoke. The silence hummed.

Aldiss smiled a bit, leaned forward. His eyes, furtive and black and bearing a hint of dark humor, flitted from side to side, searching them.

"Mr. Tanner," he said, reading softly from a class roster that must have been off camera. "Please tell us what you believe literature to be."

The boy named Michael Tanner spoke up. His voice cracked as he addressed the screen.

"Literature is an assortment of books," he said. "The canon."

"And what is the canon, in your opinion?"

"Faulkner, Joyce, Woolf. Mostly the modernists."

A shadow passed across Aldiss's face. "The modernists killed so many good things."

The boy shrank back.

"Mr. Kane," Aldiss said. "What is literature?"

"Literature is the feeling you get when you read a book," said Christian Kane, a slight boy in the second row. He wore a denim jacket with grunge patches dotting the sleeves. He tried to make himself larger than he was, bring himself to the height of those who always towered over him. It worked, but only barely. It worked because Kane was brilliant.

"Ah, a man of feelings. I like that, Mr. Kane. And tell me—what *feelings* come over you when you read Isaac Babel? Or Boris Pilnyak, who couldn't be rehabilitated and was killed by a firing squad and left for the birds to pick apart? Or Dostoyevsky? What do you *feel* when you read the scenes of Raskolnikov's axe in *Crime and Punishment*?"

Axe. The word rang out in the lecture hall, vibrated around them. Everyone sat still, waiting for the other shoe to fall.

It did not. Richard Aldiss didn't flinch, did not appear as if he had even made an error. Perhaps that one word, that casual *axe,* was meant to be dropped there. Perhaps he had planted it in his lecture beforehand, written the word into his notes. Was he this sort of man? they wondered. Was he the sort who would play mind games with his students?

"I feel repulsed," Kane said. "As does everyone else."

"Everyone?"

"Everyone who feels any empathy for the sane."

Aldiss laughed. A quick, biting *pshaw.*

"Do you know what I felt when I read Dostoyevsky for the first time?" Aldiss said. "I felt a solution. For Raskolnikov doesn't go unpunished for his crimes against his metaphorical sister and mother. He is indeed not a superman. This thing I felt when I first read that book, this *emotion,* was one of sadness. I too was destined not to be superman. I too was not meant to go unpunished."

The professor appeared to frown, that pale shadow crossing over his face again. The two guards behind him shifted.

"Ms. Shipley," he said. "Can you tell us what literature is?"

A girl in the second row hesitated. The rest of them watched her, this pretty, mysterious Vermont girl. Alex Shipley had long, straight hair that glinted in the classroom light. She was opinionated, razor sharp, and if you did not know her she could disarm you with her honesty—as was her intent. She had told no one yet (she liked to keep secrets until it was impossible not to), but she was bound for grad school at Harvard in the spring.

"Literature is love," the girl said.

"Do you believe in love, Ms. Shipley?"

"Yes."

"And so you must believe in literature."

"Very much so."

"What about the possibility of literature, like love, to hurt?"

The girl shrugged, undeterred. The camera that was trained on the students caught this, and Aldiss's eyes flicked upward to where he must have had his own monitor to view the basement classroom. He smiled: he liked this indistinct, almost rebellious, gesture. "If literature can make us feel anything," she said, "then why couldn't it make us feel pain?"

"The book as knife."

"Or arrow."

Aldiss leaned back, even more impressed. "Flaming arrow."

Another shrug from Alex. "Or axe."

Then something happened.

Aldiss's face went crimson. He straightened in his chair as if a jolt of electricity were pouring through him and clasped his hands around his throat. Then he began to writhe, still sitting upright, chair legs knocking frantically beneath him. It appeared that he was being strangled, invisibly, from behind.

The guards moved quickly. They surrounded him, both of them reaching out, only their arms and hands in the shot, trying to still him. But the professor could not be stilled. He flailed and bucked and flung himself around, the chair shrieking against the floor, Aldiss's figure shifting almost totally off camera. A tiny parentheses of foam crept from his mouth and down his chin. He was misframed now, the faceless guards at the right edge of the screen fighting with him, trying to save him. "His tongue!" one of them said. "My God, he's swallowing his tongue!"

The screen went black.

For a few moments the students in the lecture hall sat silently, wait-ing. No one seemed to know what to do. They looked at one another, shock and confusion on their faces. The screen popped with static.

"What do we do now?" a girl named Sally Mitchell asked.

Then the sound, the electronic tone from before, returned. Every-one looked toward the TV screen.

Aldiss returned, his hair wild, his eyes racked by pain.

"I'm sorry," he slurred. "I have these . . . these episodes sometimes. I've always had them, ever since I was a small boy. Not to worry. My minders here are trained medics—they won't let me expire on you." He said nothing more.

The nine stared at the box. Somehow his admission did not calm their nerves. A few of them would dream of him that night. Dreams of only sound and blurred movement: the rake of chair legs, the gargle of pain in the professor's throat.

"You have said," Aldiss went on when he was fully composed, "that literature is defined by its place in the canon. It is defined by emotion, by love. What if"—his cracked gaze swung around the room, falling on them all; and even this, this simple movement, showed the students in the night class why he was such a powerful teacher—"literature is a game?"

None of them knew how to take this. They stared at the screen, waiting for the man to continue.

"What if what just happened to me was nothing but a trick?"

The students were confused. Someone laughed nervously.

"I do indeed have a neurological condition," he told his class. "But if I did not, if the spell I just suffered was indeed a hoax, an act—would you have believed I was in pain?"

No one answered.

"Come on. Was I convincing, class?"

"Yes," a boy named Frank Marsden said from the back row. Thin, handsome in a classical way, Marsden was a drama student with a lit minor. Of all of the students in the classroom, he could tell truth from playacting.

"Absolutely," said Alex Shipley.

"What if literature were like this?" Aldiss continued. "What if a book, a novel, tricked us into believing it was real, but when we actually got into it—when we *really* read it, when we *truly* paid attention—we began to see that there was a whole world behind the pages? A universe of deeper truths. And all it took was our ability to find the rabbit hole."

He paused, let the cryptic information he had just given them settle in. "How many of you have heard of Paul Fallows?"

6

A few had indeed. They told Aldiss what they knew of the writer. They knew that no one was sure who Fallows was—not really. His first novel had been a huge success, but the more critics and scholars called Fallows into the spotlight, the more the writer refused to appear. He began to slip away like a ghost. There had been speculation, some of it published and some of it simply a part of the rumor mill at every lit department in America—Fallows was Pynchon, he was Barth, he was Eco. Or he was Charles Rutherford, the encyclopedia salesman whose photograph graced the back of Fallows's books. But to this day no one *knew;* there were no interviews with Fallows, no oral history, in fact nothing that proved beyond a doubt that the man was anything more than a pseudonym.

But even pseudonyms can be traced. Fallows had never been.

"Paul Fallows was playing a game," Aldiss said. "And in this class I want to take you into that game. The mystery we will unravel, then, will be the author himself. We will read both of Fallows's existing novels and perhaps, if we are lucky, *discover the great writer's true identity.*"

There was a moment of confused silence.

"What do you mean discover his identity?" a boy named Jacob Keller finally asked. He was an offensive lineman on the Jasper football team.

An enigma: a hulking mass, but kind-eyed and quick with a smile, his fingertips always white with yard-line chalk. He was the only member of the football team who could recite Keats.

"I mean, Mr. Keller," Aldiss said, "that your one assignment in this class will be to discover who Paul Fallows really is."

"But that makes no sense," said a voice from the back row. Lewis Prine was a psychology minor, perhaps the one student in the class who did not appear to be infatuated with books to the point of obsession. "People have been searching for Fallows for thirty years. Experts, academics, conspiracy theorists. How can we find him in our little night class at Jasper College?"

"You must believe in your abilities more, Mr. Prine."

The students looked at one another. They felt empowered, energized—and a little bit scared. Time was running out in their first class. They'd been told that the screen would go black at the hour. The feed was set to run no longer.

"Your reading assignment for the next class is the first fifty pages of Fallows's masterpiece, *The Coil*. You will receive the full syllabus tomorrow morning in the campus mail," Aldiss said. "But I want to leave you tonight with a question. Call it your homework assignment for our next class. It is a riddle right out of the great Paul Fallows."

The students waited, pens poised above notepads.

"What is the name of the man in the dark coat?"

With that Aldiss fell silent, and in a few seconds his image was gone, vanished from the screen once again.

That night Alex Shipley could not sleep.

She lay in her room in Philbrick Hall, her roommate snoring gently in the bunk above her. She stared into the darkness. She couldn't stop thinking of Richard Aldiss, of the way he had addressed them on that first night, of that fit he had fallen into. Horrible. It was all strange and horrible, and Alex didn't know why she had signed up for the class in the first place.

And yet . . .

The night class was also enthralling. It was unlike anything she had ever done at Jasper College. To have a chance to uncover the identity of Paul Fallows, no matter how impossible it sounded—that was the sort of adventure Alex longed for. It was because of the bizarre assignment that she knew she would stay with Aldiss and his class until the end, no matter what happened.

She had read the first seventy-five pages of *The Coil.* Her vein-spined paperback edition sat on the little built-in desk across the room, an orange USED sticker slapped on the side. She had sunk a bit since the beginning of her senior year. There was a time when Alex would buy only new books, when she would not think of writing in margins. But now she had to save money for Harvard, and so used books were the only option she could afford. Other students' notes sprawled away from the lines of text, chewed up every bit of white space. To her it felt like a desecration.

Her mother, who lived in the town of Darling just thirty miles away from the college, had warned her about taking Aldiss's class. *Evil,* her mother had said. The man, his class—all of it was evil. But Alex knew Professor Richard Aldiss was also brilliant. She'd read his prison writings on great American writers and had felt a lucidity there, a kinship. He spoke of books the way she felt about them—as if they were the truest forms of communication, both primitive and sacred. He once said the book was a lock, and its reader was the key. *Damn right,* Alex thought.

Tonight, though, something had changed.

Lying there, listening to the whoops and rustles of the late-night students down on the quad, Alex couldn't put her finger on what it was. Couldn't articulate it. The notion that Aldiss would change her life had dissolved when she first saw him. It wasn't that she no longer believed he would enlighten her; perhaps he and his strange ideas about literature could do that much. It was just that he was not as invincible as she had once thought. Not as stark or elegant as his writing would suggest. There was something . . . something almost fragile about the man who appeared on that screen. Something vulnerable.

Listen to yourself, Alex. Getting all mushy about a man who murdered two people in cold blood.

She thought about the riddle. Aldiss's "homework."

What is the name of the man in the dark coat?

Alex didn't have a clue what it meant. The first few chapters of *The Coil* focused on New York society at the turn of the century. It was a novel in the most traditional sense of the word. Alex knew that there were hidden meanings, not only about the narrative but also supposedly about Fallows himself, but she could not discern them. The first time she had read the classic, as a high school student, she was unmoved by the tale. *This thing?* she remembered thinking. *All that buzz for this book?*

But now here was Richard Aldiss, telling them that Fallows's novels were not novels at all but really *games*. Games the novelist himself hid behind. And Aldiss had gone further, had given them a clue that night to perhaps take them into the . . . what had he called it? Yes: into the rabbit hole.

What is the name of the man in the dark coat?

Name . . . dark coat . . . games . . .

Alex bounced out of bed. Her roommate, a girl from New Hampshire named Meredith who majored in chemistry, stirred in the top bunk. Alex, her mind roaring and her hands reaching into the dark before her, picked up the copy of *The Coil* from the desk. Then she went into the small bathroom the two girls shared—a perk for being seniors—closed the door behind her, and turned on the light above the mirror.

She flipped through the novel, skimming the pages until the words blurred together, searching for any connection to a dark coat. It only made sense: the book was their sole material in the class. No syllabus until tomorrow, no handouts. Aldiss had to be leading them to *The Coil;* he had to be.

When her eyes finally became tired, she looked up from the page and into the mirror above the sink. *Time to give up and forget this craziness,* she thought. *Somebody else has surely solved it by now, and when that person has the answer, all nine of us will—*

She froze.

There. In the mirror. An image on the back of the book itself.

Alex, moving slowly now, turned the volume around.

On the back cover was the traditional author's photograph. It was a man she knew was not really Paul Fallows. Or at least no one could be sure if it was him or not. The image had been slapped on subsequent editions of the novel precisely because of this: no one really knew the identity of the writer, and so the likeness of the encyclopedia salesman remained.

She looked down at the man's face. At his swept-back hair, the almost calculated smile. At the way his hands were crossed in his lap. And she looked at the dark coat he was wearing.

What is the name of the man . . . ?

Before she knew it Alex was out of the bathroom and moving. She pulled on her jeans and her Jasper College sweatshirt, crammed on Meredith's wool hat, and went out of the room as silently as she could, the novel still in her grip. Down the elevator and out of Philbrick, onto the frozen quad.

The Stanley M. Fisk Library was open only at the west entrance. Alex punched in the combination code and moved into the warmth of the building. The night librarian was on, a mousy woman named Daws who dressed like a character out of Austen. "Alexandra Shipley, what are you—"

But Alex was already past her and to the back section of the library. Empty now save for a few zombies who sat reading by lamplight.

Literary Criticism was here, in the back. She knew the place by heart; as a freshman at Jasper she had worked in the stacks, learned the nooks and crannies.

She found the famous study on Paul Fallows on a shelf toward the end of the stacks, in a pool of red emergency light that barely lit up the page for her to read. The book was called *Mind Puzzles: The World and Work of Paul Fallows.* Copyright 1979, published by Overland Press. Its author was Richard Aldiss, PhD. He had written the book three years before the murders at Dumant.

Alex turned to the index. Found the words she was looking for: AUTHOR PHOTOGRAPH (LIKELY APOCRYPHAL). The name of the real encyclopedia salesman, the actual man in the photo, was on the tip of her tongue. She knew Aldiss had said it in his lecture that night. *Damn it, Alex, you've got to pay attention.*

Now she turned to the appropriate page and scanned for the name in the near dark—

But something stopped her. Something froze her there, under that bloody light, the library still and quiet around her. Her pulse, which had been frantic before, strangely slowed. Alex became calm. The sweat working under her arms and on her scalp began to cool. Her entire body went rigid.

There was handwriting in the margins of the book.

Manic pencil writing, numbers and letters mixed together, symbols swirling down the page like a mad and tortured language.

What the hell is this?

Alex scanned the handwritten text. At the bottom of the page she saw a legible stack of lines. They were written differently than the rest. Darker, dug into the skin of the page, almost carved there. A cold hand. The hand of someone determined to have his message be discovered.

I OFFER CONGRATULATIONS FOR FINDING THIS MESSAGE. YOU HAVE COME VERY FAR ALREADY. NOW YOU MUST CHECK THIS BOOK OUT.

Alex's eyes scanned to the next page, where the crude writing continued. She found another set of lines written in that same pressed hand.

What she read next would change Alex Shipley's life.

RICHARD ALDISS IS INNOCENT. TO DISCOVER THE MAN WHO ACTUALLY MURDERED THE TWO STUDENTS AT DUMANT YOU MUST FIRST DISCOVER THE TRUE IDENTITY OF PAUL FALLOWS. THE TWO MYSTERIES ARE ONE AND THE SAME. DO NOT TELL A SOUL YOU HAVE SEEN THIS.

Alex, her mind on fire, walked as naturally as she could to the front of the library and checked the biography out. The mousy librarian didn't suspect a thing.

"You English majors," she said. "You always study so hard."

Alex

Present Day

7

The old man, her trusted friend, had gone blind. He lived now among his books and the memories of the college he once reigned. There was a photograph, curled with age and hanging above the walnut desk, of him with a former president. Another with a Nobel laureate, now long dead, the two men with their socks falling and drunken grins on their faces. But his prized possession was a childlike jigsaw puzzle, strip-glued and mounted to thin board, adorned with the fragmented and Cubist images of a man's distorted face. An inscription below: *To my friend Dean Fisk, we will find Fallows. Richard Aldiss.* The puzzle was dated December 25, 1985. Aldiss had made it while in prison.

Alex ran her eyes over the cluttered desk, grazed through the yellowed documents with wandering fingertips. Her heart sounded in her chest but otherwise she was quiet.

"Awful," the old man said. He sat in his wheelchair back in the corner shadows, his rheumy eyes quick and wet. "Awful what has happened to our Michael. What has happened to our college. What are you doing over there, Alex?"

Her hands stopped. Heat rushed to her face.

"Nothing, Dean Fisk," she said. "Just looking at the history in this room."

The dean breathed. Something was coming in the darkness; the air pressure dropped in the room, the feeling of electricity before a kiss, a secret.

"It doesn't exist," he said.

The words dazed her. Her eyes rose from the desk.

"I don't know what you mean," she said weakly.

"Whatever you've heard, Alex, whatever they have told you—you will not find the manuscript in this house."

"I haven't heard anything." This wasn't like lying to Aldiss; the dean was gone now, his mind turned to mush. He was ninety-four years old and wasted away. She looked at him, saw spittle glisten on his paper-gray cheeks. The full-time nurse—a middle-aged man she had met when she arrived—would be in soon to feed him.

"Those old false pieces of Fallows—it's over, Alex," Fisk went on. "You put an end to it during the night class. You."

"Of course," she said, thinking, *You're wrong, dean. It will never end.*

A silence fell, and her eyes drifted instinctively to the desk. She said, "I went to see Dr. Aldiss this morning. He says whoever did this is re-creating the Dumant murders."

"Richard," Fisk laughed. "Richard probably murdered Michael himself."

She was stunned. "You don't believe that, do you? You can't. It just isn't—"

The door opened behind her and the nurse stepped inside. A pale, deliberate man, so precise in his movements that she barely saw his hands dropping the medicines into the old man's birdlike mouth. He turned to the silver tray he'd set on the desk. A meal for a child: a piece of toast, applesauce. Fisk looked through his nurse in the way of the blind, nodding purposefully. "Thank you, Matthew," he said, and the nurse left the room, his eyes falling momentarily on Alex as he went.

When he was gone Alex said, "Dean Fisk, tell me you don't believe that Professor Aldiss murdered Michael. I know you had a falling-out years ago, but he was your friend. Your confidant. You . . ." *Helped save him,* she wanted to say.

The old man looked into the void, considering. Then he said without context, "They still play the Procedure."

She blinked. "Who?"

"The students," he said. "I can hear them on campus when Matthew pushes me over the sidewalks on our strolls. I can *hear them.*" He fell silent, and the sound of his raspy breathing filled the room.

"Dean Fisk, about Michael Tanner . . ."

His roaming eyes stopped on her. "If they are coming back for the funeral, they will need a place to stay."

"Yes."

He meant the night class students who were on their way to Jasper now. Most of them still lived in Vermont, and of course Sally Tanner was here on this campus already. It had occurred to Alex, as she made those phone calls, how easy it might be, what Aldiss had suggested. How simple to bring them together.

"I want them to stay here."

Alex's breath caught. "Here?"

"I want them to be close," Fisk explained. "This is a grieving time, Alex, and when we are grieving we all need to be together. There is more than enough space in my house. Yes, it is old. There is history here. But it is familiar to them. You can all reconnect, much like you did when Daniel Hayden—"

"Yes," she interrupted. "I'll forward your invitation."

And then the dean nodded, meaning it was time for her to leave. She went out, down a dark hallway that led to the east wing of the mansion, and moved into the heart of the old house.

The air here was musty, unstirred. As she walked the floorboards groaned, and above her the silver spindles of webs clung to the walls. Those walls had cracked, revealing skeins of plaster that seemed to point her deeper into the dark. She knew exactly where she was going; she had spent many days in this house when she was an undergrad at Jasper.

Stanley Fisk, then a spry eighty, had been her ally during the night class. He had shown her how to read the text that was Richard Aldiss, and she would always be indebted to him. If Alex was the most famous Jasper alumna, much was due to him. If he wanted the students to stay in this crumbling place, then who was she to argue?

It would make her job easier.

She took another step, thinking—

"Someone's here."

Alex spun around. Behind her was the nurse.

"Who's here, Matthew?" she asked, managing to conjure up his name as if he were a student who'd raised his hand during lecture.

"A woman. She wants to see you. She looks freaked."

She looked at him. Older than she had thought at first, his skin so pale it appeared translucent. Why was he here? she wondered. To keep the dean alive, to postpone the inevitable? And what might he know, she thought almost guiltily, of the dean's possessions?

"Tell her I'm on the second floor."

"Of course, Dr. Shipley." So he knew her name too.

The nurse left, the whisper of his tennis shoes disappearing down the hall, and Alex entered a room to her left. It was a relic from another time—two upholstered chairs covered with sheets perched in the middle of the floor, a bookshelf along a back wall, a minor Rothko hanging at a tilt. The room had been fresh once, back when Stanley Fisk ruled the campus and all the college's decisions went through him. He was known as a man of letters, which was something of a novelty among college royalty. He hosted parties that were attended by Philip Roth and Joan Didion, reinvented the literature program long before Aldiss was brought in for his strange and experimental night class. Fisk *was* Jasper College, and like this room and its pitiful furniture, the man had been all but forgotten.

I want them to stay here. There were seventeen rooms in this Victorian-style mansion that had been specifically built for Fisk in the sixties, most of them empty now. Undoubtedly spacious enough to host the students who would return. And to allow Alex free rein to follow Aldiss's instructions.

To observe without them knowing.

She walked deeper into the room, stepping into the funneled light that slanted through a window. She studied the bookshelves. More Fallows here, a spray of Aldiss prison texts. She took out a volume and shook it, maybe hoping for something to fall out. A page, a key? Nothing. The manuscript, the third Fallows—it had to be somewhere. She had been assured by Lewis Prine that it was in this house: *The person who sent me this page says Fisk has the rest.* He'd sent the page to her four years ago, not long after the death of Daniel Hayden. Scanning the book spines, Alex thought, *Did you know, Lewis? Did you know it was here when we all came to this house to grieve Daniel, damn you?*

"Alex."

She turned and saw the woman standing in the doorway, leaning as if she was fatigued, as if she had traveled a great distance. Her hair was tangled and stuck to her cheek. She had been crying.

"Sally, I'm so sorry." The women came together and embraced between the two empty chairs. Alex thinking: *How cold she is, how unhealthy, could she have killed—*

"I saw him," the woman moaned, her breath low and hot in Alex's ear. "I saw Michael lying there on the floor. At first I thought he was sleeping, but then I saw—I saw all those books, Alex, all those awful books . . ."

"Shhh," Alex said, and they swayed together silently.

Finally Sally Tanner pulled away and took a deep breath. Her knees buckled. Alex reached out, caught the woman by the elbow. Held her upright.

"The cops have been asking me questions since that night," Sally said. "This detective named Black. He thinks— He doesn't say this, Alex, but I can see it in his eyes. He thinks I had something to do with Michael's murder. Can you fucking believe that?"

Alex shook her head. She didn't know what to say.

"Black asked me something else." She steadied her gaze. "He asked about Aldiss."

Alex tensed. "And what did you say?"

"I told the truth, of course. I haven't spoken to the professor in years. Not since Daniel."

"What about Michael?"

Something glinted in the widow's eye, something hard and firm. It said, *Too soon.* Then it was gone.

"Michael wouldn't go out there. I know Aldiss lives nearby, but the class—it was over for him. He never spoke about what happened to us back then."

Then something in her broke, and she fell forward again into Alex's arms.

When the spell was over, Sally stood up and looked past Alex, over her shoulder at the books. Even those silent objects stirred her, made her tremble and turn away, her hands cupped to her mouth as if clapping quiet a scream. Again Alex thought, *Is she the one?* Then: *Don't do this, treat them this way just because Aldiss has given you another task. He could be wrong. He could be playing with you.*

"I saw him," Sally repeated. "And I will never get over it. Never."

"Sally, if you know who might have done this—"

Quickly, the widow turned to look at Alex. The light in her eyes had changed, gone to the flint of anger. Alex saw the girl from the night class in that instant, the youth springing out like a hidden figure, anger and spite stitched across her brow.

"Don't you dare," she said.

"I was just—"

"Don't do this to me. Not here, not after what I've been through. We were all different people when we took that class. All of us. And if you've come back here to be a hero again, that is between you and your dear Aldiss. I will grieve for my husband and live with what I saw in that library, and you stay the hell out of my and Michael's life."

The Class

1994

8

Richard Aldiss began his second lecture with a question.

"Which one of you found the man in the dark coat?"

Tonight the television sat atop a sea-green rolling cart labeled PROPERTY OF JASPER ENGLISH DEPT. The chalkboard was marred with palm-erased equations from an earlier class. The temperature had dropped to a record low outside, and the cold pressed in. On the screen the murderer slowly blinked, waiting for a response to his question. When no answer came, he raised his hands palms up, as if to say, *I'm waiting*.

"I was too busy with my research," a student toward the back of the hall finally answered. Daniel Hayden was a pale, unhealthily thin boy who wore his sandy hair down over his eyes. He never seemed to look at you when he spoke. He was not brilliant the way many of the others were. Instead of the cliquish way some of the nine moved about campus, Hayden kept to himself. He did not see himself as special; he did not try to dominate the others with his knowledge of books. In fact, few of them even knew Hayden *was* an English major until he appeared in the night class, wearing a Pavement T-shirt and torn blue jeans. In his front jacket pocket he always kept a rolled-up paperback novel.

"And what kind of research would that be, Mr. Hayden?" Aldiss asked.

"Research about you. About the things you did."

The professor didn't flinch. "You shouldn't be doing that."

Hayden grinned. "Don't you want to know what I learned?"

Aldiss extended his hands, palms out: *Humor me.*

"There's a true crime book about your case. It's called *The Mad Professor*. Have you read it, Dr. Aldiss?"

"No."

"I read it last night. All of it. I couldn't stop. I had to know exactly what you did before I came to class again. The author—he believes you are evil. That you might be a genius but your mind did something to you. Changed you somehow. A lot of them say the same thing."

"*Them*?"

"Your enemies. Those who believe you shouldn't be teaching this class."

"And what do you believe, Mr. Hayden?"

"I believe . . ." The boy faltered. His gaze fell away, down to the notebook that was still unopened on his desk. "I believe you were a bad man," he went on, his voice barely a whisper. "You did some very bad things. You hurt people, destroyed lives. All the information is out there. The professor-killer. The genius-murderer. They call you the Bookman."

Aldiss nodded firmly. Then he said, "Well. I didn't want to speak to you about this, but if *research* is being done without my knowledge, then it appears that we must. Let me only say this: I am guilty of sending two girls to their graves. I spend every night in this institution thinking about the troubled man I was as a young professor at Dumant University. And all I can say to you is that the mind is a locked room, conscience is the key, and some of us threw away the key a long time ago."

"Are you sorry?"

Hayden again. And in that instant the students saw, for the first time, what their professor was capable of. His annoyance at the boy turned to something else, something like rage, hot and vile just at the corners of his eyes. In the very next second it was gone.

" 'Sorry' is just one word among many, Mr. Hayden."

"But you murdered two people! You killed two innocent women and you arranged those books around their—"

"No one knows the entire story of what happened at Dumant," Aldiss said. "No one will ever know. For me to say that I am *sorry*"—the word spat into the microphone before him—"would be to go back and relive my crimes, and I am not about to do that. Not here, not now."

For a moment, it appeared Hayden had said all that he was going to say. But then he raised his gaze to the television one more time and said, "There were just the two, weren't there?"

Aldiss blinked, calmly, as if he had anticipated this very question.

"The victims they know about," Hayden continued. "The two grad students—you've never killed anyone else, have you?"

The professor swiped a hand over his mouth and said, in a voice that was as sharp as glass, "I will not be interrogated by a student."

With this the boy relented. He nodded, more to himself than anyone else, and placed his copy of *The Coil* on top of his notebook. Then he stood up and began to make his way to the television screen. There he paused and said something to Aldiss, something no one else in the class caught because his back was to them, and he walked out the door.

For a moment no one spoke.

When Hayden was gone the professor said, his voice even and calm, "And then there were eight."

There were uneasy laughs. Someone coughed nervously. A few of them chattered just to hear the noise of their own talk. After a few seconds Aldiss hushed his students by putting one long, pale finger to his lips: "Shhh, class." Silence descended.

He shuffled the notes that were in front of him on the rickety prison-issue table and said, "Now, who discovered the name of the man in the dark coat? Who solved the riddle?"

For a moment no one spoke. Then, from the middle of the lecture hall, a girl slowly raised her hand.

Alex had debated whether to say anything. Hadn't Aldiss just told them that he was guilty? Hadn't he confessed to the two murders right there before his class, with nine live witnesses and whoever else was watching the damn TV to hear his words? She thought about the book, so carefully hidden in her desk drawer back at Philbrick Hall. Of the strange and tantalizing message there. *Richard Aldiss is innocent. Do not tell a soul you have seen this.* Perhaps she should remain silent, act as if she had never even found the thing at all.

No.

To say nothing would be to possibly let an innocent man die in prison. Perhaps this admission of his guilt was part of the trick. Part of Aldiss's master plan. She knew if the book and its hidden message were real, then Aldiss was counting on her. Relying on her to follow the clues . . .

Down the rabbit hole.

She raised her hand.

"Ah, Ms. Shipley," Aldiss said, no hesitation at all in his eyes or his voice. "Tell the rest of the class what you found."

Does he know? she wondered. *Can he possibly know that I checked out the book? If so, then how is he so calm?*

"The man in the dark coat," Alex said now, trying to find her voice. Her tongue felt thick, misshapen. "His name was . . ."

"Please go on."

"The man's name was Charles Rutherford."

The professor smiled. Despite herself, Alex felt a rush of pride.

"The encyclopedia salesman?" someone behind her asked. Melissa Lee had a reputation at Jasper, both for being blazingly intelligent and for inciting a sex scandal that had been weaving its way through the lit faculty for the past two semesters. She wore all black, heavy layers of it, and her hair was streaked with alternating patterns of light and dark that made her look vaguely animalistic. Her face was death-white, a style the students at Jasper had begun calling Goth. Her eyes were painted black and her ears flashed with silver studs, and a sardonic smile always played upon her dark purple lips. Her T-shirt tonight read KILL A POET. "But Rutherford's a nobody. A pawn. He was dead a year before *The Golden Silence* even appeared, but they still slap his photo on the books because no one can be sure about the role he played. How did she . . ." Lee glared at Alex, and Alex merely smiled.

"That's the whole point, Ms. Lee," Aldiss said. "Rutherford became a flashpoint for the Fallows scholars exactly because he was so improbable a suspect. First, he died of a brain embolism in 1974. One year later, the second Fallows novel was published. There was also the problem of his clean-cut, square, midwestern image. At first, when the search for Fallows began, many believed that the Rutherford photograph was nothing but another trick. More misdirection. But as the scholars began to search for Rutherford, they found something very interesting."

"He was a writer."

Aldiss looked out at the class and found the one who had spoken. "That's right," he said. "Very good."

The boy was the football player, Jacob Keller. He was sitting just to Alex's right, and she glanced over and found his eyes. He nodded at her. *Cute,* Alex thought, *in a smart-jock sort of way.* She had seen him around campus with a few of his teammates, had spotted him down at a bar called Rebecca's a few times, sitting at a back table and tracing blocking patterns with his fingertips on index cards. Now Keller leaned over and whispered, "Me and you, Shipley, we're his pets now. The only question is where they'll find our bodies." Alex stifled a laugh, and when she looked up she saw that Aldiss had heard. He was looking right at them, and her heart caught in her throat—but the professor only smiled.

"Charles Rutherford was indeed writing a book," Aldiss finally continued. "They found pieces of the manuscript in his briefcase after his death. But it was a strange book, nothing like the stuff Paul Fallows would become famous for."

The professor looked down at his table, shuffled through more of his notes, and then came up with one sheet of paper.

"Or was it?"

A quick movement, and then the professor's form was eclipsed on the screen, replaced by a yellowed document he had held up for the camera. One rumpled page, years old from the look of it, arteries of age running through the sheet like the whorls on a palm. Alex read what was written there, saw that the font was that of a typewriter. The page was heavy with bubbled mark-outs and grayed correction tape. It appeared to be— *How strange,* she thought. It was an encyclopedia entry.

"Rutherford was writing his own encyclopedia?" said a boy in back. This was Christian Kane, the slight boy with the denim jacket. Kane was the class auteur; he wrote Stephen King–esque short stories and published them in the Jasper College literary magazine, *The Guild*. Kane fashioned himself after the famous French artisans, with upswept silvering hair and oxford shirts and colored scarves. His stories were so bizarre and violent that many wondered if he didn't live a secret life, if he hadn't somehow gleaned firsthand knowledge of his macabre subject matter back in his Delaware prep school.

"That's right, Mr. Kane," Aldiss said. "He had just begun the volume when he met his demise. Just a few entries. As you see, he was still in the A's. But this encyclopedia—it was so much different from the Funk & Wagnalls he was selling door to door. This book was unusual. It seemed to be about Charles Rutherford himself, about his own experiences, the things he did and the people he spoke to every day as he sold his wares. At first, the line between this amateurish, navel-gazing writing and the labyrinthine, puzzles-within-puzzles writing of Fallows is clear. But as the scholars began to dig deeper, they saw that Rutherford's encyclopedia was itself a kind of puzzle."

"How do you mean?" Michael Tanner asked.

"I mean Rutherford seemed to be playing a game. A game with himself, maybe—but then again maybe not. Look at this."

Aldiss held another sheet up, this one much like the first. The paper looked so old and used that Alex felt as if she might be able to smell the must wafting off of it.

"This is one of the last entries. *A, Albridge.* A tiny description of a town follows that heading. Albridge, Iowa—population two thousand. A nowhere town not far from where Rutherford lived and worked. But what's unusual is when you look at a map of Iowa—"

"It doesn't exist."

Keller again. Alex saw how quick he was, how he beat everyone in class to the answer. Whereas her mind, so tediously slow, moved much more carefully. Deliberately. She found herself looking at Keller again, glancing over and willing him to catch her eye.

"Albridge, Iowa, is indeed fictitious," said Aldiss. "It was not on any maps at the time and still isn't. In his 'encyclopedia entry,' Rutherford claims he was there. That he sold encyclopedias to a few residents. That he ate in a small diner near the town square. But none of that was real. And so, armed with this information, we must ask a greater question."

For a moment the class remained silent, hyperaware. They hung on Aldiss's voice. He was moving them toward something now, drawing closer to a connection between Charles Rutherford, the dead man whose image had appeared on the books, and Fallows himself. The only sound in the lecture hall was the electronic hum and crackle of the television.

"Why?" Alex asked.

Aldiss looked at her with knowing eyes. Eyes that seemed to pick up everything in their path, to notice everything. Eyes that had once belonged to a young, clearly handsome man. But now they looked as if they *contained* too much, like when she refilled her mother's sugar bowl at home and some of the granules poured out on the table. That was it, Alex thought: there was some of the professor pouring out, overflowing through the screen itself.

"That's right, Ms. Shipley," he said now. "The question is 'Why?' Why would Charles Rutherford make up the small town of Albridge, Iowa? Why would he claim he'd spent his days there? The only solution is that Rutherford was playing a trick on someone. That his encyclopedia wasn't an encyclopedia at all but rather a—"

"A novel," said Sally Mitchell in her too soft, too sweet voice.

Aldiss didn't respond; he only grinned, pleased that these nine (*No,* Alex reminded herself, *we are eight now*) special students were moving so fast.

"But there are always problems with the Rutherford–is–Paul Fallows theory," Aldiss said. "The obvious one being that the man was dead when the second book appeared, which blew the whole thing out of the water. The photograph on the book jackets—it meant nothing, the scholars claimed. It had been a joke. Another play by Fallows in the game."

"Did anyone at least go to Iowa and check it out?" Lewis Prine asked.

Aldiss nodded. "The scholars got to the Rutherford widow, of course. When the second and final novel, *The Golden Silence,* appeared, we—they had to know. And so yes, they flocked to Iowa. Sometimes they would just sit outside the house where Rutherford had once lived."

"Jesus," Melissa Lee muttered.

"Some of them gathered the courage to speak to his widow. At first she was polite, but then she saw how obsessed they were. To know. To put the mystery to rest. And she became angry. She and Charles Rutherford had a son, a young boy who was so ill that he had to be institutionalized for a time, and she had to think of his safety. This Fallows character, this crazy writer—he was not her husband. He could not be. She scolded them, drove them off any way she knew how, called the local police on them. Soon they drifted away and left the poor woman and her boy alone."

The class thought about this. Frank Marsden, his lashes still thick with mascara from rehearsals for *Richard III*, asked, "So Rutherford, your 'man in the dark coat'—there is no chance that he is really Paul Fallows?"

Aldiss said nothing at first. The students sat silently, waiting, the red-eyed camera mounted in the corner of the room recording everything. "I am not ready to answer that question," Aldiss said at last. "There are indeed connections between the two men. Connections that it has taken me twelve years to uncover. It is so very difficult to work with the resources this prison can offer, but I believe I am finally close to the answer. Very close. I have discovered things about Fallows that I never knew when I was outside these walls."

With that Aldiss paused, and everyone in the class sat forward.

"With the help of a few of my trusted colleagues," the professor went on, "including my old friend Dr. Stanley Fisk, professor emeritus at Jasper, I have uncovered new information. Information that no Fallows scholar has seen."

"What kind of information?" Alex asked breathlessly.

"Documents, mostly. But also clues hidden inside the two novels. Clues that you, students, will be following as this class goes forward. But these clues will not be given to you. You must earn them. This is a classroom of higher learning, after all, and in any good class the strong rise to the top. I will give you what I have discovered, but only if you earn your keep."

"Where do we start?" asked Michael Tanner.

"You have already begun. By solving the first riddle you are on your way to uncovering the writer's true identity. But know this: I am not

Paul Fallows, as some of the more sensationalist literary critics have come to believe." Again the professor laughed and the class followed suit, but theirs was stilted laughter—they had done the math, of course. It was definitely possible. "Also know that you will go nowhere without the knowledge of who Charles Rutherford was, and of the shining city he came from. The trail begins with him, and that is where we will continue on our journey."

They spoke then about *The Coil*. The opening scenes in Manhattan, circa 1900. The voyage of the woman named Ann Marie as she moves from Iowa and learns her purpose in the world. The novel was one of manners: Ann Marie comes to discover that the culture even of the greatest city in the world is not accommodating of an educated, self-assured woman. Everyone in the classroom had seen this kind of novel a hundred times before—but Paul Fallows put his own stamp on it. This book was different. There was something intense about Ann Marie's rise, something almost *destined*. A covert, sustained violence thrummed just beneath the surface of the book. At one point in their assigned fifty pages Ann Marie brings the novel's antagonist—a ghost-pale, misogynistic lawyer named Conning—into the Chelsea brownstone where she lives with an elderly uncle. After trapping the man on the second floor of the cluttered, multiroomed house, she retires to the parlor to sip Twinings with her uncle.

Aldiss kept them riveted the entire time. He led them deep into the novel, weaving in and out of the obvious symbolism and the more indirect passages, talking about the book as if it were a breathing thing. He read pages aloud, bringing his voice up an octave to impersonate Ann Marie in such an exacting way that each of them would hear his voice when they read the book in their dorms that night.

At the end of his lecture he was out of breath, sweat glistening on his brow. Alex watched the man, amazed at how much meaning he had been able to wring from the text.

"So," the professor said, glancing at the egg timer he kept on his table. There were only a few minutes left. "For next week, the following fifty pages of *The Coil* and any more on Charles Rutherford you can find. I would suggest you begin by taking a look at his hometown: Hamlet,

Iowa. Such an interesting place. And of course there are so many references to Iowa in Fallows as well. Now, are there any questions for me?"

Alex watched Aldiss. She knew her time was running out, and he had given her precious little to go on. He'd told her nothing about what to do next, where to turn. If she was going to follow the message inside the book, then she needed help from him. But how? What questions to ask, and how to phrase those questions without the rest of the class—*Do not tell a soul you have seen this*—catching on?

Ninety seconds left. Ninety seconds until the feed was cut.

"No questions, then?"

Sixty seconds. She imagined Aldiss, his long walk back to his cell, those two faceless guards leading him, the bars closing him in. The professor's life, shadows and words and the agonizing screams of other caged and damaged men. His excitement about finding something, *uncovering new information,* and all it had led to was this. A silent lecture hall, a scared girl. Alex imagined his disappointment in her, his anger.

Richard Aldiss is innocent.

Thirty seconds.

Go on, Alex. Say something.

Twenty seconds, and—

"What's in Hamlet?"

Aldiss looked at her. The professor's gaze changed, turned more serious. More intense. It was as if information was being passed only to her. As if she and the professor had entered into a conversation apart from the other students. She had the sensation that the lecture hall had fallen away and she was staring at the television screen in an empty, electric-blue room.

"I suggest asking my friend Dean Stanley Fisk," Aldiss said. "He can tell you a lot about Hamlet."

And with that the feed was cut and the professor faded out once again.

After class she walked home through the driving snow. In the distance, over the bowl of the west campus, the ice-heavy trees seethed in the dark. The campus was dead at this hour. No traffic crawled up Rose Avenue, no other students walked across the frozen quads.

Alex walked ahead of her classmates, rushing across Harper's Knoll, the geographic center of campus, then down the hill at the administrative building called the Tower where the dorms sprayed out in a web of low-slung architecture. You could hear the freshmen boys whooping from here, could see smoke pouring out of the chimneys at the Greek houses. *This is where I want to be,* she found herself thinking when she made this walk across campus every evening. *This is what I want to do with my life, to be a part of this. To teach literature at a place just like this.*

"Do you trust him?"

She turned. It was her neighbor, Keller. He wore a down coat with a rabbit-fur hood, a patch on the chest that read JASPER COLLEGE FOOT-BALL. He walked deliberately, his weight breaking through the snow, the crunch of his steps echoing off the Tower, which was now to their right.

"Aldiss?" Alex asked.

"Mmm."

"Do you?"

He said nothing.

"He doesn't look like a murderer," she said.

"Murderers have a look?"

Alex smiled. "Manson did. Dahmer. Crazy eyes. Aldiss isn't crazy."

"Crazy like a fox, maybe," he said. "Look."

Keller showed her something. Caught in a security light, flattened by his palm so the wind wouldn't yank it away, it was a piece of notebook paper. Tick marks, thirty or forty of them, tumbled out toward the right margin.

"What's this?" she asked.

"The number of times he's lied."

She looked up from the page. "And you know this how?"

"It comes from football. You block a guy, he shows you with his eyes what he's going to do. This is what being an offensive lineman is about: going in the direction that the other guy goes. It's a series of reading lies. Over and over and over again I do these little polygraph tests."

"So what, you have blood pressure cuffs on Aldiss? The security in Rock Mountain must be lax, Keller."

His turn to smile. "I'm serious. There are lots of things this guy does.

In football you get good at knowing where to move before the play even happens: your man will look down, look off. He'll say something to you across the line of scrimmage and his voice will break. These little . . . tells, you know."

"And Professor Aldiss. He has tells."

"A *lot* of them, just tonight."

"What does it mean?"

"It means he knows who Fallows is," Keller said. "He just can't get to him. We're like his legs. His legs and eyes. But to just give us the guy's identity—that would be cheating. So Aldiss is leading us on, and we're falling into it. That's what these 'riddles' are about. Little pieces of the puzzle, one by one, until we know who really wrote those books. But there's something else."

Alex looked at him. "What?"

"I don't know." The jock shook his head, snowflakes wetting his cheeks. "I haven't figured that out yet, but I'm working on it."

Alex glanced off. Philbrick Hall was just ahead, the largest girl's dorm at the college. She saw the silhouette of a girl on the top floor, stretched in a window, reading. She heard the squeal of someone's telephone, and she thought of her sick father. Wondered when that call would come.

"Maybe you're right," she told Keller. "Maybe Aldiss is lying. Maybe he does know exactly who Fallows is and he's playing this game with us. But I'm going to give him the benefit of the doubt."

"And why is that?"

"Because," she said, "I like playing games." *And I like to win.*

Alex

Present Day

9

One by one, the students from the night class began to arrive.

Alex was forcing herself to eat a bowl of soup that the dean's nurse, Matthew Owen, had prepared for her when she heard a familiar voice calling from the outer room. She got up and pushed through the swinging kitchen door. More stilted progress and decay here in the great room. And standing in the middle of it all, dust twisting down around her, was Melissa Lee.

The woman had transformed from the sharp-tongued Goth girl she'd been during the night class. Now she was sensibly dressed with straight, black hair pulled away from her angular face; the only indication of the person she had been at Jasper was one diamond stud in her nose. She wore chunky, square-framed glasses and carried a high-end duffel beneath her arm. *My God,* Alex thought, *she's a soccer mom now.*

"I hoped it wouldn't be true," Melissa said, and even her voice was different. Flat, almost affectless. A Stepford wife. "But then I saw the reporters over on the east campus on the drive in. My heart broke."

"Mine too."

She paused, something flitting in her dark eyes. Something mean and hateful. Here was the Melissa Lee from the night class. Then the look was gone and the suburban mother of three returned.

"Oh, Alex."

They did not embrace. They had not been close during their time in the class.

"A student," Melissa said. "Someone Michael had failed in one of his lit classes. That has to be what this is."

Alex said, "Maybe."

"Aldiss isn't convinced."

Alex blinked. Could this woman know of her assignment, of her visit with the professor that morning? If she did know, the others would as well.

"Dr. Aldiss knows very little," Alex said. Might as well take the upper hand while she could get it.

"And the police? What do they believe?"

"I have a meeting with the lead detective of the investigation in an hour, and I'm afraid that I won't have anything to report to him."

"Perhaps you could tell him about Aldiss and Daniel Hayden."

Alex took a sharp breath. "What about them?"

Melissa shook her head, a pitiable gesture: *There's so much you don't know about the rest of us, Alex Shipley.* "They had been corresponding with each other. This was not long before Daniel died."

"Corresponding how?"

"Letters, puzzles—Aldiss kept in touch with Daniel. He wanted something from him. It was fucking weird, and I told Daniel that the last time we spoke."

"Daniel was a former student," Alex said, realizing how weak it sounded. How desperate. "It would have been normal for the professor to contact him."

Melissa smiled. "How many times have you spoken with Aldiss since Daniel . . . since he killed himself?"

"Not since the memorial."

"Exactly." The woman put her arms around herself, drew in a great breath that made her body tremble. "God, Alex, how I would like to ask that man what he knows. How I would like to talk to him about Daniel's death to see if he might—"

"Should I show you up to your room, ma'am?"

Alex turned and saw Matthew Owen standing just outside the foyer. She registered Melissa's look when she saw the nurse, the spark in her eyes. Then Melissa composed herself and looked again at Alex.

"Strange, isn't it?" she said.

"What's that?" Alex asked.

"For the dean to invite us all to stay here. It's like . . . I don't know. I wasn't going to accept the invitation at first. But it is Dean Fisk, and no one wants to stay alone when something like this has happened. I don't care how brave you are."

"He's a lonely man," said Alex. "His health is failing him. I think he knows he doesn't have much time left, and he wanted to put the class that had made him proudest back together one more time so that we could all grieve. That's all."

"Can I see him?"

Alex glared at her old nemesis, a thought tumbling through her mind: *You will not find the manuscript. Not before I do.*

"Stanley is resting now," the nurse said from the stairs. "He will announce himself when everyone arrives."

Melissa nodded, disappointment in her eyes. "Alex, we'll chat more when I put my things away?"

"Of course."

She turned and followed Matthew briskly up the stairs, shouldering her giant duffel as if it were filled with air. She was stronger than she looked. As Alex watched her go, she wondered, *Could a woman have murdered Michael Tanner?*

The second student arrived just minutes later. He'd brought a guest with him.

Frank Marsden was a character actor. Alex had seen him on episodes of *CSI* and *NCIS* and in bit parts in movies, recognized him from time to time as a villain's henchman or, once, as the misunderstood cop who roughed up suspects in the interrogation room. He was thick and blond and ice-eyed, and he swept Alex into a one-armed embrace when she let him in the mansion. The woman at his side eyed her suspiciously, and Alex pulled away.

"My God, what's happening to us all, Alex?" he asked, his breath hot. *He's drunk,* Alex realized.

"I wish I knew, Frank."

"This is Lucy Wiggins," he said, motioning toward his guest. The woman stepped forward and offered her hand, and Alex shook. A cold grip, stiff and awkward. Lucy Wiggins—Alex recognized the name from some magazine or other, remembered one of her students going on about how gorgeous the actress was. Here, in this dark and musty mansion, the woman looked downright nondescript. She wore a black coat and a navy scarf and sunglasses pushed up into her professionally managed hair. It was probably the most Plain Jane she'd been in years. Alex watched as Lucy looked around the old house and trembled with the thought that she was going to have to stay the night in this god-awful place.

Frank stepped into the great room and scanned the bookshelf in the corner. "I just talked to Michael not long ago," he said, his back to Alex.

Alex's pulse quickened. "And what did he say?"

"He seemed fine. He just wanted to catch up. Said it was too bad we hadn't got together since Hayden. All that unholy mess. Said he thought about us sometimes. About how everybody said we hated each other when we took the night class." Marsden stopped, focused on Alex as if he wanted this next piece of information to sink in. "I never had any animosity toward Michael, Alex. You have to believe that. The others invented this thing between us. That we were jealous of each other. I love—loved Michael. I never wished anything bad on him, no matter what any of the others tell you." Then his gaze drifted off again, swept across the floor. "I was shooting a film in Canada when he called, you know, and didn't have much time. But now—now I wish . . ."

She watched his bloodshot eyes drop, a hand come up to his brow. Lucy went to him and put her arm around him. *They haven't been together long,* Alex thought. *They just met.* "Baby," Frank said to her. "Baby, baby, baby. You don't understand the history here. You don't understand what I went through with these people."

Alex waited. Then Frank turned around and smiled weakly.

"Our room," he said.

"Upstairs. Melissa's already gone up."

Frank made a face and Alex said nothing. The gray afternoon clouds shifted outside, and sunlight poured in on him for the first time. She saw how drunk he really was now. Lucy practically held him upright.

"We'll go on up," he said. "Get some rest before we start planning the memorial service."

"Of course."

They walked then, arm in arm, out of the foyer. When he got to the foot of the stairs, Frank hesitated and turned back toward Alex. He'd changed suddenly, morphed into the actor he was. A fake face, a put-on grin—none of it was the truth.

"Alex?" he said.

"Yes, Frank."

"Why are we all here together? Is it so you can watch us?"

Alex froze. She looked at Lucy again, and the woman too seemed to be waiting on an answer, some kind of explanation for being brought here.

Alex opened her mouth to speak but Frank interrupted her. He began to laugh—riotous, bellowing laughter. And then he ascended the steps, one by one, until his laughter was nothing but an echo.

After Frank and Lucy were gone, Matthew Owen came downstairs and entered the kitchen. Alex was there drinking her tepid soup, waiting for the rest to arrive. She turned and watched the nurse move to a bank of cabinets and remove a prescription pill bottle. He hadn't seen her there, and because she didn't want to frighten him she gently coughed. Owen quickly palmed the pills and turned around, his free hand to his heart.

"You scared the shit out of me," he said.

"Sorry."

His eyes held on her for a moment, then he swiped his hand over his mouth and swallowed the pills. She watched his jaw work.

"This must be an intrusion," she said. "For us all to be back here."

"Not at all," the nurse said. "Stanley's wanted to have guests over for a long time. It's just that we never thought it would be under these circumstances."

"How long have you been employed by the dean?"

The man shook his head. "Employed by him? Hardly. Stanley doesn't want me here. He just wants it to be over with. I go upstairs every day and expect to find him . . . Anyway, he's talked about it many times, even asked me to do it for him." Owen's eyes drifted away, and Alex glanced at the cabinet behind his back. "I've been employed by the college for seven years now—I was here when you all . . . when Daniel Hayden died." Alex vaguely remembered Owen, a floating presence through the rooms. She hardly remembered anything about that weekend. "I just wasn't as necessary back then. I took this job after leaving a hospital in Burlington. Too much political bullshit. Here it's just me and this old house."

"And Dean Fisk."

"Yes, and him," Owen said flatly. "Sometimes I hear him at night in the hallways, his wheelchair sliding down the floors. That's the only time he'll come out of his study. He doesn't want anyone to look at him, so he hides himself. He says it's his age, his face—they tell me he was always a vain man. But I don't believe it."

"What is it, then?"

"I think he gets off on hiding. My bedroom is on the fourth floor. Sometimes he'll call for me and I'll go room to room, looking. Searching. It's like a game to Stanley. I get tired of it, but at least I've learned every inch of this godforsaken house. And what could I say to him? He's a legend around here and I'm nobody." Owen's eyes fell away, down to the chipped and scratched tile. "That's why the place is so dark. Even when I bathe him he scolds me for looking at him."

"Do you enjoy the work?" she asked.

"Enjoy," the man scoffed bitterly, as if the word itself had a texture, a flavor. "Mostly I spend my days walking up and down the halls. It's good exercise if you keep moving. And of course I read."

"What do you read?"

"Mostly the things Stanley recommends for me. The Russians. Early British literature. Fallows, of course."

"Fallows," she repeated. "What do you think of him?"

"I hate him," Owen said, his voice dropping a notch, as if he feared Dean Fisk might hear him. "I can't understand all the fuss you people make for him."

"Fallows is an acquired taste."

The nurse laughed sharply. "That must be it," he said. "Because otherwise Stanley has wasted most of his life on the ravings of a lunatic."

With that there was a sharp clack on the door outside. Someone else had arrived.

"Ah, our own celebrity—Alex Shipley."

Christian Kane stepped through the door and took her by the elbow. He kissed her on both cheeks and then leaned back to regard her, nodding as if she had passed a test. He carried nothing but a yellow umbrella and a paperback book. He smelled of the kind of cologne Peter used and wore a corduroy jacket with a fray on the elbow. He had a three-day beard that she didn't recognize from the last photograph she had seen of him in *Poets & Writers*. The paperback was one of his own.

The writer moved into the great room now and looked around, curling his mouth at the state of the place. Then he looked at Alex and held out the book. "Page 107," he said.

Tentatively, she took the book and opened it to the page. It had been dog-eared, and one paragraph in the middle had been underlined by an uneasy hand.

> . . . *when Barker came into the library he saw what had happened there. The professor's body was on the floor, broken and discarded like a lump of rags, and for a moment Barker could not tell what he was looking at. Then it dawned on him, the horrible truth: the man had been murdered and covered with books. A pile of volumes, their heaviness sighing now against the man's dead flesh, the pages rustling as if a legion of mites had crawled inside the texts to feast. Even over the professor's eyes there was a book, the image of the cover across his face as if it were a mask. Barker stepped forward.*

"Why are you showing this to me, Christian?"

The man regarded her. Of the students she had seen so far, Christian had changed the least. He was still the suave, thin kid he had been as a student at Jasper. Now, fifteen years later, he looked less like a bestselling novelist and more like a man playing the part in one of his own stories. "Isn't it obvious, Alex?" he said.

"I'm afraid it isn't."

He sighed, slapping the paperback closed. *Barker at Night*—the fourth book of the series, written five years ago, was her least favorite.

"Aldiss never liked me," Kane said now, leaning over her. He was thin and his graying hair was tousled, his appearance almost boyish. He'd caught fire after his first novel, *Barker at Work,* appeared just two years after their graduation from Jasper. Now, after twelve novels and two Hollywood adaptations—one of them starring, in a bit role, their old friend Frank Marsden—his career had begun to wind down. His most recent novels had been published to little fanfare in crude paperback editions, and Alex thought she detected something of a fall even in the way the man dressed. Even in his slick green eyes, which had dimmed a bit since she had seen him last.

"What do you mean, Christian?"

"The professor was always bitter toward me."

"That's just the way he is."

"No," the man said sharply. "No, Alex. He was worse toward me. You and Keller and the rest of them—you were his pets. His projects. I was just a nuisance. Even Daniel got more respect in that classroom."

"I saw him this morning," she said. "He doesn't believe you had anything to do with this." *That's not quite true, is it?* she thought, flushing with shame over the lie.

Christian laughed. His teeth were yellowed, nicotine-stained, and she made a mental note to bum a cigarette later; she had run out on her short drive from Aldiss's house. "I live twenty minutes from campus," he said. "I see Aldiss sometimes. Out. He doesn't speak. He treats me as if I'm this . . . ghost. And of course with my history with Michael—"

"What do you mean? What history?"

He looked at her strangely. *Didn't you know?* the look said.

"We'd been playing the game again," Christian told her.

She gasped.

"Don't look at me like that, Alex. It was nothing. It was just a way to pass the time. Michael—he called me about it a couple of years ago. We got to talking about things. Books, my work and his, the way the college is changing. And of course Daniel. Then he asked me if I would come in and speak to one of his composition classes. Sure, I said. Afterward we went out for drinks, and he told me."

"Told you what?"

The man hesitated, realizing that he had gone too far now. He said, "That he went down to Burlington every weekend. To the State U, and sometimes even to Dumant. They were still playing down there."

"And you went with him."

"Of course I went." Christian pulled the back of his hand across his mouth. "The Procedure is still so intoxicating, Alex. So addictive. We both fell into it like old pros, even though it had been years since the night class. I started reading Fallows again, practicing. It wasn't like I was some kind of criminal. But if you put it all together, if you add up the evidence against me, then it's easy to see how Aldiss would make the leap that I had something to do with Michael being murdered." He paused then, stepped forward into her space. For the first time, Alex's heart began to thump. *One of them is responsible. One of them . . .*

"Don't listen to him, Alex," Christian said softly, carefully. "I beg of you. Whatever Aldiss told you this morning—"

"He told me nothing, Christian. We spoke as old friends, that's all."

"—whatever the professor insinuated about us, you must not believe him. You can't."

He remained in her space for another few seconds. It felt like a lifetime. Finally he pulled away and smiled wanly. He looked up at the fissured ceiling, at the streaked windows and the crimson curtains that hung heavy with dust. "My God," he said. "It's like I've walked right into a trap."

When Christian had gone upstairs to his room, Alex answered another knock on the door. Standing there was the first man she had ever loved.

He wore a bright orange rain slicker and his eyes were rimmed with grief. He was as large as she remembered him, a brute of a man who towered over her. Yet it was his eyes that had always drawn her to him: kind, somber eyes that were the gray of stone, or the page of an old book.

"Keller," she said, and the man stepped forward and took her in his arms.

Once inside, they stood together in the foyer and said nothing, which was fine with Alex.

"How's Sally?" Jacob Keller asked.

"In terrible shape. As you would expect."

They stood apart now, Alex leaning against the bookshelves and Keller with his hands in his pockets, gazing at her. She had seen him across the room at Daniel's funeral, but had only smiled at him. They'd kept their distance for many reasons, hers and his. *Married,* Melissa Lee had told her. *Coaches football and teaches English at a high school about forty miles south of Jasper. You sound like you're still interested, Alex . . .*

Thinking of the poet-in-residence she'd been seeing at the time, she had looked away.

"Brutal," Keller said now.

"Excuse me?"

"That's what the news said this morning. The Michael Tanner murder was *brutal.* They're talking about Dumant University again, Alex. They're talking about our night class. They're rehashing all that old stuff."

That old stuff—it was like a wound being scraped raw. Aldiss had warned her that this would happen.

"A copycat," she said quickly. "That's all this is. Someone who's read about the Dumant murders, someone who thinks he can get away with anything—"

"It's Aldiss."

Alex's mouth dropped open. "Aldiss? You can't believe he had anything to do with this, Keller."

"Of course I do," he said. "And so should you."

"I spoke to him this morning. I saw how he talked about Michael. I don't think he—"

"Still protecting him, I see."

Anger flashed behind her eyes. "I'm not protecting anyone," she said. "I just know that he was innocent of the Dumant murders. Cleared. You were in Iowa with me, Keller. We finished the night class together. You know everything I know."

"I know how devious Aldiss is, how deceptive he can be."

Her eyes fell to the balls of dust that traced the floor. "He didn't have anything to do with Michael's murder," she said again, softer this time.

Keller started to say something, then stopped himself. "Let's not do this, Alex. It's been four years since I've seen you. I want to talk to you again. Get to know you again. It's horrible what happened to Michael, but we've finally got our chance to start over."

The apprehension was still there, the clawing thought that Keller was one of the very people Aldiss had instructed her to watch. He knew as much as any of the rest of them about the Dumant murders, and for this reason she would have to observe him just as impartially as she would the others.

"Let me ask you something," he said.

"Anything."

"Do you read anymore?"

She opened her mouth, faltered. What kind of question was that for a lit professor?

"Of course you do," he said. "I read about you in the alumni news-letter. I know what you do for a living. I mean I'm not a stalker or anything"—Keller laughed—"but I know, okay?" He stopped, glanced off toward the window. "I couldn't do what you do. I coach varsity football at a nowhere high school, and I don't read anything. Even the books my students read I just scan, or I go off memory from classes I took at Jasper."

Puzzled, Alex waited for him to go on.

"I'm afraid if I read something I'll go back to Fallows, and I'll fall into it again. Poof—right there, right back into the labyrinth. I'll end up just like Daniel ended up."

He trailed off, and the room burned with silence. Then he looked at her again, tried to erase what he had just said with a shake of his head.

"Right now," he said, "I would like to rest a bit. I couldn't sleep at all last night. I just kept thinking about Michael and Sally and the helplessness of it all."

"Me too."

Keller smiled, but cautiously.

"Your room's upstairs," she said. "Melissa, Christian, Frank—oh, and his friend." Alex raised her eyebrows toward the second floor. "They're all up there now. I've got somewhere to be in a few minutes, but I can show you."

She led him to the stairs, and as he went up in front of her she noticed something odd. Something that spiked through her with a girlish shame.

Keller was not wearing a ring.

The last student was Lewis Prine. He was the warden of an asylum for the criminally insane in upstate Vermont and the man who had told her about the manuscript Stanley Fisk was said to be hiding in this very house. *It's there, Alex,* he'd told her again just months ago. *The third Fallows. It's somewhere in that mansion.*

Prine never showed.

10

The lead detective was named Bradley Black, and he seemed to know that she was hiding something. They met that afternoon in a fourth-floor office of the Tower with the dean who had called her to Vermont the night before. Alex could meet neither man's gaze.

"Tell us," said the detective now, his voice as slow and mellifluous as his eyes, "what Dr. Richard Aldiss knows."

"It's going to take time," she said. All the way across campus from the Fisk mansion, through the glassy, postmorning sun, she had thought, *He didn't do this. He couldn't have.* Now, sitting in Jasper College's ivy-choked administrative building with these two strange, officious men, Alex recounted the conversation. "The professor treats everything as if it's a puzzle. If he knows who murdered Michael Tanner, he will not be quick with his knowledge. You have to earn what you get from him."

"Goddamn it," spat Dean Anthony Rice. He looked at the detective. "You people are going to have to get a search warrant, go in there and—"

"No," Alex said. "That's not the way to deal with him. You're going to have to let me do this. If Aldiss knows anything, I will get it. He trusts me."

"Let's get real here, Dr. Shipley. Aldiss is toying with you. This is what he does. He got off too easy the last time. He might not have killed those two students at Dumant—"

"He didn't."

"—but he still got off way too damn easy. A lot of people at this college—people who know Aldiss very well—believe there is blood on his hands." The dean paused, and Alex knew what was coming. "And, by extension, yours."

She ignored it. "If he knows anything, then I will have it soon."

"We may not have that much time."

She bit her tongue. *No shit, Sherlock.*

"How sure are you that he is copycatting the Dumant murders?" she asked.

Black's eyes slid to Rice, and the dean nodded. Then photographs appeared on the walnut desk, the topmost crevassed and browning and the others slick and warm and fresh. Alex spread them with her fingertips. She sucked in her breath.

They were crime scene photos. She had seen the older ones before, during the night class. Stark, hectic images of two empty apartments. Someone had written the date in chalk and placed a block in the bottom left-hand corner: *January 1982*. Blood slashed up the walls in a pattern that resembled the burning butterfly of the famous Rorschach inkblot test. There were two sets of photos for the two victims, both grad students in literature. Both had been murdered, like Michael Tanner, in their home libraries. She did not—could not—dwell on these pictures.

Her eyes moved to the newer shots, taken just the morning before. They were interiors of Michael Tanner's house across campus. These were digital photos, brilliant and clean, the Rorschach pattern on the wall almost identical to the others, except here it was a dark, electric crimson. Again there were books on the floor, spread in what appeared to be the same pattern as the others. A swimming pool of books piled in the room, carefully placed and evenly spread. *They could be the same fucking room,* Alex thought. *The same victim.*

But no, she remembered. The other two were students, while Michael was—

A student as well, once upon a time. A student in the night class.

"Identical MO," Black was saying, his voice slicing into her reverie. "Murder them in their homes and cover the bodies with books. Same type of victim aside from their gender. Same pattern of education, even the same program of study: literature, specifically modern lit. Superimpose the Tanner library on photographs of the apartments from Dumant and the similarities are striking. Beyond striking."

Black paused, appraising her again in his careful way. "How well did you know Professor Tanner?" he asked. He made a show of flipping through his notes, the dry flick of the Gregg notebook the only sound in the room.

"Pretty well. Michael and I got together often at academic conferences. I always thought he was one of the most brilliant men in the comparative literature field, and that's including any of my colleagues at Harvard."

"Did he ever speak to you about Richard Aldiss? Did he show any signs that he may have been holding on to the class? In an unhealthy way, I mean."

"No. Never."

"What about e-mails? Correspondence about the class, about Aldiss or the Dumant murders."

Alex shook her head. "We all wanted to forget, Detective. The night class . . . it changed us. Some of us in profound ways. It wasn't something we wanted to dwell on." Her mind flashed to her old friend Daniel Hayden and what happened to him, and then she shook it free. "It happened, and there's no taking it back—but nobody wants to relive it."

She watched something pass over Black, something like the answer to a question that had not been asked. Alex knew it was that one phrase, the damning word right in the middle of it, ticking like a bomb: *changed*. She thought again of her meeting with Aldiss that morning.

"I want to see the library," she said.

"Impossible," said Rice.

"You're going to bring me back to Jasper to be your messenger, Dean Rice, and you're not going to tell me all you know? That's called tilting the playing field."

"It's called due process. Tell us more about Aldiss."

"The professor believes Sally Tanner is innocent." A lie, but it was worth a chance. Fuck them if they wouldn't share. A look passed between the two men.

"Has he spoken with either Tanner recently?"

"Your turn," she said.

Black sighed and said, "You're a tough one, Dr. Shipley."

She smiled.

"This killer," Black continued, "he studied the murders at Dumant. I mean studied them intensely. Learned them. He was not just tipping his hat to those crimes, he was *re-creating them*. Everything, down to the flares on the Rorschach bloodstain and the books and the time of Michael Tanner's death—everything was the same."

Re-creating them, Alex thought. The phrase was like a flash, a pinpoint of hot light. She blinked twice, hard, trying to sweep it away.

"Aldiss knows more than he's saying," Rice finally broke in. The dean sat forward, steepling his chin in his fat fingers. He was constant movement, the perfect antithesis to the still, methodical Black. "And he knows we know. We won't go on with this dance too much longer, Dr. Shipley. Tell him that. Tell him that if he has been in correspondence with someone who is interested in the Dumant murders, if he has been a *mentor* in any way with someone, then he will be dealt with. Deliver that message to him, will you?"

"Richard Aldiss doesn't take kindly to *messages* from interim deans," she said.

Rice reddened, looked off toward the office's only window. Wind rattled the pane. For a moment the three of them sat silently.

Then Black said, "Thirty-seven hours have passed now. That's a world in terms of a murder investigation. If you can't get Aldiss to open up, then we will."

"I'll go back to him later this evening."

"We will be looking forward to your report," Black said, standing. "And in the meantime, Dr. Shipley, it's nice of you to keep Dean Fisk company. You and the others."

His gaze held on her.

The detective stood and walked her to the door, and in the corridor he stopped. "You will let us know if you find out anything of interest during your stay in the mansion."

"Of course," she said, and she began to walk away.

He caught her by the arm.

"They're saying things about Aldiss."

She turned to face him. "Who, Detective?"

"The people at Jasper. Teachers, students. They say he's changed. He isn't the person he was when they brought him in to teach that class."

"Is that right?"

Black shook his head. "All I'm saying is be careful. You might think you know Aldiss, you might think all you did back in '94 was the right thing to do. But this guy . . . I don't trust him, Dr. Shipley. You never know what kinds of tricks he has up his sleeve."

"I just want to find out who killed my friend," she said hotly. "If Aldiss can help me with that—and I think he can—then we have to use him. He is our best resource right now, and tonight I intend to go back and get some answers."

"And if he's not who you think he is?" Black asked.

"Then I don't deserve anything I got for solving the night class riddle," she said, turning away from him and beginning her walk down the cold hallway. "My whole life is a sham."

The Class

1994

11

Dean Stanley Fisk lived in a peeling old Victorian that sat on a hill high above campus. Fisk lived there alone now, his wife of forty years having passed away the previous semester. Rarely did you see the old emeritus out. Ribbon-cutting ceremonies, black-tie charity events—these were the things he was good for now. Mostly he stayed to himself, surveying the grounds of the Dean's House and keeping watch over the college he once ruled.

Now Alex knocked on the front door and heard the professor inside. The muted shuffling of footsteps was followed by a soft, lilting voice: "Coming."

The door was flung open and a man stood in the threshold, blinking out the sunlight. At eighty years old, Stanley Fisk was a slumped man with energetic blue eyes. He wore a Jasper sweatshirt and a bathrobe that hung limply across his boyish shoulders. He had always been known around campus as an eccentric; Alex noticed a smudge of what seemed to be mascara slashing away from his right eye and thought, *This is the man whom Richard Aldiss's fate is resting on? Holy crap.*

Fisk pushed his reading glasses up into his cotton-white hair and said, "Can I help you?"

"Dean Fisk, my name is Alex Shipley. I'm so sorry to bother you this early, but—"

"Early? Dear Lord, I've been up since dawn. What can I do for you?"

"I wanted—I needed to talk with you about something important."

The old man cocked his head to the side. "Go on."

"It's about Richard Aldiss. About the class he's teaching this semester. He said something last week, and I believe he . . . I think he might have been leading me to you."

At first there was no movement from the old man, no tic of recognition. Fisk merely stood in the doorway and looked past her, where the Jasper architecture rose up from the crescent of campus and blended with the tree line fifty yards away.

Then, his voice slow and even, he said, "You found our book."

Alex exhaled. "That's right."

A smile broke across his face. The age lines seemed to disintegrate and, suddenly, Alex found herself looking at a much younger man.

"Well, come inside in that case," he said, moving to the side so that she could step past him. "We have much to discuss."

The living room was an homage to the old man's existence. A quilt had been thrown over the sofa, dog-eared books were stacked on the parquet floor, a withered apple tipped on its side on an end table. Clearly he spent his days here. The rest of the house was probably preserved in dust.

"We didn't know if anyone would ever find it," Fisk said as she sat down across from him. "We worried that the clue was going to be too obscure, or somebody else would check out the book. Someone not even enrolled in your class. I went back, you see. Checked the records and everything. No one had taken that book out for more than five years. Five years it had remained in the stacks. And so we decided to go for it, plant the message there and see what happened. If there was a stir, we could just deny our involvement and try again some other way."

"The two mysteries," Alex said. "Fallows and Aldiss. The book says they're one and the same."

"That's right. But that is for another time. I'm not sure what Richard has planned for his class. I wouldn't want to spoil anything." He laughed, a cold rasp that emanated from deep in his chest.

Then he looked at her, his eyes pinched. She felt as if she was being evaluated.

"Do you understand the consequences of the message?" he asked. "Do you comprehend the weight of this situation, Ms. Shipley?"

"I think . . . I believe I do, yes."

"You should. Truly, you should. You are going to help clear Richard's name from those two awful crimes at Dumant University and get him out of that place. And *that* . . ." Fisk held her eyes. "That will be a glorious day."

"But what if he actually did it? What if Professor Aldiss really did kill those two students?"

"You're still skeptical."

"He confessed," she said. "Right there in that classroom last week. He confessed to everything."

"Another ruse," Fisk said. "Richard is a unique man. At first he was angry, furious that they would pin these horrible crimes on him. Everyone was convinced that he was guilty. The Fallows over the eyes, the relationship he had with the victims—it was too perfect. Richard became despondent. For years he sat in Rock Mountain, and his silence, his writing on so many matters not related to Dumant, convinced them that he was guilty and the verdict was correct. Now, now that he's found this new information, he is being careful to give them exactly what they want. Ironic, isn't it? He must embrace guilt in order to curry favor, to be *allowed* to teach his class." Fisk's voice fell away, and he looked past her into the dense shadows of his home, his own sort of prison. "He wants everyone who is watching—and the nine of you are not the only ones watching, you have to know that—to believe he is merely teaching a literature course. But it is so much more than that. So much more."

Alex thought about what the old man had just said, about the possibility of it.

Dean Fisk picked up on her silence. "Let me ask you this, Ms. Shipley. Do you believe our justice system is flawless, and that every man and woman who is imprisoned is guilty?"

"Of course not."

"How many men on death row alone were exonerated just before their executions? How many accused innocents have given false confessions? What happened to Richard is real life."

She looked away. "I'm sorry."

Fisk smiled. "Good heavens, there's no need to apologize. I know how difficult it is for you, to be thrown into this."

You couldn't begin to imagine.

"But it is also necessary. Your responsibility now is great, and I trust that you will do everything you can—no matter how bizarre it seems, no matter how difficult it might be—to follow Richard's clues and prove his innocence."

With that, Fisk caught his breath, the excitement slowly ebbing from his ancient frame. Then his eyes widened, as if something had just occurred to him.

"There's something I want to show you," he said. "I think it will put all your worries to rest."

He led her to a room at the end of an unadorned hallway that seemed to stretch on forever, like one of the corridors of a campus dormitory. The room itself was no bigger than a storage closet. A desk in the corner, an old beetle-shaded lamp that poured pale yellow light across the walls. And on the floor were stacks of cardboard boxes, each labeled ALDISS.

"I became interested in Richard's situation in the mideighties, not long after his imprisonment," Fisk said. "I wrote him a letter one afternoon telling him I enjoyed an essay he'd written on Dante—I have a weakness for the *Purgatorio,* just as Richard does—and he kindly responded. That began a correspondence we have continued for many years."

"So you know him well?"

Alex watched as the old man measured his words. "The more I came to know Richard, the more I realized that he could not have committed those crimes. It was simply not feasible. I felt a kinship with him, a connection I could not begin to explain. Richard's mind is fierce. Much fiercer than either of us can understand. His years in Rock Mountain have muted him, dimmed him somewhat. But years ago, when I first went to visit him there—his intelligence was simply immeasurable. Here."

Fisk removed from one of the boxes a series of newspaper clippings. He spread them out in front of Alex on the small desk.

"These are the 'facts' of his crimes," the old man said. "But as you read, I want you to pay attention to two things. Call them inconsistencies. First, look at how his colleagues at Dumant spoke of him."

"And the second thing?"

Fisk smiled. "You will know it when you see it," he said. "You're a sharp one. You found our book, didn't you?"

Alex began with the earliest clipping, which was written in January of 1982. The story was about the shocking murder of a female graduate student. Shawna Wheatley had been attacked with what appeared to be an axe. Wheatley was severely mutilated in a fashion the writer called "sickening," and over her face had been placed a single book: Fallows's *The Coil.* There were quotes in the article from the girl's boyfriend ("I don't know what kind of monster would do this to a person") and the Dumant University president ("We intend to invest all of our resources in stopping this sick human being"). No suspects had been questioned at press time.

The second article was dated the next day. A second body had been found. Abigail Murray, another grad student in literature, was murdered in her campus apartment. Again the murder weapon was assumed to be an axe; again the murder was vicious and again a solitary book (this time it was Fallows's *The Golden Silence*) had been placed over the dead girl's face.

The next piece was a general story about the manhunt for the killer. It contained all the language that one would expect from an unsolved case narrative. There were no persons of interest, there were very few leads, and the Dumant campus was frightened. Alex read the phrase *serial killer* for the first time.

By the middle of March, there was a break.

On March 17, 1982, Dr. Richard Aldiss was questioned by police. There was a brief article, accompanied by Aldiss's faculty photo, about the event. At that time the police were simply "interested" in Aldiss, who had taught Shawna Wheatley in Modern Lit and had been seen speaking to Abigail Murray on many different occasions at the Dumant Commons. The tone of the article was almost flippant, as if the writer disbelieved the very notion that the wildly popular Aldiss could have been involved.

Then things took a turn. Aldiss was arrested in early April, and the next article was a reaction piece. There was a series of quotes, most of them from Dumant professors. The comments were not flattering. "Richard is very bizarre," said one professor, who refused to be named. "He was always difficult to get a read on," said another. "When you were speaking to Richard, it was almost as if he was calibrating his personality to what you wanted it to be. A real chameleon." There were other mentions of Aldiss's connection with the victims, and the crime scenes themselves— particularly the damning coincidence of the Fallows novels the killer had draped over the girls' faces. Alex began to realize that the professors who spoke did so in the past tense. They had already convicted Aldiss.

The last piece was published a year later. It was a blow-by-blow account of the investigation and Aldiss's arrest. Alex read closely; there might be something here she needed to remember.

> Authorities became interested in Prof. Aldiss when an anonymous tip came in through the Dumant crime hotline, and the professor was brought in for questioning. After several hours, Aldiss admitted he knew something about the murders, but would say no more without a lawyer present.
>
> While awaiting counsel, Aldiss grew defiant and many times he referenced a character from classic literature, Fyodor Dostoyevsky's Raskolnikov. (The very book, it has been noted, was found among the strewn texts in Shawna Wheatley's apartment the night she was killed.) He became enraged that anyone would punish him for what he had done, and at this point of the interrogation investigators "saw the professor's capabilities firsthand." At one point he dared to declare, "You should look into Shawna Wheatley," as if to suggest that the young woman deserved exactly what she got.

Alex's eyes wandered over the article for a few more seconds. Then she turned to Fisk. He was standing behind her, leaning against a shelf and smiling wryly, the dean's streaked mascara like a shadow on his face.

"Well?" the old man asked. "Did you see anything that seemed out of place?"

"The other professors were definitely suspicious of him."

"Of course they were. But being eccentric doesn't make one a murderer. If that were the qualification for being a criminal, then everybody in academia would have a body in his closet."

"But Aldiss has never appealed his conviction. Not once. If he is innocent, wouldn't he have tried to find a way out?"

Fisk shook his head, that pitying look on his face again. "If only it were that easy, Ms. Shipley. What Richard has been doing is biding time. Waiting for the right moment, until he has all the information in front of him."

"And now he has it."

Fisk smiled. "He does."

"What did he find?"

"Alas, I do not know. Richard and I . . . I want to get closer to him, but he is a difficult man. All I know is that he is telling the truth about his innocence. I know that as I know my own name. Who actually committed those crimes? I have no idea." The man's rheumy eyes focused on her again. "Now, the second thing. I told you there were certain *points of interest* in the articles. The conspiracy at Dumant is one. And the other?"

Alex looked again at the yellowed strips of newsprint. Scanned them, trying to pick up something she'd missed before. But she could find nothing in the column of old words that seemed to stand out. Nothing whatsoever.

"I'm just not seeing it."

"Look, Ms. Shipley. Look as closely as you can. If you are the one student Richard is going to depend on this semester, if you are going to go through with this, then you need to be able to see things that are at first not there."

Alex didn't want to fail this test. Not here, not in front of the legendary dean. She worried that if she failed, they might lose interest in her. Fisk and Aldiss might pick someone else, and everything she had learned, everything she had done to this point, would be for naught.

Where the hell is it? What does he want me to see?

She stared at the text, at the grainy crime scene photos that accompanied the early articles. The Rorschach bloodstain on the wall, the books strewn across the floor. The avalanche of books in Abigail Murray's apartment, the starkness of the shot, the nakedness of the room. The smiling face of Richard Aldiss, being led away in cuffs after his arrest.

Where is it? Where?

Her eyes went to the final article, the story of how Aldiss had been discovered. The tip that led to his arrest. The professor's admission.

Alex looked up.

The confession, she thought. *Aldiss admitted he knew something.*

"'She deserved exactly what she got.'"

"Go on," Fisk urged.

"The way he said it. Aldiss told them that they should 'look into' Shawna Wheatley. The reporter mistakes him, I believe. I think Aldiss meant it literally. He meant that they should investigate something *about* Wheatley. Check her out, because she might lead them to the real killer."

Fisk beamed, and Alex felt a rush of pride. "Very good. And in time Richard *was* able to find information about Shawna. Of course no one at Rock Mountain knew he was looking. No one could know. But he uncovered the information he needed. And it turned out to mean everything."

"And you really don't know what he found," Alex said, emboldened now, "or you just won't tell me?"

Fisk hesitated. Finally he said, "You asked before if this has to do with Paul Fallows. Well, as I said, I do not know who committed this crime. But I can tell you this much: what Richard has found has everything to do with the writer. Everything. Paul Fallows is the key. Find his identity and you will find a killer."

12

That night.

The lecture hall at times seemed larger than it really was. Desks had been pulled into small, tight rows. They would arrive early and talk with one another about their studies, the social life at Jasper, the grad programs they had applied to. With only a couple of exceptions, they were not the best of friends. Over their three years at the college they had competed more often than not. A few of them, like Alex, were content to do their scholarship in silence; but others wanted nothing more than to work their way into the best grad programs and professorships in the country. When you came from a tiny place like Jasper, total dominance in your field was the only way to get noticed.

They were nine again. Daniel Hayden had returned.

"Couldn't stay away, huh?" said Michael Tanner. "You miss him?"

"Yeah," Hayden scoffed. "That's it."

As always, there was an uneasy silence just before the professor appeared. The screen wobbled and Aldiss was there again at his table, hands clasped and eyes straight ahead. He could have been anywhere, that concrete room was so nondescript. He could have been down the hall in an empty classroom for all they knew.

"Now," he began, "are you starting to see the patterns in *The Coil*?"

"I'm coming to understand that the novel is a kind of allegory," said Christian Kane. "The city—it's so strange."

"The New York City of the novel is very strange indeed," said Aldiss. "This book is about Ann Marie, our heroine, breaking away from Iowa, coming into her own. Instead, what does she find?"

"She finds a kind of . . . labyrinth," said Sally Mitchell.

"Very good." Aldiss nodded, pleased. "That is exactly what the setting of *The Coil* is like for its last two hundred pages. Our reading so far just brushes the surface. Everything in this book is a mirror, a reflection of something else. Ann Marie doesn't go off into a jungle so much as she walks into a house of mirrors. Everywhere she goes Fallows is throwing up obstacles for her." Aldiss stopped, then cocked his head to the side as if he was thinking. "Obstacles, yes. But what is the writer really doing, class?"

No one answered. A few students looked down, as if they couldn't even face the professor without an answer to his question.

"Come on," Aldiss said, the tone of his voice getting sharper. "What is Fallows doing here?"

"He's tricking her."

It was Jacob Keller. He blinked slow-lidded at the screen, his look one of casual disinterest. But this was far from the truth; Keller was perfectly engaged. He always was.

"And why do you say this?"

"Isn't it clear?" Keller asked. "He is trying to do everything in his power to keep her from succeeding. He's the master and Ann Marie . . . well, she's like a rat in a maze."

"A rat in a maze," Aldiss repeated, as if he had never heard the phrase used to describe this novel. But it was clear it worked: it fit the patterns and themes of the book perfectly. "I think you're exactly right. The literary critics have said over time that the novel is a feminist text. But as you see Ann Marie struggling through this city-labyrinth, you begin to wonder if Fallows isn't—"

"Trying to drive her mad."

He swung his head to look at Alex. "Exactly, Ms. Shipley."

"So what you're saying," put in Melissa Lee, her smoky voice barely audible in the room, "is that Fallows isn't a feminist at all. In fact he is the opposite of that. He hates women and is trying to dominate his main character."

"What I am saying," Aldiss said, "is that Fallows is in no way a *generous* novelist."

"Then what is he?"

"Haven't you seen, Ms. Lee? He's a trickster. This city of obstacles, all of these pitfalls Ann Marie must overcome—think of the crazy uncle who continues to hide himself from her in the rooms of his mansion—have an edge to them. All good novelists give their characters hurdles to overcome, but here it's as if Fallows is teasing his heroine. As if he intends to drive her to the edge. And of course he does. But that is for another time."

The class shifted; again, they had hung on his voice, his exegesis of *The Coil,* and now that he had moved on they were snapped out of their trance. The line that connected Aldiss and his students through the TV screen was severed again.

"What does all this say about Paul Fallows himself?" he asked.

"It says the man was a liar."

The class turned to face the student who had spoken: Daniel Hayden.

"Aren't all novelists liars, Mr. Hayden?" asked Aldiss.

"Some are more accomplished than others," the boy shot back. He spoke now with confidence; the uneasy, defiant kid from the last lecture was gone and had been replaced with somebody more brazen. Somebody with something to prove.

"Of course. But to accomplish a lie you need two things: the skill of the teller and the naïveté of the listener."

"Skill," scoffed Hayden.

"So you disagree that Fallows is good at what he did?" Aldiss's eyes shined now. He was enjoying this back-and-forth. "At what he does?"

"I believe people should tell the truth."

"Do you?" Aldiss goaded. "Always tell the truth?"

Hayden dodged. "Even in fiction there needs to be a context. Where is the context in these games Fallows is playing?"

"It's in the texts themselves."

"What texts?" asked Hayden, his voice rising. He held his copy of *The Coil* up, shook it like a doll. "This thing isn't real enough to be a text. The author won't even come forward and claim the damn thing. It's like some kind of forgery."

Aldiss began to speak, stopped. His tongue came out, swiped against his lips. The classroom had an intensity now, a pulse. It was as if Aldiss had drawn closer to them, as if he had stood in the front of the room and taken a literal step toward the boy.

"Well," the man said, "in my mind a good lie is the same as a good story. Without embellishment there would be no artifice, and what is embellishment but—"

"Do you lie, Professor?" Hayden asked.

Aldiss drew back. "Pardon me?"

"It's a simple question."

"I do. I have. But it's a habit, like many other habits I once had, that I have tried to break since I have come to this prison."

"What kinds of lies did you tell?"

"Oh, come on, Daniel," said Melissa Lee. "Let's get on with it."

On the screen Aldiss smiled. "No, no, let him talk. I find the boy *interesting*. My lies . . ." Aldiss's eyes closed to slits as he thought back. "I used to tell my students at Dumant stories that were not quite true. In that way, I was like the great Paul Fallows."

"What kinds of stories?"

"I told them that I had lived in Europe," Aldiss said. "This is not true. The strangest place I have lived was Iowa." The class laughed.

Hayden didn't laugh. He looked at the screen and muttered something else. No one in the class caught it, or if someone did, they didn't dwell on it. It was just two words: *the Procedure.*

But Richard Aldiss caught it. And he smiled.

Alex

Present Day

13

On her way back to the mansion Alex called Lewis Prine's cell. That familiar voice, recorded in a flat monotone: "This is Dr. Lewis Prine, warden and chief psychiatrist at Oakwood Hospital. Please leave a message at the tone. If it's an emergency, you may contact Administrative Services. Thank you." There was a short pulse, and then Alex said, "Lewis, I'm starting to worry about you. We're all here, staying in Dean Fisk's house for the night. Michael's memorial service is tomorrow morning. We're waiting for you. We would . . . I would really like to see you. Please call." She pushed End and walked on across the quad.

When she returned to the house, everyone was in the great room, telling stories about Michael Tanner. As she entered, the tales abruptly stopped, and each of the five former classmates looked at her as if she had caught them revealing their innermost secrets. In the middle of the group, a blanket around her shoulders and shivering wickedly, was Sally Tanner.

She knows, Alex thought. *She knows what I'm up to.*

"Hey, guys," she managed to say.

"Anything?" Sally asked, her blue eyes now devoid of anything but hope.

Alex shook her head. "They're still looking. Detective Black is a good man, Sally. He will find out who did this."

The widow made a face. "Black. The bastard." Christian Kane pulled her to him, and for some reason this gesture made Alex jealous—that she hadn't been around the others in so long, that she had gone back to Harvard after Daniel's death without keeping her promise to stay in touch. She looked at Keller and he glanced away.

"Let's talk about the good times," Christian said. "Michael would have wanted that."

"Yes," slurred Frank Marsden. "Absolutely." He was sitting off to the side, Lucy Wiggins clutching his arm.

"Do you remember when Michael asked Aldiss if he was sure about a quotation from Fallows?" asked Christian.

"I remember," Melissa Lee said. "That was pure Michael."

"It was, wasn't it?" It was Sally who had spoken, but there was nothing in her voice. Nothing at all. Alex wondered if she even really remembered the moment.

They went on like that for the next half hour, trading stories about their murdered friend. Most of them were minor instances from the night class where Michael had challenged Richard Aldiss's authority. He was brilliant even then, as they all were in their own way; when he'd accepted the position at his alma mater just a year out of graduate school, Alex had called to congratulate him. She remembered the tone of his voice, remembered thinking, *He's not happy to be back there, not excited to return to that place—and I don't blame him.*

As they spoke, Alex watched them. Observed them.

"I remember something else Michael said once," Christian was saying, and Alex focused on the writer, on his sharp academic's jaw and his eyes that never settled. Again she remembered what Aldiss had said that morning, the task he had given her. Could this man be responsible for the murder? Could Christian, with his ratty clothes and desperate ambition, possibly be the one who—

"Good evening."

Alex turned and saw Matthew Owen pushing a wheelchair into the room. In the chair—it was outdated and canvas-backed and somehow fitting for the shambles of the mansion around them—was Dean Stanley Fisk. The sight of the man shocked her. He was shrunken, slumped and childlike in a heavy robe. He wore sunglasses and a thick patina of foundation. His face was powdered and his lips had been daubed with a bright crimson. The dean's head was covered with a blond wig that swept over on top and was parted at the side, the look pitifully aping the style he'd worn as a lit professor at Jasper. Owen pushed Fisk inside and left him there, sitting just outside the circle of former students, and went to stoke the fire that had gotten low. Night was coming on.

"I am so sorry about what's happened," the dean said in his lilting voice. "Michael and Sally are dear friends of mine, and I am as devastated about this as you all are."

"Dean Fisk," Melissa cut in. She wore a black sweater over her shoulders, and the porcelain whiteness of her face reminded Alex of the girl she had been in the night class. On her lap was a book, pinched open with a slender finger. It was one of Christian's. "Do you believe Richard Aldiss had anything to do with this?" Her eyes flicked toward Alex.

"We must keep our minds open to any possibility," the dean said.

"They say Aldiss changed after he was released from prison," Frank offered. He sat on the sheet-covered sofa, a sweating glass of something toxic in his hand. The hand trembled slightly, ice singing against the glass. "That he got darker, took a house not far from campus, and started a new book about Fallows. A book he still hasn't finished."

At the sound of the writer's name there was a hush in the great room. Owen got the fire lit and a knot of sparks blew out from the hearth, making Alex jump.

"They should at least investigate him," Melissa said. "There's too much history for them not to."

"History," spat Sally Tanner. She was still wrapped in the blanket, still shivering as if the fire weren't raging just a few feet from her. It threw a shadow on her face, a black scar running down the woman's sharp cheekbone. She was no longer a twenty-one-year-old with her life stretching ahead of her, and Michael's death had turned her bitter. She too had taken something, drunk something—her eyes fluttered in the half-light and her words were slurred. "There is no history now. It's over. Everything Richard Aldiss did, everything he accumulated, all his fame—gone. Now he's just a pathetic old man living out there with his memories."

"No." Alex realized too late that she had spoken aloud. "He's still a genius. He still has his mind."

Sally laughed, rage burning in her eyes. "Of course *you* would think that."

Alex bit her tongue and looked away.

"Lewis," said Dean Fisk from his wheelchair. "Will he not be joining us?"

"Prine probably went batshit crazy," Frank said, "working with those nuts."

"Frank." Playfully, his date squeezed his arm.

"I'm serious, Lucy. Have I ever told you what Lewis does? He's the warden of this prison, this castle where they keep very bad men. I don't know how he does it and stays sane. Really I don't."

Frank faded off, realizing that he might have gone too far. He finished his glass of poison.

"Tomorrow," Dean Fisk said, "we will have a memorial service on the east quad in front of the Tower. Alex will give the eulogy, and anyone who wants to speak about Michael may do so." On the sofa Sally sobbed, the sound dry as dead leaves. "I am so pleased that you have agreed to stay with me. You do not know how happy it makes me to hear the voices of the best and the brightest in my house again."

His swiveled his head and blindly searched for Owen, and Alex saw a brief look of disgust come over the nurse. Then Fisk turned his wheelchair and began to roll out of the room. Owen caught up with him and pushed the old man into the shadows of the house.

When the dean was gone Sally stood up and said, "I better get going. It's almost Rachael's bedtime." She was referring to the Tanners' daughter, and Alex shook her head at the thought of the little girl growing up fatherless. Alex knew how hard it was at any age.

The others hugged their widowed friend, and Sally stood among them, quivering as if she might slip off the edge of the world. She finally composed herself and walked out, nodding coldly as she went by Alex.

The rest spoke more freely when the specter of the woman was gone; their stories got rowdy in the makeshift wake. Alex tried to parse the conversations, find a piece of information that might help her with her task. But there was nothing here. It was implausible to her that one of these people would betray Michael, let alone murder him. They appeared to her as they had at Daniel's funeral: made awkward by grief, trying their best to fill up the silences that would lead them to imagine the body, the library, the blanket of books. *They're just old friends, Alex. Aldiss has led you off, he's conned you. When you go back tonight you must—*

Behind her there came the chirp of a cell phone. Sally, pulling on her heels by the door, flipped the phone open. "Hello?" she said. Then she listened, and Alex watched the woman out of the corner of her eye. "I can't talk right now," she whispered. "It isn't a good time." She slapped closed the phone and went out into the evening.

Alex excused herself and walked slowly upstairs to her own room.

The talk of Aldiss before had stirred her. She knew the professor was innocent of the Dumant murders. After all, it was her investigation that had proven beyond any doubt that Aldiss could not have committed those crimes.

But what if there had been a mistake? What if Aldiss had been manipulating the night class, and now he was manipulating the murder of Michael Tanner?

No. Aldiss was innocent this time as well. He was innocent and someone in this house held the answers that would lead her to Michael's killer.

Alex moved down the dark corridor. The house was quiet up here on the second floor, just the slight trill of the others' talk reaching her. She walked deeper into the house, her hand on the wall leading her into the dark. One step at a time, the planks announcing her every step. *Is it up here?* she thought. *Did he hide it in these—*

Her cell vibrated.

"Hello?"

"Dr. Shipley, this is Detective Black."

A heat rose to her face. *They've found something.*

"Can you meet me on the east campus in twenty minutes?" Black asked.

"Of course. What's this about?"

"Nothing much," he said. "I just want to show you something that I think you'll find interesting."

"I'll see you soon." She ended the call.

Alex continued down the hallway. She was thinking, *Answers.* There were many reasons to return to Jasper, after all, reasons that were at least a little selfish. With her heart thumping and her blood roaring, she stepped into a room off the main corridor.

It was another book-filled room, shelves sagging under the weight of volumes that had not been touched in years. This room, like so many others in the mansion, had almost been overtaken by tomes. But Alex could see a pattern: instead of letting them run wild, Fisk had attempted to order them into schools or eras. In this he was nothing like Aldiss.

She stepped over the threshold and turned on the room's only lamp, approaching the shelves with reverence. She traced a hand over the spines, making sure to look closely between the books to see if a manuscript might be hidden there.

She began with William Wordsworth and the Romantics, Whitman and the American poets, Hazlitt and the critics, then on to the modernists. This shelf was more bare but still diverse: Eliot, Oppen, Pound. Alex traced her fingers across the books, allowing her senses to lead her, the others' laughter echoing up from below.

Where are you? Are you real?

Alex continued through the stacks. There was nothing here. Nothing at all. She had looked throughout the second floor, checked every room, and still she wasn't even close. The manuscript was a farce, another promise by the scholars that turned out to be—

She stopped. She was still in the modernists, looking at the studies on Fallows. There was Benjamin Locke's famous text on *The Coil*, and of course Stanley Fisk's own treatise on Fallows the feminist. And there were two Aldisses side by side, the volumes he had written in prison on Fallows. She stared at the shelves, at the way the books had been arranged. The order she had noticed before—it was disturbed here. The book called *Ghost* had been eased out over the lip of the shelf, its wrinkled dust flap clinging staunchly onto one loose tendril of spiderweb.

She reached out and gingerly slid the book off the shelf, and as she did she heard a click. A small, rasping bite just beneath the text. She looked closely at the empty space on the shelf. An opening had been created behind Aldiss's *Ghost,* a carved notch in the wall roughly the shape of a mailbox. Curved inside the space was a manuscript.

Heart fluttering now, Alex put her fingers on the paper and pulled.

"Alex?" Startled, she spun around. "What are you doing up here?"

Keller stood in the doorway. He was leaning against the threshold, a beer in his hand. A flash, then, to when they were students. Her knees would have weakened under different circumstances.

"I—I'm not doing anything. Just looking at Fisk's collection."

He stepped into the room. Said, "So. Lucy Wiggins, huh?"

Alex turned her back to the shelf, hoping beyond hope that Keller hadn't seen the secret space. "I know. Isn't it wild?"

"Different than I thought she would be." He sipped his beer. "I saw her on *CSI: Miami* a few months ago. Googled her. Married with children, sitcom star in the nineties, rehab a few times. The usual. I wonder if she knows Frank's married."

"How could she not?" Alex rolled her eyes. Then, "They look happy."

"So they do."

He came deeper into the room, swept past the pale lamplight. "You're going back to see Aldiss tonight, aren't you?" he asked.

"After I meet with the detective, yes."

"What do you hope he'll say? That he knows who killed Michael? That he has all the answers? How could he, Alex?"

"Aldiss is smarter than us all."

"Of course he is. He's also more dangerous."

She looked away. "I have to go back."

Keller waited.

"I have to go back because if he had anything to do with this, then everything we did in Iowa doesn't matter. Don't you see that, Keller? Don't you understand?"

She watched him breathe. The alcohol was burning in his cheeks a little, and he took another drink. He said, "Melissa says Daniel didn't kill himself."

Something dropped inside her. "What do you mean?"

"While you were meeting with the detective she knocked on my door. We talked. She says she spoke to Daniel sometimes. Says she went with her family once to Manhattan and he came to meet her. She spent the day with him, meeting all his cop friends."

"And?"

"And he was fine, Alex. Happy. Not a man who was apt to blow his brains out in the front seat of his squad car."

Alex thought. The temperature in the room seemed to have dropped, the cool night pressing in. There was the feeling again of running wildly along, of being pulled in every direction at once. She steadied herself on the bookshelf. "What does it mean, Keller?"

He shrugged. "Daniel had a stressful job. A detective? With the NYPD? Maybe the atrocities he saw became too much to handle . . ." He trailed off, couldn't find the words. "Or maybe Melissa is right and all this—Daniel and Michael and all the rest of it—has something to do with Aldiss."

A flash of anger behind her eyes. "Impossible."

"Listen, Alex," Keller said, taking a step toward her. "Listen to me. You have to be careful out there. You have to watch him, pay attention to him. Close attention. If he is lying as everyone in this house except you believes, if he has anything remotely to do with Michael's and Daniel's deaths, then this is a pattern. And you could be putting yourself right inside that pattern." He stopped speaking. He was looking at her as intently as he ever had, but she couldn't hold his gaze. She looked away, back to the secret space, which gaped open not six inches from Keller's hand. "You could be next."

14

Detective Bradley Black was waiting for her when she crossed over Harper's Knoll. He was reading a paperback novel—she knew instinctively, by the way the pages bent, by the aged-brown tinge of the book, that it was Fallows's *The Coil*—and he folded the book into his pocket when he saw her.

"I wanted you to see," the detective said, falling into stride beside her. "Wanted you to get at least one look at it without that asshole Rice around."

She stared at him. "You mean Michael's library."

He nodded. His boots echoed sharply over the quads as they walked.

"I appreciate it, Detective. I really do. But I don't need your charity."

"Yes, you do. You think you're a hero around this place, and in some ways you are. I expect them to rename the library in your honor when Fisk kicks the bucket, slap a bronze statue right out there on the great lawn. But there are a lot of people here who think you saved the ass of a man who wasn't innocent."

"And what makes you think I care what people think?" she bristled.

"You've got a tattoo on your shoulder."

"So what?"

"There are two kinds of women," he said, a smile touching his lips for the first time. She wanted to like him. "Those who have tattoos and those who don't. Those who do know they are the center of attention. They know people are staring at them, trying to read them. To puzzle them out. What does it say?"

She felt the six-year-old tattoo burn her shoulder blade now, remembered the drunken night she'd gotten it in Cambridge. It was a string of bluing words written in the most ornate fashion the pierced and goateed artist could pull off: "*Un buon libro non ha fine.*"

"I have no idea what that means, Professor."

"A good book has no ending."

They walked toward the fringe of campus. Black kept his eyes down at the concrete. She had the feeling that he wanted to say something but couldn't quite find the words.

"If this crime is just like the other two," he finally said as they passed in front of Bacon Hall, where Michael Tanner would have taught his undergrads, "the killer will not be satisfied with one. There were two murders at Dumant, two victims."

"I know that, Detective." Then she gentled her voice. "I remember."

Black stopped. Something caught his gaze, a blackbird tearing away from a beech on the quad. He tracked the animal's movement until it was a crumb in the sky, and then he said, "We studied you. Back in police school. The others—they laughed it off. An English major solving a murder? Some joke. But I was always fascinated by what you were able to do."

She looked more closely, studied his face. "Is this an invitation, Detective?"

Black started on ahead of her. He had a way of not looking at you as he spoke, of connecting even as he remained elusive. She reminded herself to be careful around him. "Dean Rice says you're unpredictable," he said. "That you have no regard for the rules. That some of the things you did during the night class could have gotten the Jasper brass in trouble. That you could have gotten you and that boyfriend of yours killed."

This stung her, but she said nothing.

"But if you want to know what *I* think, I think this investigation could use a little unpredictability. You could be our go-between with Aldiss, you could do what you did back in '94."

She reached into her pocket for the nicotine gum, slid a piece between her fingers, as if it might take effect through touch alone. "Tell me one thing, Detective."

"Anything."

"Why are you harassing Sally Tanner?"

The man tumbled away again, followed the air with his eyes. "In a murder, the spouse is always the first—"

"Don't give me that bullshit," Alex said. "This isn't some lovers' spat. This crime was calculated, scripted. Whoever did this is trying to create some twisted work of art. That's not how Sally was—is." Alex bolstered herself. "Please. She's suffered enough."

The man's mouth went tight. "She was sleeping around on Michael," he said. "Driving downstate, maybe seeing another professor. Or perhaps even a student."

"Are you sure?"

He nodded. "She was gone every weekend to Dumant University."

Alex remembered what Christian had said earlier. *The Procedure,* she thought. *Sally was playing it too.*

The detective measured her. Finally he said, pointing off toward a grid of police tape in the distance, "Let's move on. It's getting late."

Michael and Sally Tanner's house was a modified Cape Cod on Front Street. A dog barked shrilly in the neighborhood and a Jasper Police cruiser sat in the drive, its flashers languidly throwing blue light over the house.

Two cops sat on the hood of the car, sharing a bent cigarette. They eyed Alex as she approached.

"Davidson," Black said. "Warren. Meet Dr. Alex Shipley."

"Pleasure," the shorter man said.

The other man's eyes held low.

"Go on," Alex said. "Say it. No need to save it for later."

The cop's jaw tensed. Beside her Black coughed into his fist. Then he tugged on her coat and they went for the front door.

"Are you ready?" Black said at the front door.

She looked at him and nodded. "As I'll ever be."

They went in.

A lamp stood on the floor, shadeless, its bare bulb painting the walls white. The dust had been disturbed, and Alex covered her mouth with the collar of her trench. As Black had told her that morning, the house was not as clean as the apartments at Dumant: there was a gash on one wall, dark and ugly. An investigator had circled it with chalk. In one corner a chair had been toppled. In the kitchen the tablecloth had been pulled to the floor and dishes were scattered, some of them broken into a thousand glittering pieces. *You fought him, didn't you, Michael? You fought that bastard and you nearly won.*

"Sally Tanner arrived home that night around nine," Black said. "Found the place wrecked like this. Then she made her way to the library."

"My God," said Alex.

"Of course no one heard anything. No struggle, no racket. The students who rent across the street were having a party to celebrate the end of midterm exams—nothing. It was like the killer was never even here." Black shifted in place. "Except for the disturbance in the kitchen. And this."

He led her down a hallway. A couple of techs stood at the far end, speaking in low voices. Their eyes flicked to Alex, held for a second, then dropped away. Everything was a secret in the house of death.

Black entered a room at the far end of the hall, and Alex followed. *He thinks I'm ready for this,* she thought. *He thinks what happened during the night class prepared me.* She wanted to say something. To tell him she wasn't ready.

She wasn't at all ready. But she was there, inside that horrible room.

The bloodstain. It was the first thing she noticed. The police had chalk-circled this as well. The Rorschach butterfly wings, the burning fire spreading away from the shape's edges—so meticulous, as if someone had used a paintbrush to put it there. But also so simple that it could be the work of a child.

"Notice again how precise he was," Black was saying, his voice spinning up from a great depth. "It's identical to the Dumant apartments, down to the shape on the wall. And the books . . ."

Alex studied the books. At first there was a chaos to them, but when she looked closer she saw how careful the pattern was. They had not merely been dropped to the floor but had rather been *placed* there painstakingly, like the instruments on a surgical tray. But she couldn't focus, didn't want to focus—the books were worse, somehow, than if she had seen Michael Tanner's body.

"The one covering his eyes," she said, her voice strangled. "What was it?"

"Fallows," Black said. "*The Coil.*"

Of course.

"He wants us to be thinking about Dumant," Black went on. "This thing is a carbon copy, a kind of rehashing. A revision. Will you help us, Dr. Shipley?"

"Yes," she said weakly. This apartment, this room particularly—it had convinced her. Her throat was bone dry, her hands clenched and nails digging into her palms. Before, it had been a tragedy; now, standing here in the middle of these books, the tide of them around her, she saw it for what it was: a revulsion. Anger, quick and tight, rushed to the surface. She wanted to spit, to tear the covers off the books and demand answers from them, to hide away the terrible meaningless image of the inkblot on the wall that seemed to be an eye now, a camera staring at her. Into her. "Yes, I will."

Black nodded and Alex stood up, sweeping over the damage in the library one last time. *How could no one have heard him struggling?* she wondered as she stepped past the detective. *Why didn't anyone save him?*

Black glanced up from where he crouched. "Where are you going?"

"I have to see someone."

"And who would that be?"

"Richard Aldiss," Alex said, and then she left that awful room and the ghosts it refused to give up.

The Class

1994

15

When everyone was ready, Aldiss sat forward and scanned the lecture hall, as he often did at the beginning of his classes. His faceless guards, as always, stood watch behind him. The black legs of their trousers were slick and pressed.

"We have fully begun our journey now," he said at last. "We are on our way toward discovering who Paul Fallows really is."

"Why don't you just tell us?" Melissa Lee wore a Pixies T-shirt and tattered pants slung with a man's necktie for a belt. The girl's black lips glistened, her dark, oily hair hung over piercing olive eyes. "If you know his identity, as you claim you do, why don't you just reveal it to us?"

"I agree with her, Professor," said Michael Tanner, who sat beside Lee. He was a skinny, frail boy made frailer because of his baggy sweater and sharp features. There were rumors about Tanner and Lee—in fact, there were rumors about Lee and almost every guy on campus, and a few women as well—and Alex noticed how close their elbows were, how near they sat to each other. "Just tell us who you believe he is. This charade, this . . ."

"Game."

It was Keller who had offered up the word, and no one objected. Not a mystery, as the class title suggested, but something much more complex. Something dictated by the whims of Aldiss himself.

"That's right," Daniel Hayden said. "This is a *game*. And it's becoming a bit tedious, don't you think?"

"I disagree."

There were only three women in the class, Alex and Lee and Sally Mitchell. It was Mitchell who had just spoken. A quiet, mousy girl—not as opinionated as Alex nor as scandalous as Lee, Mitchell was the forgotten star of the English department. She was a Burlington girl, and like Alex she was branded because of this fact. But unlike Alex she was often invisible on the campus, absent from the frat parties and the spontaneous Front Street gatherings the English profs often put on. She, as much as anyone in the lecture hall, maybe even as much as Daniel Hayden, was an enigma to the rest of them.

"And why don't you tell us what you think of my methods, Ms. Mitchell," Aldiss said. He remained frighteningly composed.

"I think giving the information would be too . . . easy," the girl said.

"Who agrees with her?"

Aldiss waited. Three students raised their hands: Alex, Lewis Prine, and Frank Marsden, the actor, in the front row. Almost everyone agreed that to see Marsden act was to see a boy who fell completely into his role, who *became* the character he was playing. Tonight he was fresh from rehearsals; he sat wearing full makeup, his eyes dark with shadow.

Aldiss looked at the boy. "Do you enjoy my class, Mr. Marsden?"

"Very much so."

"And what exactly do you like about it?"

"I like the fact that it's so unexpected. That anything can happen."

Aldiss was pleased by this. "Mr. Prine?"

"Call it intrigue," the boy said.

Aldiss scanned the room, and his eyes fell on Alex. "And you, Ms. Shipley," he said. "You also enjoy this chase I have you on?"

She didn't exactly know how to answer. *Enjoy*—it wasn't the word she wanted. "I understand why you're doing it this way," she said.

Aldiss cocked his head. "Do you?"

"I think so, yes. To just give us Paul Fallows's identity, to hand over the information you've uncovered while you've been in Rock Mountain—that would not only be too easy, it would be wrong."

"I think you understand my methods quite well," Aldiss said. "I have waited for twelve years to get to this point, I believe I can hold out for a few more weeks."

He laughed, and a few in the class did as well.

"Plus, I do not know for a fact that the person I believe to be Paul Fallows is really him."

The class buzzed. No one quite knew how to take this announcement.

"What do you mean?" Tanner asked. "I thought you had new information, Professor. Stuff that has never been seen before."

"That's right," Aldiss said. "But what we are working with here are possibilities. Equations. You may come to the end and find that my information was flawed. That the person I believe to be Fallows isn't him at all. It has happened to the Fallows scholars again and again over the years. I believe I am right this time, but . . ."

For some reason, this admonition scared Alex. Terrified her. How could he not be sure?

"Does it even matter?" It was Lee again. The girl looked at Aldiss with a challenge in her eyes.

"Does what matter, Ms. Lee?"

"Finding Fallows. Will the world change if we do find him? Will it mean anything?"

"Of course it will. It will mean everything."

Alex nodded, then stopped herself. She mustn't get too close to him. How dangerous it was to join his side, to form a relationship with this man. The image from Dean Fisk's newspaper articles flashed through her mind, the libraries of those dead girls . . .

The professor went on: "If you find Fallows, then you will have solved one of the world's greatest—"

He stopped. "Professor?" Hayden asked.

There was a quick, choking sound, and Aldiss lurched forward onto the table where his camera must have been mounted. The speed of his movement startled Alex. Aldiss's face banged off the metal surface. His eyes opened impossibly wide and then he slumped down out of view, the camera jostling and twisting downward in the movement. Now the lens held on Aldiss's one open eye. It was as if he had seen something beyond words, something so terrible or beautiful that he could not understand its meaning.

"I'm . . ." he gasped, and then nothing.

The guards bent forward, batons tipping downward. They were still mostly hidden, but one of them stooped now and the camera caught him. The line of a jaw, a downy tuft of pale stubble, one frantic eye caught in the frame—and then he was gone.

The TV went black.

"What the hell?" Christian Kane said.

"Not again," said Keller.

Alex held her breath. She didn't want to be left like this. Not after the information she'd gathered from Dean Fisk. Not after those photographs of the crime scenes. She felt as if she was close now, as if the message in the book was finally real.

"Are we supposed to wait for him?" Lee asked, annoyance in her voice.

But before someone could answer, the box screeched and the image reappeared. A different man was sitting at Aldiss's table. He wore a gray suit and tiny glasses that shrunk his face. The man stared solemnly into the camera.

"My name is Jeffrey Oliphant," the man said in a slow, looping voice. "I am the warden at Rock Mountain Correctional Facility. I regret to inform you that Dr. Aldiss will not be able to continue tonight. He has been taken back to his cell and is being checked by our medical staff. He suffers from a rare neurological condition, as he has told you. Certainly nothing to be alarmed about. If he is able, you will continue your course on the next scheduled night. Thank you for your cooperation."

Again, the screen went black.

Now what am I supposed to do? Alex wondered.

She walked home with Keller.

The air was not as cold as it had been the previous week. Students were out now, walking the quads, some of them sitting out on the campus benches. It didn't get much better than this in January in Vermont.

"Still think he's lying?" she asked Keller. She was already feeling close to him. Silly, yes—she admitted it. A girlish game she was playing with herself. It had only been one walk through the snow. But she felt like she could trust him.

Almost.

"Hard to say," Keller said. The snow had begun to melt and the walkways had turned to slush, the drifts pooling out and soaking down the quads to a dark, viscous mud. "I actually feel sorry for the poor bastard."

"You shouldn't," Alex said. "He murdered . . ." She stopped herself.

"I know, I know. Those dead girls. It's just that he's so pathetic, trapped there in that cell with his guards. And what happened tonight. Can you imagine?"

"No."

"Me either. I think I would just off myself. Just get it over with." Then Keller stopped, seemed to consider something. "Let me ask you something."

"Have at it."

"Which one of us is Aldiss's favorite?"

She thought about the book back in her room. "I don't know," she said.

"I think it's Daniel Hayden."

"You can't be serious."

"Look at the kid, Alex. He was never really going to leave the class. He's just like Aldiss—he enjoys playing these games and seeing how many people he can get to go along with him. It's all an act with this guy. He's the only one there who . . ." *Isn't like the rest of us,* she knew Keller wanted to say.

"I guess."

"You're still not convinced."

Alex thought, imagined the faces of the students. Of the way they interacted with Aldiss and of the way he manipulated them. A strong word, but this was the feeling she got: that he was playing with them somehow, keeping them going with his promise of Fallows. His carrot on a stick. "I just get the feeling that Aldiss doesn't like any of us," she said. "Not really. The whole class creeps me out."

"You mean Unraveling a Literary Mystery isn't your very favorite class?" he said in a mock-serious way, his accent thick and proper. Alex had to laugh.

"It's not that," she said. "It's just that I feel weird when I'm in that room. I don't know. It sounds stupid."

"No," he said. "Go on. What?"

"I feel like Aldiss is toying with us," she said. "Like he's the puppet master and we're his puppets."

"You can stop any time, Alex. You know that."

She looked away. "I know. And I guess I'm just being paranoid. But there's still something underneath it all. *Simmering.*"

"Simmering? What's this, Julia Child 101?"

She shoved him, felt his muscle beneath his flannel shirt. Felt something else flicker deep in her belly.

A moment of silence spooled out. She saw Philbrick Hall ahead.

"We should study together sometime," Keller said.

"Yeah," she said. *Yeah? Dumb-ass!*

"What about tomorrow night? We can read Fallows together. The magnificent, mysterious *The Coil.* We can unravel the mystery together."

"That sounds nice."

"My stomping ground, then," Keller said. "Rebecca's. Seven sharp."

"I'll be there."

Keller nodded and left her on the walk. When she got inside her dorm, she realized she hadn't been breathing.

16

The next morning, Alex returned to Dean Fisk's mansion on the hill. The old man was waiting for her this time.

"Tell me about Iowa," she said when they were seated in the great room. "Professor Aldiss said we should begin there, in Rutherford's birthplace. Did something happen there?"

"Iowa is where many of Fallows's characters are from," Fisk said. "And there you have Charles Rutherford as well. It was always believed that Iowa was ground zero, the middle of the map. If you were going to find Fallows, that's where you would begin."

She noticed the hesitancy in his voice. "But . . ."

"Richard disagreed. At least at first. He felt that Iowa was a smoke-screen, just like the 'author photograph' of the encyclopedia salesman. Fallows wrote about New York City, about Europe. He mailed his manuscripts from European postmarks. It was as if the entire thing was a farce, as if Fallows had deliberately chosen this nowhere place in the middle of America to start his characters' journeys. It was pure Fallows: the fact that it looked like it meant something suggested that it didn't."

"And the town where Rutherford was from?"

"Hamlet. A void."

"Did Aldiss go there? Before, I mean?"

"He did. He and Locke."

"Locke?"

Fisk was surprised. "Richard hasn't told you about Benjamin Locke? Ah, you haven't even begun your night class, then."

"Who was he?"

Fisk sat back on the sofa, crossed one leg over the other. "Dr. Benjamin Locke was a cult figure at Dumant University," he began. "Dumant was where Richard did his undergrad and then became a professor, of course. Locke was a kind of renegade professor. The women at Dumant loved him, the men wanted to be him. He was a fixture in the burgeoning student movements of the early 1970s, wore bell bottoms and love beads to his lectures. I met him once, I think it was in '71. He was more student than professor, but you could see the genius almost drifting off of him. He was much like Richard in that way."

"And he was Professor Aldiss's teacher?"

"That's right. Locke taught critical theory. You have to understand: Locke was firmly in the Raymond Picard school. He treated literature as if it were simply a series of mathematical patterns, and it was the reader's job to unlock those patterns and crawl into the hole. Get right in the book's insides."

Into the hole, she thought. *The rabbit hole.*

"It was as if Ben Locke were tinkering with a machine of some kind," Fisk went on. "In front of his classes he would cut the covers off his books and X-Acto the pages away, physically destroy the volume so that he could examine it piece by piece."

Alex thought of the pages Aldiss had held to the screen during the night class.

"I suppose Richard saw a kind of art in that," Fisk said. "A sort of truth. Of course they were inseparable the moment Locke saw how powerful Richard's mind was."

"Was it Locke who turned Dr. Aldiss onto Paul Fallows?"

"Yes. At that time Fallows was an unknown, but Locke soon changed all that. It was 1972. *The Golden Silence* hadn't yet appeared, and many believed there was nothing special about Fallows. A more modern version of Edith Wharton, perhaps. In fact, it was Benjamin Locke who was the first scholar to posit the theory that Paul Fallows might have actually been a woman."

Alex thought about that. It fit with the hundred or so pages she had read of *The Coil*. There was something almost feminine about the writing.

"You said that Benjamin Locke changed the perception of Paul Fallows," she said. "How did he do that?"

"He did it very carefully," Fisk replied. "He formed an elite group of students. A small, selective group of Dumant's finest lit majors. They called themselves the Iowans."

"And Richard Aldiss—"

"Was one of them, yes. Of course he would be. It was there, in those secret meetings in the home of Benjamin Locke, that the mythology of Paul Fallows was born."

"But what did Locke teach them? If not much was known about the novels at that time, then what could the professor possibly have been able to give to his group?"

"He gave them the beginnings of an obsession, Alex. Imagine them there." With this, Fisk leaned forward, and Alex followed the man's always moving fingers, the way they stained the wall of the great room with their mad, intricate shadows. "These students learn that the one existing novel, *The Coil*, was not merely a book but . . . something else. Something like a treasure map. A map that was so new and untapped that no one had really taken the time to puzzle over it. They would be the first. Think about how immensely powerful they must have felt."

Alex thought of the night class, of that smothering, windowless basement room. Of the feeling that overcame her when Aldiss appeared on the television screen.

"Yes," she finally said. "I think I know how they felt."

"And so it was easy to see how they fell into it," Fisk continued. "I mean totally fell into it, free will and all cast aside. If the so-called Iowans were obedient to Locke before, they were now in his thrall. He not only became a mentor to them—he became a sort of spiritual guide."

"Did they begin a search for Fallows?"

A slow, deliberate nod. "It was during Richard's final year of grad school. Locke showed for a meeting one night looking ashen, pale. The students knew that something must be wrong. When they confronted him, Locke told his students what had happened."

"What was it?" asked Alex, getting swept up now. Losing herself in the dean's story.

"Locke had been contacted by Fallows himself."

Her mouth dropped open. "What do you mean, 'contacted'?"

Fisk leaned forward. Strands of thinning hair fell down and clung wetly to his forehead. He was exhausting himself by telling this story.

"The writer had called the professor on the telephone," he said. "He told Locke that he'd heard about his group and he would like to meet the students in person. This, of course, was shocking even then. Fallows was already known as a recluse, a man who never showed his face or granted an interview. The photograph of Charles Rutherford on the back of *The Coil* was already being called into question. When this man calling himself Fallows requested an audience with the professor and his students—well, that was enough to terrify Ben Locke."

"He thought something didn't add up."

"Very much so. Wouldn't you? You had spent three years digging into one novel, tunneling into it and prying it open, and the reclusive author suddenly wants to see you? Locke was afraid. He admitted to Richard that the writer had sounded strange during their conversation. Off, somehow. Not like a man but a . . .'"

"What?" Alex asked. Heat gathered beneath her arms now; her heart roared.

"A recording," Fisk said. "A machine of some kind."

"Christ."

"Yes. It was all very disconcerting. Nearly all of the Iowans refused to go, even though to meet Paul Fallows and discuss *The Coil* would have been beyond their wildest dreams."

"What about Professor Aldiss?" she asked. Almost despite herself she thought of the professor as he would've been as a student—powerful, even sexy. He would have been above the obsession that drove the Fallows scholars. Something swelled in her, a kind of shameful energy. She swallowed it down harshly.

Fisk smiled. "Of course you know the answer to that already. He was the only one who stayed by Locke's side. Richard would not be dissuaded. He very much wanted to go, whatever the risks. He is not a murderer, Alex, as I have told you, but he is a very brave man. A confident man, so sure of himself and his own notions that danger . . . well, he never considered danger. He just wanted to get to the bottom of the Fallows search. He had been working on the novel with Locke for long enough, and he craved answers."

"So what did they do?"

Fisk paused. The light had swung again, and the living room was almost completely dark. The only artificial light was cast by a small lamp in the corner.

"Richard will have to tell you that story."

"Dean Fisk, please."

"I promise," the man said again. "You will learn the answers to these questions. Either Richard will tell you, or you will discover what lies in Hamlet on your own."

Alex thought again about the small Iowa town.

"So, Hamlet is where Aldiss is leading us? Leading me, I mean. Is that the purpose of the night class, to have me retrace his and Locke's steps so that I might be able to find what they could not?"

At first Fisk did not speak. When he did, his eyes were away from her, distant and somber, his face drawn.

"Yes," the old man said. "That's exactly what is happening."

Alex

Present Day

17

This time Richard Aldiss was waiting for her.

He had wine ready, an immaculate dinner of stewed hare and ex-
otic vegetables on china that spread across a stark white tablecloth.
There were two chairs, one on each side of the small circular table, and
through the nervous flame of a candle Alex watched the professor smile
at her in the half darkness of his little kitchen. At her place setting was
an envelope that read, *To Alexandra.* She had refused to open it.

"Poor Michael Tanner," the man said when they were seated.

"They're still searching," Alex said. "The police have been watching
Sally, but they haven't charged her with anything yet."

"And is it your opinion that quiet Sally killed her husband?" he asked
bluntly. He tore at the rabbit with his fork, a tortured smile stretched
across his face.

"No." The word out there, she drew herself quickly back. "I don't know."

"'No,'" the professor repeated in a perfect imitation of her voice. "'I
don't know.' Which is it, Alexandra?"

"I haven't had time to observe them all yet." She took a cautious
bite. It was luxurious, but she refused to show Aldiss her pleasure. "But
I will. They're staying in Dean Fisk's—"

"Fisk," spat Aldiss. "Has the old man trotted out his mythical manuscript yet?" Aldiss laughed, but his eyes didn't leave her. Alex looked off into the shadows of the kitchen. "Give me something of substance."

Alex looked at him through the candle's flame. *Bastard.* "I saw the house."

The smile curled upward. He rested his fork on the plate with a gentle *tink,* steepled his hands beneath his chin. "Go on."

"You said before that you felt that the person who did this was someone who knew Michael."

Aldiss nodded almost imperceptibly.

"I think you may have been right."

"Of course I was," he said. His hands moved. She watched his fingers dance from glass to knife to cloth and then back again. Glass, knife, cloth. His heart was racing, his mind whirling. She knew it. "You were describing Michael Tanner's house."

But Alex didn't continue. She could feel the balance of power shifting ineluctably away from her, and she couldn't let that happen. Not again.

"Your turn, Professor," she said, her gaze steady on him. "Were you in touch with Daniel Hayden before his death?"

"Don't be ridiculous," Aldiss said. But it was too quick, too abrupt. "I am not interested in the past, Alexandra. I could fall silent right now. I could close myself like a book and end this lesson, and where would you turn then? To your hapless detective? To your conspiracy-theorist friends?"

She glared at him, heart thudding. Finally she nodded and said, "It was Dumant. Michael's house, the crime scene—everything was the same except the kitchen."

Aldiss went still, looked up at her quizzically.

"There were dishes all over the floor. They had been broken, pulled from the table and strewn across the room. Shards of glass everywhere. The chairs had been toppled and there were marks across the walls."

Aldiss thought. Then he said, "How many plates?"

"What?"

The professor sighed. "An easy question, Alexandra. How many plates were there?"

She tried to remember the kitchen, the strewn glass. But it was futile. She could remember nothing but the library, the books, the awful silence of the place—

"I don't know," she said shamefully. "I can't remember."

"You will," Aldiss said, his smile tightening. "You will dream of those rooms tonight, and you will remember. When you dream, make sure you pay attention. I am wondering if there weren't others in the house with Michael."

"Others?"

Aldiss said nothing, took a deep drink of the wine. When he put down the glass his lips were stained a dark red.

"The books," he said. "Tell me about them."

"At first I thought they were random," she said, "but when I looked closer I could see that there was an arrangement there. He was careful, precise. He wanted us to know that the murder was as much about his process as it was about Michael's death."

"Randomness does not exist. Not with this man. His obsession with the Dumant murders will have created a situation for him of unsustainability. He is writing a kind of sequel, you see, and in any sequel the writer cannot reach the point where his art matches the original. It is an impossible task."

"You mean he's going to go off the deep end?"

"I predict so, yes. He will rattle apart, because what he is doing is not his. It belongs to the real Dumant killer, the one that you—"

"Yes," she said, and looked quickly away.

"None of this belongs to him," Aldiss repeated. "This is a man who will feel an incredible amount of inferiority. He will be angry. He will burn with anger, radiate with it. He is in someone else's playground now. Someone else's mind. He is a thief, and all thieves are caught eventually. But . . ."

"Yes, Professor?"

"The damage will be done," Aldiss said softly.

Alex sat, staring at the man. His smile pulled apart into an O, and a hand drifted to his face so slowly that she could follow it all the way across, over the tablecloth and almost through the licking candle flame and to his cheek, where it sat on the flat, dead skin, fingers spidering the mandible closed. She looked away as the man worked on himself.

"You're thinking about something," Aldiss said finally. "Something I've said—it doesn't fit with your theories of the crime?"

"No," she said. "It's just . . . Can I ask you a question, Professor?"

She saw him hesitate, the black hearts of his pupils crushed flat as he drew his gaze down on her. Then he said, his voice knife-sharp, "Only if you plan to be polite this time."

"Did you ever hear of anyone being murdered while playing the Procedure?"

The vein in Aldiss's forehead jumped. He considered the question before he spoke. "It was played in different ways on different campuses," he said at last. "We each had our own set of rules."

"And Benjamin Locke. What were his rules?"

Aldiss opened his mouth to speak but stopped himself. Then, his voice smooth and measured, he said, "I don't want to talk about this right now."

She nodded, her eyes passing over him and into the hallway. There was a room there, its closed door setting off alarms inside her.

"Where is she?" Alex asked.

"You mean fair Daphne," the professor said. "Safe. She has her own life, her own friends." He stood and walked across the kitchen, passing through a knife blade of moonlight. He was not wearing shoes, and his bare feet smacked against the gnarled linoleum. When he passed behind the table he stopped, hovered above Alex. He was inches away from her now.

"Talk to me about Dumant," she said with her back still to him. "About what happened there."

"Is this a crisis of conscience, Alexandra? Do you not believe in your own findings during the night class? Do you doubt my innocence after all this time?"

"I believe in what we did in Iowa," she said, her voice faltering. "I believe . . ." *In you,* she wanted to say.

"The person who committed those crimes is dead," Aldiss continued. "You remember what happened. You were there. What you and your boyfriend discovered while you were in Iowa was true. It was all true. It was the one thing you have done correctly and thoroughly since you have been under my charge. You helped me reclaim my life, and I will never forget that."

She turned and faced him. "Why have you never spoken about it?"

Aldiss said nothing.

"You've never spoken about anything before," she went on, gathering courage now. "About your previous life, the one before Dumant. Before Fallows and Locke and—"

"*Stop this!*" Aldiss shouted, and Alex shrunk back. The smile held but his eyes brimmed with rage. Some of the wine had sloshed out of the flute and stained the crease of his hand. "I have no intention of talking to you about any of this. You are still my student, Alexandra. You will remember that you are beneath me in every way imaginable."

The thought came to her like a flash: *At least I don't prey on my students.*

Aldiss's eyes lit up. He'd read the direction of her thoughts. "Yes," he hissed. "Say it. *Please.*"

She didn't. She refused to give him the pleasure.

The man moved out into the living room and sat down on the couch. He had thrown a yellow sheet over an end-table lamp for ambiance, and he sat in its sickly glow, staring into the maze of shadows on the other side of the room.

"In Fallows," he said softly, "there is a moment where the narrative turns. The scholars call it a *volta,* this moment where the novel becomes something else. In *The Coil,* you remember, we go from a novel of manners into a character study of Ann Marie. We begin to see that she is not as powerful as she seemed at first, that she is a scared Iowa girl lost in the big, bad city. In *The Golden Silence* there are many voltas, sometimes multiple turns on a page. Remember that that book is full of trapdoors."

Alex stared at the man. The feeling of being back in that basement classroom, of being a student again and waiting desperately for Aldiss to fill in the blanks, was palpable. "Professor," she said. "Why are you telling me this?"

Aldiss looked at her. "It's about to turn, Alexandra."

"What do you mean?"

"This is not about poor Michael Tanner and his broken dishes. This is about something else entirely. It's about something older than the night class or the Dumant killer or any of that. I thought at first that the man who is doing this—I thought he was weak. To steal another's crime is not flattery; it is not literary at all, no matter how much our invisible man wants it to be so. It is destruction." Aldiss took another sip of the wine, the final liquid in the cup spinning down toward his ruined mouth. "This man isn't continuing something. He's trying to finish it."

Alex looked at him. She felt weak, suddenly. Dizzy. "I'm sorry, Professor," she said. "Excuse me."

She went out into the hallway and found the bathroom she had seen earlier. She stepped inside and closed the door, turned on the light, and looked at herself in the mirror. It was streaked glass, bone-gray with age. Alex leaned on the sink and took a cleansing breath, splashed cold water on her face. *Finish it,* she thought. *Finish . . .*

Her cell phone vibrated in her pocket. She took it out and looked at the face. She had two texts. One was from Peter; she didn't open it. The other was from Dean Rice:

Report back to us when you are finished with him.

"Asshole," she whispered to herself, turning off the water. When she returned to the living room, Aldiss was still sitting on the sofa. His face was flushed with drink and his hands were clasped in his lap. His shirt was open at the collar and she saw the puzzle tattoo in the delta of his throat and chest, just the topmost edge of it. He followed her with his eyes as she sat down.

"Are you afraid in that house with them, Alexandra?" he asked.

She lied. "No."

"You should be. What I said this morning—I am even more sure of it now. The killer was part of the night class." He paused, twisting the flute between his fingers. "Do you have a weapon?"

"No. Of course not."

"You will need one. Just in case. I can get that for you."

She shook her head softly. There were a million things roaring and collapsing through her, but all she could think about was Keller. Keller, standing before those shelves, urging her to be careful.

"You're thinking of something, Alexandra," Aldiss said. "Tell me."

She gathered herself. "How do you know it was someone from the night class?"

Nothing. Silence spun out.

"How do you know? You must tell me how you know one of them murdered Michael, Professor. You can't just put me up in that house, make me observe them all like some fucking Judas without telling me!" Alex was on the edge now, pushing him as hard as she had ever pushed. She felt a burning in the pit of her stomach as hot as a red wire. It was desperation. "Something happened," she continued. "Something went on between you and one of them to cause you to think this way of them. Was it Daniel, Professor? Is he the connection?"

Aldiss's eyes registered a hit, but again he said nothing.

"This is ridiculous," she said. "They're going to come for you, Professor."

Aldiss laughed.

"They're going to come out here and destroy your books and papers, rip the place apart seam by seam. And Daphne—they will find out what she knows. You will end your life the way you would have if you had never met me—cast in a net of suspicion, believed to be a murderer by most of your own colleagues. This, here, everything you've built—it will become Rock Mountain all over again."

He swung his gaze toward her, only one side of his face visible in the lamplight. The smile wavered. "I did not kill Michael Tanner."

She waited a beat. Then: "If you know who did—"

"I know. It was someone from the night class. That is all I can tell you."

"But *who*?" she said, shrieking now, her hands thrown up in front of her. "Which one of them?"

The man was silent. The smile split apart, revealed teeth.

"Good night, Professor," Alex relented. "And good luck."

Then she was walking to the rental. The night was high and clear, the lake behind the house shining in the moonlight. She got in and started the car, felt the heat pour over her chilled face. For a moment she sat in the drive, cursing herself, pounding the steering wheel. *Fuck fuck fuck, Alex! It was a simple thing, the easiest job in the world, and you wrecked it. You—*

Something cracked against her passenger window.

Alex looked over, saw Aldiss's face at the glass. She rolled the window down.

"Here," he said. "You forgot this on the kitchen table."

The professor passed her the card he had given her earlier. Alex took it and slipped it between the covers of one of the books on Fallows she had brought on the trip with her but had yet to take out of the car. Then she rolled the window back up, reversed down the driveway, and drove out of Richard Aldiss's life for what she hoped was the very last time.

18

It was just after eleven o'clock when she returned to the mansion. She found Christian Kane smoking outside. She walked up the drive, scanning the windows of the Victorian for Keller's room, wondering if he was still awake.

"How is the good professor?" Christian called as she approached. The writer's cigarette flared in the shadows.

"Adamant about his innocence," she said.

"No heads in the closet, then?"

"I'm afraid not." She nodded at his cigarette. "Bum one?"

He knocked a smoke out of the pack and handed it to her, lit it as she leaned close. She smelled liquor on him, wondered what they had all talked about while she was away.

Now the man watched her, his arms crossed to fend off the wind.

"If I told you something," he said, "do you promise not to tell the rest of them?"

Alex regarded him. "Of course, Christian."

"I plagiarized from Fallows."

"What?"

The man shifted, his breathing faster than it had been. Alex saw that he'd been wanting to tell someone for the longest time but didn't have the courage. Now, back at his old college with one of his friends murdered, he'd brought himself to the confession. *Maybe there's more there,* Alex thought.

"Not word for word, nothing like that," he said. "I simply stole his style, his rhythm. In my last novel, *Barker in the Storm.* I got stuck. Maybe I had this crazy notion that people would be playing the Procedure to my novels, I don't know. I was going with Michael every weekend to Burlington and Dumant, we were deep inside the Procedure. I was getting swept away by it, I was losing myself, Alex. My editor started calling me, asking when the next book would be ready. I kept telling him, 'Soon. Soon. Soon.' Months turned into a year, and I almost lost everything . . ." Christian trailed off, looked away into the shadows as if he'd heard something. Alex followed his gaze but saw nothing but darkness, only the flickering spread of the college down below them. "One day I went into my library and I took down *The Golden Silence,* started reading through it. And I thought to myself, 'This. This is it.' So I read a few passages and tried to emulate them. It was like stealing from Fallows. And it felt . . . my God, Alex, it felt so good. I felt powerful again, like when I first started writing. It was magnificent."

"Someone will find out," Alex said. "The scholars—they catch those kinds of things."

He smiled darkly. "I hope they do. I hope they find me out." Again he looked into the fringe of trees, took one last drag on the cigarette, and flicked it into the brush. "And I hope I'm punished."

Inside the house the crowd had dispersed. She found Frank Marsden and Lucy Wiggins by the fire, snuggled tight and talking in low voices. She went into the kitchen and drew a glass of water from the tap. Stood there drinking, listening to the silent old house and thinking of Aldiss. Of his persistence about one of her friends being guilty. Someone who was here.

Laughter, then. Coming from somewhere in the darkness.

"Hello?" Alex said. She waited.

Nothing at first. Then the laughter again, trilling and feminine. Alex stepped deeper into the room.

A man's voice. Familiar, but she couldn't place it. She took another step.

There was a door beyond the refrigerator. The laundry room, perhaps—she had never explored this part of the dean's house. She took another step, then another. Finally she reached out and pushed the swinging door open and saw—

Melissa Lee knelt before the nurse, Matthew Owen.

Embarrassment rushed through Alex, but she didn't turn. She stood for a moment, hidden in the darkness, the door cracked open. She saw Melissa's face in the man's lap. Saw Owen's head upturned, heard the low moan of his pleasure. When she looked down again she saw Melissa watching her, a kind of wicked amusement in the woman's eyes.

Not such a soccer mom after all, Alex thought. Quietly, she stepped back into the kitchen. Then she walked out into the great room, into the flushing heat of the fire, and ran right into Frank Marsden. He was drunk but solid, and she was nearly knocked to the floor.

"Alexandra," he slurred. The fire's reflection burned in his eyes.

"Hello, Frank."

The man smiled and said, "Lock your door."

"Excuse me?"

"That's what they're saying on campus." Frank got close to her, the liquor on his breath strong and thick. Some mad vision of revenge burned in his eyes. "Lock your doors tonight. Whoever did this to Michael—the guy's still out there."

"Is that you, Alex?"

She was upstairs now, her heart pounding from what she had seen in the kitchen. At the sound of the voice Alex stopped midway down the corridor and looked into the dean's study. The room was mostly dark, lamplight streaming weakly across the old man's form. He sat in his wheelchair, the limp wig hanging askew on his head, his lipstick smeared and his breathing thick and wet. She waited for him to go on.

"Your eulogy tomorrow," he said. "Do you have something planned?"

She didn't, but she was going to try to get her thoughts down in her room before sleep. That was how she always wrote her lectures: exhaustion coming on, the conscious mind being peeled back and laid bare, inhibitions stripped away.

"I'll be ready," she said.

"Good. Sally is broken, I think. There are police watching her every move. It's a horrible thing. She will need some relief, some proper remembrance of him."

"Of course."

The dean shifted, pulled back out of the light. "And how was Richard tonight?"

"He didn't do this, Dean Fisk."

"He told you that."

"I know him. I know he's not capable." *Do you have a weapon? I can get that for you.*

"We change," the man said, and then he coughed harshly into his fist. When the spell was over he repeated, "We change. My falling-out with Richard was the genesis of it. When you finished the night class and he was released from prison, I began to see the man's capabilities. I started to see him for who he really is."

"He isn't like this," she said. "This is . . . evil."

"An overused word. I believe it is much more simple than that."

"Simple?"

"I believe Michael had found something. Discovered something. And his killer was forced to silence him. It is pure Shakespeare, to snuff the truth with the greatest silence. 'Truth is truth, to the end of reckoning'—the reckoning has come to Jasper, Alex. Michael had fallen upon the wrong secrets."

"Secrets about Fallows?" she asked.

"More than likely, yes."

"I know he'd been playing the Procedure again. With Christian."

"Yes," Fisk said, his blind eyes moving more quickly now. "As I said to you earlier, Matthew tells me that he sees them playing it on his walks across the east quad. The students. Rudimentary versions, mostly on weekends. Nothing complex enough for Michael to be interested in. But it is here on this campus. It has spread."

She wondered about the significance of what the dean had just said. "What does it mean?"

"It means that Richard is perhaps more connected to this college than he is letting on. And that makes him a suspect."

Fisk slumped back in his wheelchair. His face was ashen and doughy, the bald scalp pink and irritated. Alex bid the dean good night and left the room. She no longer felt exhausted, even though it was getting late. Instead, her senses were sharp and her mind was calm, precise. She walked purposefully down the hallway and entered the library she'd been in hours earlier.

Once again she felt her way across the shelves in the weak light, searching for the modernists. Easily she retraced her steps to find Aldiss's *Ghost*, the marker she had given herself to find the secret space. She pulled it off the shelf and—

The manuscript was gone.

She reached into the space and groped madly in the darkness, splayed her fingers across the dusty shelves. She ran her hands over the spines, pulling out book after book, her heart hammering and sticky sweat pooling beneath her arms. *No,* she thought. *Please, no.*

Anger. It all came out in that instant, the bitter, gnawing frustration. Michael's murder and the task Aldiss had given her and all the rest of it.

Keller, she thought. *Goddamn him.*

She spun on her heel and left the room. It was pitch-black in the hallway now, and for a moment she couldn't find her way. Her thoughts were still swimming, the fact of the manuscript being stolen blurring her vision and making her stumble into the tattered wall. So much darkness here.

A sound. A footstep behind her.

Alex turned and put her palms to the wall, bracing herself in fear.

"Hello?" she said into the shadows. "Keller, is that you?"

She listened, her pulse pounding in her jaw. Nothing.

She began to walk again but stopped. Something moved, the form of someone darting across the room at the end of the hall.

"Who is it?" she called. "I can't see anything. I can't—"

Again there was stillness. *Damn it, Alex, you're creeping yourself out.*

She backed again into the darkness, palm over palm against the curling wallpaper, until she found her room. Then she went inside and shut the door. Locked it.

For a moment she stood there, breathing, with her back to the door. Cursing herself for being here, for putting herself into this situation.

Then she went to the bed, opened an end-table drawer, and found a pen inside. There was her copy of Christian Kane's *Barker at Play,* and she put the paperback on her knees and began to write in the margins of a page what she had learned so far.

Melissa Lee. Distance from campus: lives in downstate Vermont. Motive: unclear. Still using sex as she did as a student—for power, leverage?

Frank Marsden. Distance from campus: resides mostly in California. Motive: possible dislike/jealousy of Michael Tanner, just as in night class.

Sally Tanner. Distance from campus: lives here. Motive: possibly found something of interest on her husband, something incriminating (re: Fallows?).

Lewis Prine (hasn't arrived yet; remember to call again before sleep). Distance from campus: lives and works in upstate Vermont. Motive: connection with last existing Fallows manuscript. May be right about its existence and it being hidden in the Fisk mansion.

Christian Kane. Distance from campus: close. Motive: became involved with Michael Tanner while in the Procedure. Included a crime scene in one of his novels that matches the Dumant/Tanner scene. Seems overly willing to absolve himself from the situation.

Jacob Keller. Distance from campus: close. Motive:

She sat back and looked at what she had written. She wondered again if Aldiss was right about one of her old friends. Wondered if Keller could somehow be involved. Inexplicable, but still . . .

She went back to her notes:

Jacob Keller. Distance from campus: close. Motive: stole Fallows manuscript.

She put the pen down and looked at the six names. As she studied them a vision appeared: the crime scene photos she had seen earlier that morning. Michael's body, broken and destroyed, the— What had Keller said? The *brutality* of it. The awfulness of it. And someone here, one of the people she had once trusted and studied with in the night class, might be to blame.

Almost at once exhaustion fell over her. She felt herself falling, tumbling softly down—

Another sound from the hallway. Alex sat up in bed, her senses alive now. Readied.

She stared at the door. Heard it again: a scuffling noise, the sound of someone walking. Approaching.

"Who—" Alex began, but she was cut off by a knock.

She went to it and pulled it open a crack. "Yes?"

"Hey, it's me." Keller.

"Tired," she said.

"Yeah. Of course." Disappointment in his voice. "Something came for you."

"What?"

"Here." He handed her something through the crack. It was an envelope, thick and chunky, nothing on the outside but ALEXANDRA SHIPLEY in a jagged, slashing hand. "There was a knock on the front door. We thought it was another reporter, so we didn't answer. When Christian went out to smoke, he found this on the porch."

"Thanks, Keller."

"No problem."

The man hesitated there at the door. She thought about letting him in, and then she remembered Peter, her boyfriend back in Cambridge. She remembered the missing manuscript.

"Good night," she said, and closed the door.

Alex took the envelope to her bed and opened it in the pale lamplight. Tipped its contents onto the bed: a book. It was a Fallows, a first edition of *The Golden Silence*. She turned it around, saw the photograph of Charles Rutherford on the back.

What is this?

She opened the book and saw what was inside.

The pages had been cut out. The text had been carved into a precise shape, and an object had been placed inside the space that was left. It was a perfect fit, the gun falling out slowly into her hand when she turned the book upside down.

She had her weapon.

The Class
1994

19

When Alex arrived at the Fisk Library that Wednesday evening to finish her Fallows reading, she opened *The Coil* and found a note inside. It had been written on a small strip of paper, no larger than a sliver of glass. It read, *Find out about the Procedure.*

Her backpack—had she left it somewhere on campus? Mentally she retraced her steps that day: lunch at the Commons, 1:00 p.m. with Dr. Mew (Japanese Literature After the Bomb), afternoon study session in Lewis Prine's dorm room, back to her dorm to retrieve the Fallows. Someone had gotten to her book.

She looked around, paranoia tickling the back of her neck. There was a group of students leaning over a physics text two tables over. A lone reader in a lighted cubicle on the other side of the library. A few others drifting lazily through the stacks. Other than that the library was empty, quiet. She fingered the note.

Find out about the Procedure.

Alex had heard the term somewhere. Had Aldiss said it in one of his lectures? Had she read it somewhere? Again she scanned the library. A boy lifted his gaze to look at her. He was a floppy-haired sophomore, a Kappa Tau she'd danced with at a party—she glanced away. There was the loose feeling of something coming unraveled, a thread tipping from a spool. The Procedure—had she seen it in a book? She stopped, her hands absently crinkling the note into brutal origami, her breath coming fast. *A book,* she thought. *That's it.*

She was up and moving, her backpack slung over her shoulder. Outside, into the biting cold, and over the lawn toward Philbrick. The day was ending, the trees shot through with bloodred sunlight. The old Alex would have stopped and observed this, maybe appreciated it. The silent quads, the way the snow diamond-sparkled on the ground. But this was the new Alex, the girl who'd been changed by the night class. By Aldiss. She pumped her legs harder, walking fast, wind striking her cheeks like a thousand needles. She entered the dorm, breathing in the blast of warmth, and took the elevator up to her room.

The book was exactly where she had hidden it.

Mind Puzzles by Richard Aldiss. For a moment she stood in the empty room, thinking about how her life had changed because of this. One little volume, a collection of pages held together by cheap glue. A flimsy thing—and yet so powerful. So profound.

As she had done that night in the library two weeks ago, Alex searched the index. It was easy to find: there were over ten references. PROCEDURE, THE. She scanned the subentries and picked one: RULES, VARIATIONS OF. Her hands trembling, she turned to the page.

It was a game. That much was clear right away. Alex ran her eyes over the text, making sure her back was to the door in case her roommate returned. But this game—it was unusual. It was only played by what Aldiss called "the enlightened," those Fallows scholars adept enough with the texts to keep up. And there was something else; something about the tone Aldiss used to discuss the Procedure. A certain demure quality she had never seen in his other work. About this the professor had cared deeply. He wanted the reader to understand that this game, these pages, were important.

One section particularly struck her.

A game, yes, but the Procedure is not some innocent children's pastime. Half memory contest, half puzzle, the objective is this: to reenact scenes from Paul Fallows's novels as perfectly as one can. There are levels of complexity—from the true Masters to neophytes who are simply looking for a new experience on campus—but the form and function of the Procedure is always the same. It is a method of deconstruction, a method of understanding the texts in a completely new way outside of a dusty lecture hall. Of tunneling inside the pages themselves.

There was a photograph accompanying the section of text. It showed a group of students on a campus, their '80s fashion clearly evident, talking to one another. There was something about their faces, about their stance and their manner of dress, that struck Alex right away. *They're acting,* she thought. *It's like they're in a production. A play of some sort.*

She continued reading. She read about the variations of the game, how it had been invented (at Yale, perhaps by Benjamin Locke—though this was disputed), its rules and objectives. "Some believe you cannot understand Fallows," Aldiss wrote, "unless you learn how to play the Procedure. That you cannot truly know the two existing novels unless you become enlightened in the game. And if one does not know the novels, if one does not fully understand them, then how is one to even begin his search for Paul Fallows?"

Alex dug deeper into the book. References to the Procedure cropped up often. There were other photographs of players; there was a crude diagram of how the Procedure was scored and who was declared a winner. But one thing became apparent as she read: *you never knew when it began.* The Procedure could begin anywhere, at any time, and the player never knew. A line from Fallows would be dropped and the player would have to respond accordingly, in character, the way the dialogue had appeared on the page. This was the game; this was the contest of wits and memory. One simply had to be ready to begin.

"It could be happening now," Aldiss wrote. "It could be happening to you, wherever you are, and you would simply have to react."

That night she was late to class. She slipped into the basement room and found her seat. She looked at the others, scanned the small windowless lecture hall. Which one of them had slipped the note inside her book? Which one had sent her to do the research on the Procedure? When she reached the front row she froze; Michael Tanner was staring right at her.

For a moment neither of them acknowledged the other. Alex could feel the measure of her own breathing, her pulse hammering. The boy continued to look.

Did you do it? she mouthed, checking the others. No one was listening. Jacob Keller was laughing at some joke Daniel Hayden had told. Christian Kane was scribbling something, probably another of his weird stories, in his red notebook. Melissa Lee was catching up on her reading. Alex looked back at Tanner, saw that he hadn't heard her question. He leaned forward.

Did you leave the note in my book?

But his only response was a question of his own. Alex followed his lips.

Do you like this class?

Instinctively her eyes flicked up: the screen was still black.

No, she replied.

Neither do I, he said. *No one does.*

Then a shadow twitched on the wall and Michael turned quickly away. When Alex raised her eyes, Aldiss had already appeared on the screen. Had he seen them talking? But the thought was quickly swept away by the man's appearance.

He was disheveled, his hair in wild tufts and his eyes purpled with exhaustion. The collar of his orange uniform was off center, as if he had been yanked into his seat by one of the guards. And there was something else, something even more curious: the man had *drawn closer to them*. Perhaps the camera had tightened in on his face, maybe his steel table had been brought forward a foot or two—something had changed. The professor had become the focus, the absolute center of the room. In the corner, near the foam-tiled ceiling and cradling the western wall, the red eye of their own camera bore down on them.

"I'm sorry," Aldiss began, his voice broken and slurred, "for what happened the last night we met. My spells . . . they come upon me so suddenly that there is nothing I can do to stop them. When I was a child I called them fugues. I was horribly ashamed of them, and the other children used to tease me. I was the Go-Away Boy, the Sleeper. I would hold them in, squeeze the blackness inward like a breath. My fugues were rooms I walked around inside. But that . . ." He looked away, toward the unseen walls that imprisoned him. "That was too horrible." The room was silent; they remembered him that night, his face seizing and that one eye descending toward them, nearly colliding with the camera and holding, pausing on them in those last seconds before the connection dissolved to black. Finally Aldiss smiled, waved a hand idly across the lens. "Enough of that. Let us talk about why we're really here: Paul Fallows. Tell me what you've found."

No one spoke. The TV screen flickered, maybe from the wind or some movement in the professor's small cinderblock room. A line of static pulled down like a curtain and the professor appeared again, his hands folded before him and his alert black eyes on them. He hadn't shaved, and a graying stubble freckled his cheeks.

"Nothing?" Aldiss said. "Surely you've been doing something with your days."

"How do you hunt a man who doesn't exist?" asked Lewis Prine. He was sitting in the back row with his head leaned against the concrete wall.

"I assure you Paul Fallows exists, Mr. Prine. He has always existed."

"But how do we know that?"

"Because I have told you that it's true. Is that not enough?"

"No," said Melissa Lee, jumping in before Prine could speak.

"And why not?" asked Aldiss, smiling more sharply now. He rested his chin on his right hand, and they could see that he had written something there. A fugitive word snaking over and around the webbing of his thumb. Aldiss did this sometimes, wrote his class notes on his body, but like everything else about him the words were elusive. A date, a motif, a page number, everything always just out of the camera's view.

"Because you're . . ."

"Here?" he asked, extending his arms. The guards, only their torsos and legs visible, shifted as they did each time Aldiss moved. "Is that what you mean, Ms. Lee? The fact that I am imprisoned in this place makes me less trustworthy? Less capable of being correct?"

She looked up, met his eyes fiercely. "Yes."

"There's also the fact of how much information we have at this point," put in Daniel Hayden, challenging Aldiss as he so often did. "It isn't much."

"What more would you like me to give you?" Aldiss asked.

The boy said nothing at first. He watched the screen intently, as if the box itself might instruct him on how to proceed. Then he said, his voice measured and calm, "Your trip to Iowa. Tell us about that."

Aldiss didn't flinch, but something changed in his face. Something cracked on the right cheek, a fissure of dark skin there like a piece of string being pulled taut. "And that is relevant to Fallows in what way?"

"In every way," said Hayden. "Isn't the beginning as important as the end?"

"The beginning," Aldiss repeated, drumming his fingers on the steel table. "I was a student just like all of you when I went to Iowa in search of Fallows. But what I've discovered at Rock Mountain is so much more important than that. I was a child then. I didn't know where Paul Fallows was, I didn't know *who* he was. All I knew was what my mentor, Dr. Benjamin Locke, supplied for me. Now I am much wiser."

"Locke," Tanner said. "Who was he?"

Aldiss's eyes fell away. "Someone who knew more about Fallows than anyone alive. But, like so many other scholars, Locke was consumed by the writer. The search became everything to him, and eventually it destroyed him."

Alex thought about what Dean Fisk had told her, about the scholars the Fallows search had wrecked. She thought about Aldiss in his lonely cell, about the two graduate students at Dumant University who had been murdered. All for this, these meaningless words. Almost independent of her conscious mind she reached out, touched the lined and crinkled cover of *The Coil*. Its cold inanimateness brought her back to the night, to the basement room and all its mysteries.

Ask him about the Procedure.

Before she could catch herself the question was out, dropped into the conversation like a bomb: "Did he introduce you to the Procedure?"

Silence. On his screen Aldiss drew back—a wince, or perhaps a flinch. The man had not expected this. "More research?" he asked, his tone cool.

"Well," Alex fumbled, "I—I didn't mean to . . ."

"What is it, Professor?" Lee asked, saving Alex from the shame of doing battle with him. Now that something had been uncovered, some new thread of the class, Lee felt a need to unravel it. "What is the Procedure?"

Aldiss looked off toward the edge of the frame. This was a common gesture: his glancing away, his biding time. Everything with the professor was deliberate, measured. They waited for him to continue.

"The Procedure was a game," he said at last. "A game played with the novels of Paul Fallows."

"Do you mean like a role-playing game?" asked Sally Mitchell.

"No," Aldiss said quickly. "It was much more than that."

"How was it played?"

Again Aldiss seemed almost cautious. He lifted a hand to his hair, swept some of it back out of his eyes. The wind screeched above them, feathering the picture and making the professor appear, in texture and shape, like a thin shadow. He sighed. There was no choice now; he had gone too far.

"The strange thing about the Procedure was that you didn't know you were inside it until you realized something had changed," he began. "To be part of the game you had to be chosen. I remember when I was chosen as a student at Dumant. I remember the pride I felt, to finally be one of them . . ." Aldiss's voice fell away, and he looked again past the camera's edge. When he continued his voice was more measured. "A message written inside a book told me the game had begun. But as far as I could tell, nothing had happened."

Three rows away from the television, Alex sat forward. *A message inside a book?* She focused more deeply on the professor.

"You mean the Procedure hadn't really begun?" asked Frank Marsden. He was again dressed as Richard III, his eyes dark and his hair colored with shoe polish.

"No, it had begun. This is the thrill of the game—*you never know.* You never know exactly when real life ends and the Procedure begins."

Aldiss waited while the class digested this. When everyone was quiet, he continued.

"After the initiation, you wait. You wait until they are ready. Three weeks after I found the message in the book, odd things began to happen. My friends—they were not behaving in normal ways. They were . . . it was as if they were playing parts in some theater production. This, students, was the Procedure."

"And these parts," said Hayden, his gaze leveled directly at the screen. "You were supposed to respond to them accordingly. To pick up the loose threads of these scenes and become a character from Fallows."

"That's right. It seems silly, yes—but trust me, when the Procedure reaches the highest levels there is *nothing* silly about it. I will always remember: we were at a campus coffee shop one day, and someone looked at me and started speaking lines right out of *The Golden Silence*. For a moment I didn't know what was happening. I was lost. I panicked. Finally this person just got up and left. Another message appeared in one of my books the next week, this time in a copy of Derrida: *WE'RE DISAPPOINTED IN YOU, RICHARD*."

"You lost," said Keller.

"That first time, yes. But I got my next chance a couple of weeks later. We were walking down a campus street, the five of us who called ourselves the Iowans, and someone started saying lines. I recognized the passage—it was from deep inside the novel, when Ann Marie has moved into the mansion with her uncle. I fell into my own role, saying the lines and using the gestures exactly from the text. It has to be exact; the player has to show a mastery of Fallows, down to the very last detail. And that second time I knew from the others' faces—I had won."

"And what happens if you win?" Mitchell asked quietly.

Aldiss turned his gaze up. Something had changed in his face, eclipsed the hard-set tension from before. His eyes flashed. "You are accepted," he said. "The Procedure ends and you become one of the elite."

"And if you lose?" asked Alex. "What then?"

Aldiss's eyes dropped again. The faceless guards rocked.

"Then you are shunned. And as a Fallows scholar, to not be inside, to not be one of them—that is a fate worse than death."

The professor said nothing else. Seconds later the feed was cut.

20

Later that night she met Keller at Rebecca's. He was there when she arrived, his note cards spread out on the streaked table, a football field cut apart by grid lines and *X*'s and *O*'s. When he saw Alex across the smoke-filled room, he waved her over.

"Just a little homework," he said as she sat down. The place was loud, jangling. Good.

"No problem."

"Order you a beer?"

"I'll take a Number Nine."

"Magic Hat," Keller said, impressed. "Excellent choice." He called the waitress over and ordered for them.

A couple of awkward moments passed. This wasn't like being in the night class with him, Alex thought. This was something else entirely. This was a real date. It wasn't as if she were a homebody at Jasper; she got out as much as anyone else. But since Harvard had accepted her, and since her father had gotten worse, there just hadn't been much time for this sort of thing. She felt foolish, out of her element.

"So, the Procedure."

She looked up, realized Keller had spoken. It was hard to get a feel for how big he was, how solid his frame was until you were sitting close to him. There was no softness at all on his body. But he was also good-looking, with kind, quiet eyes and a mouth that always seemed to be bent into an ironic smile.

"What about it?" she asked. Their beers came.

"Stupid, isn't it? To get caught up in books that way? It's almost like they wanted to find a hole and slip right into the Fallows novels."

"I don't know," she said, thinking, *a rabbit hole* . . .

Keller cocked his head. He smiled, intrigued. Alex had caught him off guard. "You thought the game sounded fun."

"I can understand why he did it," she said. She looked beyond him, saw Melissa Lee in a corner booth. She was talking to three or four other English majors, and Alex was surprised to see Michael Tanner among them. Lee caught Alex looking, and Alex turned back to Keller, her cheeks burning.

"I think it's high nerd," Keller was saying. "But I do want to hear more about his trip to Iowa with this guy . . . what was his name? Locke."

"I thought you distrusted Aldiss."

"I sure as hell do. But I also want to see where this thing is going, Alex. I want to find out what he knows, what he found out inside that prison. He's hooked me, which is exactly what he intended to do with this class. But still . . ."

"Say it," she said.

"It sounds corny."

"Come on, Keller."

"It's like things just aren't what they seem with this guy."

She laughed, and Keller flushed.

"Maybe it's just me." He lowered his eyes to the table, pulled his beer into the cradle of his arms. "Maybe I'm just paranoid as hell."

"You're not paranoid."

"So you feel it too?"

Tell him, she thought. *Tell Keller about the book, about the message there. Tell him that Aldiss is innocent.* She opened her mouth but nothing came out. She put the bottle to her lips and took a long drink.

"I did some digging," he said.

"What kind of digging?"

"I've found some things. Today, in the Fisk Library."

Alex sat forward, but Keller didn't offer her anything. He just sat there with his arms crossed and stared at her blankly. The jukebox was playing Screaming Trees, and there were a couple of drunken sorority sisters on the dance floor. The place was getting louder.

"Well?" she said. "Spill it."

Keller grinned. "Nope."

"Keller! I thought we were coming to study tonight."

"Is that what this is?" he asked, that smile hanging in place. "Studying?"

"What else could it be?"

"Unraveling mysteries," Keller said, lowering his voice and doing a pitch-perfect imitation of Aldiss. He took a deep drag from the beer, his eyes glistening. It was at that moment that Alex realized something: she was having fun.

"Are you going to tell me what you found in the library or not?" she asked.

"Not yet."

"If you don't show me, Keller, then I'll—"

He leaned across and kissed her. It was quick, silent, the table's feet sliding gently and their bottles sloshing as if a train had blown through on the tracks outside Rebecca's side exit. Alex was left dazed.

"I'm sorry," he said.

"No. No, I didn't mean—"

"Here."

The boy reached down and pulled something out of his backpack. It was a thick satchel, I LOVE VERMONT stitched on the side.

Keller tossed a book on the table. It slid across the slick surface and bumped against Alex's arm. She picked it up, inspected its cover. She had seen it before, many times. It was Fallows's *The Coil.*

"Not funny, Keller," she said, thinking about how fast he'd moved toward her, about the gentle push of his breath against her lips. "I have one just like this back in my room."

Keller ignored the quip. "At first I didn't believe him," he said. "Thought it was just another one of Aldiss's tricks. But then I started reading this thing. I mean really reading it, Alex. Reading it the way the professor talks about in class. Working with it. Working *into it.* Deconstructing it."

"And?"

Keller breathed in. He reached forward and touched the book—but it was a careful touch, as if the thing were charged with electricity. "Aldiss was right. There are things . . . Jesus Christ, Alex, there are things in here that tell us where to find him."

"You mean Fallows?"

A nod. "Yeah, I think so. It's like a—"

"Map," she said, remembering what Stanley Fisk had said earlier.

"That's it. *The Coil* is a goddamn map."

She touched the book's cover now, ran her fingers over the cool surface. The image was disorienting, bizarre. A woman in a city, but it was a strange city. The skyscrapers cast no shadows; the streets all ran in zigzag patterns toward the middle of the metropolis, where there lay a black, vine-choked heart. The title of the book swept upward, the words composed of tendrils and branches that grew from the smothered heart:

THE COIL
BY PAUL FALLOWS

Alex said, "Show me what you found."

"Like I said, I went to the library this morning. Thought I would do some reading, you know, get caught up for tonight's class. But I read a few pages and started to get tired. Sleepy. We had a game Saturday and I'm still not recovered."

"Don't tell me you dreamed of this thing."

"It wasn't a dream," he said firmly. "I laid my head down on the table. I was there in the reading room and . . ."

"What was it, Keller?" she asked impatiently.

"Here."

He turned the book on its side and pointed. There, right at the edge of his finger, was an imperfection on the page. The mark was barely noticeable, just a small formless dot. It was so tiny that Alex thought it was a smudge of ink, and she tried to brush it away.

"No," Keller said. "It's permanent. Typed onto the page. I thought it may've been just my book, a mistake from the printer or something. So

I went into the stacks, found the library's copy of *The Coil.* Same thing. The same smudge in the same exact place."

"What the hell is it?"

Keller didn't say anything; he simply opened the book near the smudge and pointed. She could see the tiny speck of ink floating on the outside margin, nothing more than a granule.

The fact hit her like a punch.

"It's a placeholder," she blurted.

"Exactly." Excitement gleamed in Keller's eyes now. "Like a bookmark or something. It has to be this page, because the following page doesn't have the mark. Page 97."

Alex read.

It was a scene from the heroine's home in Hamlet, Iowa. She is planning for her trip to New York City, the voyage that will be her liberation. Alex read the whole page twice, but found nothing of substance there. Nothing at all.

"I don't see it, Keller," she said. "It's just a scene to me. Just words."

"Look again."

She sighed. She hated these tests. Aldiss, Fisk, and now Keller—test after test, gauntlet after gauntlet. Nothing could be simple.

Once more she read. In the scene Ann Marie is explaining to her mother that she is going to New York City, and that that decision is final. There was an apartment for her on the East Side, an elderly uncle who would take her in. At the bottom of page 97 Ann Marie says, "This is what I want to do, Mother. I'm leaving Hamlet tomorrow." The page ends. Nothing.

Alex was almost ready to throw up her hands, tell Keller that she hadn't found anything there. She clearly wasn't as smart as he was. Of course there were other things on her mind, she might tell him. Other, darker things she had found out about Aldiss and—

But then. Then she saw.

The mark. The shape of it. The tiny granule, the shadowy blur at the edge of page 97. It looked just like . . .

It was pointing.

Pointing at a line in the middle of the page. The edge of the mark extending inward like an arrow toward the text, drawing her eye there now. It was unmistakable, and Alex scolded herself for missing it the first time.

A map, she thought again. *And every map has a legend.*

She stared at the mark, then put her fingernail on the page and drew her eye directly to the corresponding lines. As she did this, she saw Keller smile.

The lines read,

> . . . *in this century a woman needs to be at the center of every-thing, Ann Marie thought. She needs to be the heart of the matter, the absolute center—Plato's liquid gold.*

Alex read the line a second time, then looked up at Keller. He had the beer bottle to his lips, but the smile held.

"'Plato's liquid gold'?" Alex said aloud. The phrase practically jumped off the page.

Keller shrugged. "Got me. That's where you come in, Ms. Harvard."

"I've never heard that phrase before in my life," she said.

"Then I guess we're stuck."

"But the mark has to mean something, Keller. It has to."

He shrugged. She looked at him, thinking.

"Let's work this through," she said softly. "Who was Plato?"

"Alex."

"I'm serious, Keller. Who was he?"

The boy sighed. "Classical philosopher. Greek dude, had a sweet beard. Socrates was his Aldiss and he was Aristotle's. Freed some people in a cave."

"What else?" Alex asked.

Keller stared at her. Shook his head.

"There has to be something, Keller. There just has to be."

She moved it through her mind, looking for those connections. Keller had found so much, had discovered the marking in the book and this strange line with its bizarre language, and she knew the tumblers were clicking into place. She knew something was happening, could feel it happening. But it would not happen by magic; the door to Paul Fallows's identity would not simply open by itself.

Plato's liquid gold, she thought again. Her eyes were closed and she had her fingers on her temples, massaging. It was what her father did when he was in deep thought, the way she had seen him do it when the headaches began. *Come back now, Alex,* she said to herself, and thought of oil. Thought of Texas. Made connections that were so definitely *not* Greek that she felt herself losing sight of the line and the text and the marker and everything else—*and shit. Just shit.*

Plato's liquid gold, Plato's—

"Aldiss," she said.

Keller looked up. "What?"

"Something you said earlier. Something about Socrates being Plato's Aldiss. What did you mean?"

"Socrates was Plato's mentor," Keller said. "Aldiss is our mentor now, isn't he? Our guide?"

Guide, she thought. *Teacher as guide.* There was something there, some kernel inside the realization she knew she needed to make the next connection. If she could just isolate it, squeeze it out of there, extract it.

"Where are you going, Alex?" Keller asked, snapping his fingers. "Still with me?"

"Plato was a guide."

"Yeah, so?"

"Plato taught Aristotle in Athens. He taught his classes—where did he teach his classes, Keller?"

He made a face. She'd lost him.

"He taught his classes outside. Remember Humphries in HUM 101?"

"Ugh. Hump Fries. The Antichrist."

"Humphries told us that Plato always taught his classes outside," she repeated. "And what's outside in Athens?"

"Statues?"

"Come on, I'm serious."

"Okay, okay. What's outside . . . the same things that are outside at Jasper College, I would imagine. Flowers, grass, trees."

She looked at him, eyes wide now. "That's it: trees."

"What are you getting at, Alex?"

She leaned over and picked up her own book bag and pulled out her *Norton Anthology of World Literature.* Her fingers moved confidently through the pages; how many times had she searched through this very book, how many treasure hunts had she gone on as her professors waited? She had become so good at it, at finding the answers to back up her theories, that some of her professors accused her of having memorized the heavy book.

Now she was looking for a particular work. It wasn't by Plato; it was by Homer.

When she hit the page and began to scan the lines, Keller leaned forward. She could feel his suspicion hotly on her cheek. "Wrong work, girl. That's not the Greek we need."

"Shhh."

She went on, taking in line after line.

"It's in here somewhere," she said, frustration edging into her voice. "I remember Humphries talking about Greek nature one day when our class was reading *The Odyssey.* There was something about trees here, something about—"

Alex stopped. She'd found her old note.

"What?" Keller asked, suddenly interested. "What did you find?"

She read aloud: "'The girls stood still, each urging the others on. Then they led Odysseus to a sheltered place where he could sit down as Nausicaa, the daughter of the great-hearted Alcinous, had ordered. On the ground beside him they laid a tunic and cloak for him to wear, and, giving him some soft olive-oil in a golden flask, they told him to wash himself in the running stream.'"

Alex stopped, looked up at Keller. He still didn't understand.

"Fallows's lines," he said. "They didn't say anything about any of that."

She stopped him by touching his hand. It was a simple touch but she felt the spark of it—and she could tell that Keller did too. He looked up at her quietly.

"Look at my note," she said. "Notice what the professor said about that passage."

Keller took the book in his huge hand and turned it. Then he read what Alex had written as an eager freshman in the margin of the text. She saw him mouth it silently, watched his mouth draw the phrase out:

Liquid gold.

When he met her eyes again, she saw the hope in them. "What does it mean?"

"I think it's something to do with that part about olive oil," Alex said. "Olives. Plato taught his classes outside and often used olive trees as symbols for his students. Maybe Fallows was trying to nest the symbolism deep inside the text so that it would be difficult to draw it out. That's a starting point, Keller. It has to be. But where it leads us now, I have no idea."

"I think I might."

She blinked. "What?"

"Let me say first that you're good, Ms. Shipley," Keller said. "Real good. But let me show you what I can do. Today I went back to some of the old maps in the Fisk Library and I found Hamlet, Iowa. It's the town where Charles Rutherford lived and died."

"Our encyclopedia salesman whose picture is on the books."

"Right. I was just looking around at some of the streets, trying to get a sense of what Aldiss might be talking about when he tells us that to find Fallows we have to begin with Rutherford. And I found—"

"Liquid Gold Street."

Keller smiled. "Close, smart-ass." He turned the map and put his beer bottle on one corner. They both stood and stared down into Iowa. It was an old map, photocopied and smeared, the sweep of a river blurring into the grid of streets. All of it framed by the expanse of a pixelated disc that was labeled in a giant dark font: HAMLET.

What she wanted was on the south end. She followed Keller's finger along the grid, into the grid, and for a frantic moment she imagined herself there, in this town, walking these very streets. Then she came out of it to the flurry of guitars in the room behind her and saw that he was pointing to a jutting river road that curtained off the southern edge of town. Her breath caught.

Olive Street.

"It was where Rutherford lived," she said, getting caught up in the rhythm of their conversation now. Each signpost, each connection seemed so clear now, so elemental. Her heart banged in her chest.

"Exactly. This is why Aldiss mentioned the town that first night,

Alex. There's no question now. He's trying to tell us something about Hamlet."

They both fell silent, thinking about what it could mean.

"But what does he want us to find here on Olive Street that he never could?"

Keller downed his beer and slid the bottle away, picked up the novel and studied the cover image. The black heart, the woman standing before her maze. Unlike Alex's earlier, his appraisal of the book had a coldness to it. A kind of suspicion.

Finally he said, "I think I found the answer to that one, too."

"You're on fire today, Keller."

He removed another object from the satchel. It was a photograph.

He held it out, but as soon as she reached it he yanked it away from her. She thought it was another one of his games. Thought that maybe another kiss was coming. But when she looked at him she saw how serious he was and her own smile fell away.

"You can't ask me where I got this picture," he said.

"I—"

"Promise me, Alex. The person who gave it to me swore me to secrecy. He believes, as I do, that the night class is something bigger than it looks to be on the surface. But he wants to help me. To help us. Just please, don't ask me his name."

"Okay. I promise."

He handed the photo across the table to her. It was of a man standing in front of a small clapboard house. She had seen him before, but he looked different. Much different. Aged, yes, but somehow darker. Darker eyed. Somber. A lot like Richard Aldiss.

But the man in the photo was not Aldiss. Not even close.

"What the hell?" Alex said. It came out in a choke.

"It's him, Alex. There's no doubt it's him. Look at the date."

She did. On the bottom right-hand corner was a date stamp: 1/11/94.

The man was Charles Rutherford. He had been photographed just four days ago.

Alex

Present Day

21

Lewis Prine was already running late for Michael Tanner's memorial service when his Saab's engine began to whine. For miles he ignored the sound by thinking instead of coldblooded murder. How death carved a line from past to present, ripped out the seams and blurred everything painfully together. On the Burlington border, tears cooling on his cheeks, he rolled down the window and let the wind destroy what hair he had left.

Soon the vehicle began to shimmy and a gray scrim of smoke broke across the windshield. He pulled over on some Vermont back road and tried to call Alex Shipley on his cell. But there was no service out here in the middle of nowhere, and anyway he was past the point of no return now: the memorial procession would be starting soon, the mourners gathering on the Jasper quad. (Lewis knew from his work with violent, damaged men that the killer would likely be among them.)

Maybe it was better this way, he thought. A psych minor, a failed psychologist, and then the warden of a hospital for the criminally insane, he'd never truly been one of them anyway.

It took half an hour to flag down a passing car, another forty-five minutes to make it into a town called Orwell, where a mechanic patched up the engine with a stoic warning: *She won't last long*. Soon he was back on Route 2. As he passed into Jasper and saw the winking tops of the campus buildings in the distance, Lewis wondered if all this—his lateness, the car trouble—would somehow make the rest of them suspicious. They had always been like that, discerning and cold toward him. *A busted radiator?* they'd scoff. *How just like Lewis this is.*

It was crazy, as insane as something one of his prisoners would say, but he began to concoct a story in the rearview. A lie about why he was running late. A kind of careful alibi.

He parked and ran up the hill to the Fisk mansion. If he could catch the others before they left for the service, then he could convince them that he really cared. That he had always respected Michael and what had happened to him was such a mindless tragedy. By the time he made it to the front door, his shirt was stuck to him with sweat and his breath was coming in sharp, heavy gasps.

He knocked but got no answer. Lewis remembered the house well from his undergrad days: Fisk would often entertain the English majors, the nine who'd been chosen for Aldiss's night class. It had always given Lewis a pathetic sort of pleasure to be here in this house with the others. It was as if, on those evenings as they sipped crazy-expensive wine and talked of great literature, he truly belonged. Until he received the manuscript, those times were few and far between.

The manuscript.

He thought of it now. Of how it had come to him, that one brittle page, the promise of more. The anonymous guarantee that the unpublished Fallows was here, in the very house that loomed before him. Lewis wanted to speak to Alex, to see if she'd found the rest. If he could somehow resurrect Fallows, he thought, bring him back from the dead, then maybe the others would change their minds about him. Respect him as an equal.

He went around the side of the house and peered in. The window, dark with grime, barely permitted a view inside. Still, it was unmistakable: a figure moved behind the glass.

"Hey!" he shouted, rapping on the casement. "It's Lewis! I'm here! I've made it!"

He went quickly around to the rear of the house, checking his watch again. The seconds bore down on him, chipped away and made him break into a sprint, bound up a cobbled porch and to a back door only to find it—

Open. Standing wide, inviting him in. His first break today.

He stepped into a foyer. Jagged slats of sunlight curved down onto the hardwood floor. He smelled it: must and decay and disuse. The passing of time. The fact of his age, of Daniel's suicide. Of Michael's senseless murder. Strangely, he recalled one of his patients, a man who'd strangled his three-year-old daughter and then set her body on fire, saying, "You think bad thoughts too, Dr. Prine. This is how you and me are alike. This is how we're the same." Lewis pinched his eyes closed and went deeper into the house.

His footsteps echoed. A lamp was on here in the great room, scattering light—but there was something else. They'd been here recently. A blanket was twisted on the couch, black embers stacked in the fireplace.

"I made it," Lewis said into the room, aiming it in the direction of the figure he'd seen from outside, his voice resonating hollowly back to him. Now the alibi: "One of my patients. There was a situation back at the hospital. But I'm finally here. Is anyone there?"

He turned to leave but heard it again. The soft whisper of footsteps. The groan of a board. He waited.

Then the shadows unclenched and someone stepped into the room with him. A familiar face.

"I didn't think anyone was still here," Lewis said. "Are you—are you going to the service?"

"No hello for an old friend, Lewis?"

The figure materialized fully, hands out as if to say, *There's nothing to be afraid of. It's just me.* Regardless, Lewis was uncomfortable. He was already late, the service was about to start, and they hadn't even been that close. Not as close as he was to the others, anyway.

He tried to regain his composure. "God, it's been years."

"Too long. Friends should make it a habit to talk from time to time."

Lewis looked down, checked his watch again. Heat bloomed beneath his arms. Why were they both standing here? It was time to go; they could catch up later.

"Michael was one of the true elite, wasn't he?" his companion mused. "Maybe the best. Better than you, Lewis. Even better than Shipley."

Lewis blinked at the undisguised vitriol.

"You know what comes next, Lewis." A step closer. "What have you done with the manuscript?"

This was insane. Lewis reached out, as if he might physically ward off the accusation. *How could you know? Does everyone know?* It was only a page, he wanted to say, one page he'd been sent four years ago—but nothing would come. His throat was constricted, raw. The time banged painfully against his wrist, and all he could think was, *You think bad thoughts too, Dr. Prine. You think bad thoughts . . .*

"Do you believe Michael died because of Fallows, Lewis?" The voice sharp now as a piece of cut steel. "Do you really think you should have entrusted the manuscript to Alex Shipley, of all people?"

Lewis looked away. The room seemed to have gotten smaller, tightened in on him. His back was toward a wall. There was no door, just the scorched maw of the fireplace he'd seen earlier. He tasted ash in his throat.

"And then the house turned, became a hall of mirrors."

Lewis didn't understand the shift in conversation, the blank look behind his friend's eyes. But there was something about the line, something familiar . . .

"The house engulfed the man, turned inward and began to chew him, windows like teeth approaching—"

"No," Lewis said weakly, finally recognizing the lines from the unpublished Fallows. From the page Lewis had been sent. "Please don't do this."

"—and chairs upturned so that their arms reached out and caught him. Pulled him down, drove him under—"

There was nowhere to go now. He stumbled, fell heavily into the chair that had appeared from nowhere, cutting him off at the knees. He was trapped.

"I'm not one of you!" Lewis shouted, looking up in terror. "I'm different from everybody else in the night class and I always was! I'm different, goddamn it!"

But as Lewis Prine said these words, all he saw was a familiar face from years ago bearing down on him, and a great and deep truth roared through him. The knowledge was hard and fast and incontrovertible.

They had never been friends at all.

22

"Ladies and gentlemen," said Dean Rice from the podium, "scholars and distinguished guests of Jasper College, we are gathered here today to remember the life of Dr. Michael Tanner."

A cold, ugly morning. On the walkways a few students made their way to class, craning their necks to watch the service with morbid curiosity. One of Tanner's former students sobbed; a reporter snapped a photograph. Alex had spent the morning thinking of what to say about her murdered friend, and the more she thought, the more ill she became. There was no question now: they were gathered here because of her. Because of what she had discovered in Iowa; because she had finished the night class and put all of this in motion.

She wriggled at the thought. Her stomach churned.

As the dean continued with his introduction, Alex scanned the faces on the makeshift stage beside her. Christian Kane sat in his chair looking nervous, fidgeting like a child in church. Melissa Lee was beside him, her posture prim and straight, girlish ovoid sunglasses hiding her thoughts. Next was Frank Marsden, who had arrived late and now looked lost without his lady friend. Alex glanced out at the crowd but she could not see Lucy Wiggins anywhere. She forgot about the actress and focused again on the stage. Sally Tanner was dressed in black, a lace veil hanging over her eyes and her jaw tight with sorrow. Last was Jacob Keller, who had just slipped into his seat and was trying to look as if he'd been right on time. He appeared solemn and calm now, his head canted as if in prayer. Finally, at the end of the stage were two more chairs. The first was Lewis Prine's; the other was meant for Dr. Richard Aldiss. Both remained empty.

Dean Rice said her name, and Alex stepped up to the microphone and gazed out at the quad. The people there had pressed in, reporters flashing a volley of photos from the back row. She opened her mouth but nothing came out. *Come on, Alex,* she told herself. *You do this every day at Harvard.*

It was then that she felt a heavy arm around her. Keller had joined her at the podium. "It's all right," he whispered. "I'm here."

This emboldened her.

Alex leaned close to the mic and said, "A good friend of mine told me once that death allows us to focus more deeply on life. If we focus on Dr. Michael Tanner's life, we see a man who was indebted to scholarship. We see a family man"—she cast a look at Sally, who glanced away—"who truly loved his wife and daughter. We see a professor who believed in the theories and the practice of good literature. A man who'd given up years of his life for this college, and who died here trying to make a difference."

She paused. Keller pulled her closer.

"I met Michael Tanner fifteen years ago. We took a class together, a class that would change all of us forever. Even then, I knew Michael was a brilliant man, but it was more than that: he was kind. He believed in righteousness and . . ." The crowd shifted. They were not paying attention to her as much as they were *searching* her: looking at her as if they might tease something out of her. A group of students stood in the front row, their faces wolfish in the patchy sunlight. *We know who you are,* they said silently. *We know, we know, we—*

Alex balled up the eulogy she had written in her room the night before. Then she gathered herself again and said, "The Procedure is a dangerous game." There was a look of confusion in the crowd, murmurs of uncertainty. "If anyone is playing it, then you must stop immediately. Michael knew this as well as anyone. If not for the Procedure, he might still be—"

At that moment someone cried out in the distance. The sound had come from the steep hill that led up to the Fisk mansion. The mourners turned and searched the fringe of campus, looking for the voice.

It was Detective Black. He was running toward them.

All Alex could do was simply watch the man approach. He ran across the east quad and entered the crowd, pushed his way to the stage.

"What is the meaning of this, Detective?" Dean Fisk said. He had rolled his chair forward. His blind eyes scanned the crowd madly.

"There's been another murder," Black said breathlessly. "The body was found in your home just a few moments ago. Everyone needs to return there immediately."

There was a group of policemen standing on either side of the arm-chair, looking down at the body of Lewis Prine. He sat stiffly, his hands clasped over his trenchcoat. The fire had gone out and the room smelled of ash. On the tables, glasses and bottles from the night before made a lonely cluster, some of them smeared with lipstick, others toppled on their sides. And in the middle of the room was the dead man, looking as if he were nothing but a bystander to it all.

So he decided to come after all, Alex thought. *He just got to campus too late.*

Prine's head was cocked back as if he had fallen asleep sitting up, and draped across his face was a book, a paperback that was stained now with dark blood. It was Christian Kane's *Barker at Night.*

"I swear to God," Christian was saying somewhere in the midst of people in the room. "I swear I had nothing to do with this. I'm being framed. I'm being framed, goddamn it!" His voice was tinged with hysteria, and the others regarded him coldly. Sally Tanner had fallen limply into Frank Marsden's arms, and in her face was a breathless shock. *No,* she mouthed soundlessly. *No, no, no.* Beyond her Lucy Wiggins stood by the fire, her arms cradled around herself, trembling in fear. And Keller stood beside Alex, his eyes jumping from the dead man to the wall and back again. Like Alex, he couldn't look at Lewis without re-membering Iowa.

"A bullet wound," Black was saying, "just behind the right ear."

"I have no guns in my house," Fisk said defensively. "If you find the weapon, then it was brought here by the killer."

"My men are searching," Black said, and Alex thought of the book she had hidden in her room. The object within and the place where she'd left it that morning. Black caught her eyes and she looked quickly away. "What we need to do now is get everyone who was in the mansion this morning back here. Prine was murdered then, either just before or just after everyone left."

"But someone would have seen him," the dean pleaded. "We would have surely run into—"

"Which way did you leave the house, Dr. Fisk?" Black asked.

The dean gestured to Matthew Owen. "Through the kitchen," the nurse said.

"So it is possible," deduced Black, "that when you left you simply did not encounter Lewis Prine. The man was running late, and when he arrived, someone here, someone who was staying in this house, murdered him."

Fisk scoffed. "Impossible."

"After the murder of Michael Tanner," Black said, "we have to examine every possibility." The detective looked at Alex and said, "You visited Aldiss last night."

"He hasn't been here," she said. It was too quick, too defensive. "He wouldn't come to a memorial service. It isn't his style."

"Every possibility," Black repeated.

Then the man backed into the hallway and said something to Dean Rice, who looked pale and shaken. The dean nodded and left the house.

"Is everyone back from the service?" one of Black's lieutenants asked.

Alex looked around. The great room was a swarm of activity now, cops and technicians working within the wide space cordoned off to preserve the crime scene; it had taken the former students nearly an hour to work their way free of the people at the service, past the crush of reporters pushing forward against the stage. Through the grimy window she could see a clutch of reporters. Rice was giving them some sort of statement.

Aldiss was right, she thought. *He was exactly right about all of this.*

"Is that everyone?" Black asked again.

"Everyone," said Keller, still fixed firmly at her side, "except for one."

Alex scanned the room and noticed that someone had indeed not returned from the service. When she saw who it was, a mix of anger and confusion swept through her.

"Melissa Lee," she said aloud.

Black nodded and motioned to the lieutenant. "Find Lee and bring her back here," he said. "Everyone who stayed in this house last night is a possible target—and a suspect."

The Class

1994

23

When the students arrived the next night in Culver Hall, they found the classroom empty. The television cart had been pushed to a back corner and on the chalkboard someone had written NO CLASS— PROF. ALDISS HAD BLACKOUT.

The nine students went back out into the night. They walked together, the wind burning their cheeks. The campus rested, the high windows in the Tower throwing grids of yellow light onto the quads. The wind screamed through the corridor of dormitories on the west campus. For the longest time no one in the small group spoke.

It was Melissa Lee who broke their silence.

"The game," the girl simply said.

"What about it?" Keller asked.

"We should play. Here, tonight."

The others stopped walking. Lewis Prine said, "I don't know if that's such a good idea, Melissa."

"I have a friend at Dumant," Lee continued. "Russian lit major. She says they still play the Procedure on weekends. It's nothing—just something to do for fun. We've read enough of *The Coil* to at least fake it." Her eyes jumped from face to face. She wanted this.

"I don't understand it," said Sally Mitchell quietly. "It all sounds . . . cliquish."

"Come on, Sal. Do you think there's anybody else at Jasper who could play this game? No, only us. We're the best. I think this is what Aldiss was telling us the other night. He was urging us to start our own game. To begin the Procedure on this campus." Lee fell silent. They were in front of the Fisk Library now, a lone streetlamp illuminating their group.

Finally Daniel Hayden spoke, the boy's voice clear and sharp in the night: "I don't want any part of this," he said. And he turned and left. The others watched him go, his footsteps crunching away over the ice, and when his figure was merely a speck on the dark quad, Lee said, "Anybody else scared?"

No one moved. It was an agreement.

Twenty-four hours later, Alex pulled on her gloves and slipped outside. She stopped on her dorm's front porch and looked across the campus into an unsettling blackness, unusual for a winter's night. Where was the moon?

She walked, her breath steaming in her eyes. She kept her head down and went instinctively; every turn on the campus she knew by heart. It took her three minutes and seventeen seconds to reach her destination.

The party was already throbbing. The Alpha Sigma Tau house was crammed full, students clumped into the living room and standing before a blazing fire. Someone bumped against her, offered her a cup. It sloshed over into her bare hand, scorching cold. Alex took it and drank. The music raged.

She looked for Keller. She had begun to do this out on campus, at these random parties: search the room for his smile. Sometimes she saw him and sometimes not, but always she looked and felt empty when she couldn't find him.

At the back of the house now. A set of tall windows looking out over the vast east campus, the darkness here more unstable. A few students were sitting on floor cushions, playing truth or dare. Keller wasn't among them. The song—Throwing Muses' "Cry Baby Cry"—ebbed away and another replaced it.

Someone brushed past her again. "Hey," Alex said, the drink still burning her throat. She looked up, but the person had bled into the crowd.

No. Not quite. They had left something.

A note. Another piece of confetti dropped into her cup, swimming upward, four words bleeding away just as she read them.

Culver Hall. It begins.

Alex felt her throat constrict. Again she looked around, laughing despite her fear. She'd forgotten about the Procedure in the day's studying, blotted it out with Fallows. The real Fallows, not the legion of subtext: *The Coil,* the end of that strange book coming on now, the meaning she knew was there taunting her, just out of reach.

Maybe you need to get deeper, she told herself now. *Maybe you need to go where Aldiss went.*

Alex left the house, went back out into the cutting wind. She made her way to Culver.

The building was as black as the night. Nothing moved; nothing rustled.

At first Alex didn't see anyone. The drink, the smoky frat house, the fear she felt knocked through her, tremored her limbs. Made her legs weak. The cold became sharper, the moonless night more bottomless. She wondered if she'd been tricked, if this was Lee's way of pulling a prank. *That bitch,* she thought—and it was then that she saw a shape flit against the building's dark facade. Someone was coming.

Frank Marsden appeared before her, a loopy smile on his face. "Miss Claire?" he said.

Alex wanted to laugh. To be doing this here, tonight . . . it was ridiculous. And yet another part of her wanted to keep it going, to see if she could play the game Aldiss had spoken about in his lecture. To see if she was worthy. She remembered his words that night: *The strange thing about the Procedure was that you didn't know you were inside it until you realized something had changed.*

"Yes, sir?" she said.

"Welcome home, my dear lady," Marsden went on, falling into the part like the actor he was. "Welcome to . . . Fuck." He shook his head and brought up a paperback book he'd brought with him. It was *The*

Coil. Marsden had brought a penlight, and he shone it on the page. Finally he said, "Welcome to Hamlet, Iowa. Is there anything I can get you?"

Alex opened her mouth to speak but nothing came out. Nothing but a girlish little squeak that made Marsden shift and Alex flush with shame. She remembered the scene but couldn't find the words. The details. Now everything left her, got sucked away as if some kind of vacuum lock had been cracked, and a feeling of panic swept over her. She didn't want to go to the book, to show Marsden that she'd already forgotten. *Then you are shunned. And as a Fallows scholar, to not be inside, to not be one of them—that is a fate worse than death.*

"The book," Marsden whispered, offering his copy. She smelled whiskey on his breath; it was all a game, she told herself, nothing but a deviation from midterm exams on a Thursday night. Just a little fun. She tried to relax. "Your line."

Alex took the book from him, opened it. Found the scene and read, "You can show me where—"

"No reading," Marsden said. "That's one of the rules. Sorry, Alex."

She lowered the book, closed her eyes. "You can show me where Ann Marie is staying. It has been so long since I've seen her."

Marsden said, "Right this way."

She followed him. And as she did she noticed something: other people, some of them strangers and some familiar. Ten or twelve Jasper students, each passing her on both sides of Rose Street. She saw Lewis Prine. "Evening, ma'am," he slurred, tipping an invisible hat.

It was the scene. The scene exactly, down to the crowded street and the people swarming by.

Fallows. They're replicating it, re-creating the book here, on this campus.

For some reason, the realization filled her with dread.

Alex followed Marsden around Culver Hall, past trees glazed with snow. Branches smacked at her face but she walked, and soon they were on a different quad. In front of them was Turner Hall. This was Melissa Lee's dorm. The students called it the Overlook, after the hotel in *The Shining.*

Inside then, into the warmth. More students here, extras and outcasts. Some of them drank from plastic cups, some were already drunk

and going off script. The scene in *The Coil,* the tiny four-page movement Lee had chosen for this game, contained only some of it.

Someone called out, "What the fuck is a Procedure?" Another two
students kissed, tongues flashing. Someone was playing the Doors on a
portable stereo, "The End" filtering through it all. Frank Marsden, still
in character and stumbling a bit, led Alex to the staircase. She followed
him up.

The door to Lee's room had been cracked, just as Fallows described
it, and inside there was the heavy smell of marijuana. Soft, acoustic
music played, and as Alex entered she saw Lee sitting before a cardboard
box wrapped in tinfoil: the "mirror scene," one of the more important
in *The Coil.* Aldiss had highlighted it, had finely gone over it with them,
had talked about its themes and details at length. Now she was here,
in this simple dorm room, inside those pages. Alex's pulse quickened.

The others were here: Sally Mitchell, Michael Tanner, and Keller.
Her heart skipped when she saw him, but she brought herself back.
They were waiting for her, sitting off to the side and not moving
through the room—a little different from Fallows's original version,
but it would have to do. They were too far in now.

"Alex," someone hissed. It was Keller. The seriousness of his face
disarmed her; she wanted to tell him to not take it so seriously, that it
was nothing more than a game—but that wasn't true, was it? Now that
she was here, inside the scene, it had taken on an urgency. A pulse. The
boy motioned to her. "Your line."

Alex came back to the room, the scene. "Ann Marie," she croaked.
"How long has it been?"

"Hello, Claire," Lee said, her voice accented, perfectly fake. "So nice
of you to come all the way to Iowa to see me. I want you to meet my
father." She gestured to Tanner, and the boy nodded. "And this is our
maid, Olivia."

Mitchell said, "How do you do?"

"And this is Mr. Berman, Esquire."

Keller extended a hand. This was wrong: Berman, the officious
lawyer, did not come in until later. Alex paused but Keller remained
there, his eyes wandering off. *Stoned,* Alex thought. *They're all stoned.*
She shook the boy's sweating hand and he smiled sloppily and then sat

down again. The CD skipped on the stereo. Lee turned for the first time to face Alex, her lips an old-fashioned bright red and antique turquoise earrings hanging in her ears. Her hair had been pulled up into the style of the time, but she still wore her Pearl Jam T-shirt, her Doc Marten boots, her chipped black nails.

"What brings you back to Iowa?" the girl asked.

"Business," Alex said.

"What type of business?"

"Business about . . ." Again she was frozen. The room seemed to spin wildly. She willed the words, but nothing would come. The others seemed to be waiting on her, urging her to continue. "About . . ." She reached for the book on Lee's desk-cum-boudoir.

"No," Lee said, pulling the volume away. "Don't. You know this, Alex."

Alex bit her lip. *Damn you.* She tried to think of the scene, to remember her lines. But it wouldn't come. Fallows's text swirled just out of her reach.

"I . . . I can't . . ."

"I thought you'd been accepted to Harvard," Lee said. "I thought you would be better than this." The girl's dark eyes judged her cruelly. *She's taken something. She's not herself.* Smoke curled from somewhere, making the air thick. Alex coughed, and then the ball in her throat became bigger and she coughed again. Soon it was coming out in thick, violent bursts and she was bending over. Keller was there, rubbing her back, saying, "Are you okay, Alex? Do you need me to get you a glass of water?"

"Let her go, Keller," Lee said. "She's fine."

Alex stood up, shame burning her face. She'd failed; she'd failed Aldiss and all the rest of them and she shouldn't be here. She didn't deserve to be. She turned and went out into the hall, where Nirvana was throbbing, and down into the lobby. The scene had broken loose there, and she saw Lewis Prine gibbering in a nonsensical language as the extras stared at him in perfect silence. They had been in tableau.

Alex rushed through the crowd and burst outside, gulping air.

For a moment she stood alone in the snow, the wind burning her face. Then she walked away. She was finished for tonight. Done. To hell with them and their stupid game.

Thirty steps to Culver Hall, and then she slipped down the same back way and out toward Front Street. Soon she would be home and she could forget about this, put the Procedure behind her and get back to her books. It was a stupid thing to have done, and she regretted ever having—

"Shawna Wheatley and Abigail Murray."

Alex stopped. Sitting on a bench, his face half bathed in the glow from a security light, was Daniel Hayden. She watched him for a moment, saying nothing.

"You've heard of them?"

"The two victims," she said tentatively, her breath frosting the air. "The students Aldiss was accused of . . . the girls he killed at Dumant."

"The others are too busy playing their games," the boy went on. "But not me, Alex. I've been reading up on Aldiss. Studying him. What he did to those two girls . . . I can't get past it. I want to drop the night class, stay as far away from him as possible, but I have to stay with it. I have to see how it ends."

"Why are you telling me this, Daniel? It's late and I have an early class tomorrow."

He looked up at her, his hands trembling on his lap. "Because I know what you're doing," he said. "I've seen you on campus. You're doing research too. Why do you think I left the note in your book last night?" She started to speak, but Hayden waved it away. "I was trying to lead you," he said. "To point you in a certain direction. My dad was a cop, so I know a little bit about murder investigations."

"Daniel, I still don't understand why you're—"

"I'm telling you this so you can do it the right way, Alex. Your research, whatever you've been doing at the Fisk Library and up on the hill with the old dean—you need a focus. No more flying blind. You have to start at the beginning. Go back to his victims. Go back to Dumant University. That's where Aldiss was born."

24

The microfiche reader was antiquated and shoved to a back corner of the library. The light in the tiny, closet-size space streamed yellow and weak. Cobwebs glinted in the corners. Alex had the place to herself.

She fanned through the alphabetized strips. *You have to start at the beginning,* she thought. The shame she'd felt earlier at having botched the Procedure was all but gone now, replaced by the information Hayden had given her. It meshed perfectly with what Fisk had said—she had to go back to the root, to the two victims themselves. She had to follow Aldiss outward from there. She'd been doing it the wrong way, trying to use the text to solve the riddle. Now she saw her mistake.

A for Aldiss. F for Fallows. H for Hamlet. D for Dumant.

Dumant University. 1982. The murders of Wheatley and Murray. The beginning.

She took out the W strip and put it on the machine.

W for Shawna Wheatley, the first victim.

Alex had been able to find articles on Richard Aldiss, on the Dumant crimes themselves and on the man's vast scholarship—but about his (*No, Alex,* she thought, catching herself, *not his but someone else's, the real killer's*) victims there was little. The only photos she'd found were the ones Fisk had shown her.

She moved the wheel through the sheets of microfiche, tracking words with her eyes. *Killer. Investigation. Upheaval. Campus. Methodology. Aldiss.* She stopped only now and then—on a photograph of a young Aldiss, an aerial shot of the Dumant campus with a black circle where Shawna's body had been found—but mostly she moved through the information, looking for anything about Wheatley.

"Ms. Shipley?"

Alex, startled, turned to see the librarian in the door.

"Yes, Ms. Daws," she said. "Everything's fine."

The woman left Alex alone.

She shook her head, clearing the exhaustion. It was nearing midnight now and so much had happened. She thought again of Melissa Lee, of her eyes in that false mirror, of Keller's pitying hands on her back.

"Come on," she said aloud, clearing the thoughts. "Focus, Alex."

She thought of poor Shawna Wheatley. Everybody was searching for Paul Fallows, trying to uncover the identity of the writer, but no one was trying to find the truth about Shawna. No one was looking for an answer to what had really happened to either of those two students at Dumant University.

Alex closed her eyes, remembering something. It was something Fisk had shown her that day, a small piece of those terrible articles on the Dumant crimes.

You should look into Shawna Wheatley.

It was what Aldiss had said when they brought him in for questioning. She'd always felt there was something strange about it, something buried inside those words that might lead her to answers. *Look into,* she thought, pinching her eyes fiercely, nails digging painfully into her temples. *Look into . . .*

She almost missed the article by scrolling too quickly.

It had been written in the fall of 1981, just months before Wheatley was murdered.

A simple story about a graduate fellowship in literature at Dumant. A hometown-pride angle, the mother quoted. In the accompanying photograph Wheatley wore thick glasses and a turtleneck sweater, her smile wide and innocent. The microfiche reader whirred in the small, dust-filled room.

"Who are you?" Alex asked aloud. "Who are you really, Shawna?"

She looked at the story again. Read each word, her eyes stinging. Nothing. There was nothing there.

But there had to be. She was on the last microfiche sheet now.

Goddamn you, Aldiss, she cursed silently. She was exhausted, getting loopy. Losing herself. *Goddamn you for doing this to me. To her.*

Promising herself this was it, Alex read the story one last time.

It was then that she saw it. Just a few throwaway lines at the bottom of the page. She leaned close to the screen, the cheap plastic chair scratching the floor beneath her.

> *Recently Shawna began her dissertation. Under the tutelage of her favorite professor, she has begun to read books in ways she never imagined. "Dr. Aldiss has taught me so much," she said. "He wants me to go to Iowa for research, just like he did when he was a student here. If I can find someone to go with me, I might just make that trip."*

Trembling, Alex stared at the screen. The girl had fallen away; all the texture in the small, cramped room had dissolved. She was alone. Completely alone. Someone walked past the door, heels clicking. She barely heard it.

Someone to go with me . . .

Alex reached forward and turned off the machine and the room fell dark.

At just after one in the morning she knocked on Keller's door. The football dorm smelled of pizza and vomit and aerosol deodorant. Someone had hung a jockstrap on the fire spigot. She waited, her mind racing with unanswered questions.

Keller pulled the door open, blinked into the harsh corridor light. His eyes were glazed with sleep, his hair spiked into tufts. He was shirtless and Alex made herself focus on his face, his bloodshot eyes.

"Alex, if this is about the Procedure, then—"

"The photograph you found," she said. "The one of Rutherford. I think I know what it means."

"What are you talking about, Alex?"

She told him in one breathless rush. She told him everything she had learned about Shawna Wheatley that night.

When she was finished, Keller asked, "What do we do now?"

She didn't have to think. The answer was obvious, right there on the tip of her tongue. It had been obvious the moment she'd found the article on the microfiche reader, maybe even earlier than that—when she'd seen that strange photograph of Charles Rutherford in the bar, or when she'd read those time-withered newspaper articles in Fisk's treasure room. All she'd needed was Daniel Hayden to push her in the right direction.

"It means," Alex said finally, "that we have to go to Iowa. Aldiss is leading us there."

Alex

Present Day

25

After the murder of Lewis Prine, the remaining classmates had been locked in an upstairs room of the Fisk mansion.

It was early afternoon and the sun knifed in through curtains the color of feathered pages. There was another fireplace here, two massive shelves flanking the hearth, and a wooden clock hanging above it all that had stopped on some long-passed 3:38. Christian Kane was mumbling frantically about his innocence; yes, it was a book—his book—that had been placed over the dead man's eyes, but *what did that really mean, what did it mean when everyone in this house had a copy, what did it mean when*—

"That's enough, Christian," Keller said, and the writer fell quiet like a scolded puppy. The nurse, Matthew Owen, stood to the side, hands kneading the handles of Dean Fisk's wheelchair. Sally Tanner and Lucy Wiggins stood on opposite sides of the room, the widow frighteningly composed and the actress tracing nervous ellipses across the furred dust on the mantelpiece while Frank Marsden watched her unblinkingly, a shadow of disbelief on his face. And inside a clot of shadows Alex observed them all as Aldiss had instructed, wondering which of her classmates had turned.

A young cop guarded the door, his arms crossed and a look of vigilance on his face.

"Look at him," Keller whispered to her. "The kid's scared shitless. No wonder they didn't send him out to talk to Aldiss."

She would have laughed under different circumstances.

"Why hasn't Melissa returned?" Fisk asked. Behind the old man, Owen continued to massage the handles of the chair, his movements almost hypnotic. Alex tried to shake off the lurid memory of Melissa's head in his lap, of the way he—

Owen turned his gaze on her and she looked away.

"No one knows," Keller said. The woman still hadn't returned from the memorial service.

"Melissa didn't have anything to do with that . . . thing downstairs," Christian said, his voice on the edge of panic. "She couldn't have."

"She talked a lot about Daniel," Frank said. Lucy stopped moving her finger through the dust and stepped away from the dead, blackened fireplace. "She seemed a little obsessed with his death."

"What do you mean?" Keller asked.

"I mean she seemed convinced that his death wasn't a suicide. She talked to me a little last night, before bed. I wasn't thinking clearly. We had some drinks on the plane and then again when Sally visited and my mind . . . you know. I didn't think much of it. But now, given what happened to Michael and Lewis— My God, do you think she might have been right and Daniel was the first one?"

"Daniel killed himself," Sally said flatly. She was standing alone in a corner, lips pursed and eyes hot as coals; grief had untethered her from the rest of the group. "He was upset about a case he was working on. He put his service revolver in his mouth. He was a detective in New York City, under enormous stress—let's not complicate Daniel's death just because of this."

"Melissa says Daniel was happy," Frank put in, his voice soft and even. "She says—"

"Melissa *says* a lot of things," Sally said, glaring at the man. "Let me ask you this: did you trust her when we were students?"

The man shifted uncomfortably.

"Well?"

"No," Frank said softly. "No one did."

"The woman has a psychological problem. Michael told me that himself."

Alex sat forward. "Sally, do you think Melissa committed these murders?"

The woman regarded Alex coolly. Her arms dropped to her sides and she looked at Alex as if to say, *How dare you ask me that question. You of all people . . .*

"It's a good question," Dean Fisk said quietly from his chair. "Do you suspect her, Sally?"

The woman straightened. She was turning something over in her mind, trying to get her words exactly right. Finally, her voice measured and cool, she said, "Michael told me that Melissa called him sometimes. She was having problems in her marriage. I—well, of course I got jealous. I remembered her reputation when we were in college. I mean who doesn't? But she kept calling, and Michael kept taking her calls. He would disappear to his library to talk, and I would put my ear to the door to listen. They would talk for hours sometimes. We got into these terrible fights about it." Sally shuddered, whether at this memory or at what had happened in the last seventy-two hours, it was unclear.

"What did he say about her?" Christian asked. He had suddenly brightened, glad perhaps that the group's focus was shifting now to Melissa and off the horrible sight of Lewis Prine.

"He thought the woman needed professional help," Sally said. "He'd called Lewis about her, and Lewis shared the same thoughts: they believed she struggled with reality. That she was a compulsive liar."

"You can't be serious," Frank protested.

"She isn't right, Frank. Melissa wasn't like the rest of us, and you know that's the first thing Aldiss—"

"Aldiss?" Alex couldn't help herself.

Sally glared. "You asked me if she could have done this, Alex. The answer to that is no. I do not think Melissa did this. I think—and have thought since I saw . . . what I saw in my husband's library three days ago—that Richard Aldiss killed my husband. But Aldiss couldn't do it alone, so he got one of his 'protégés' to help him." She looked at them all in turn, jabbing a finger at each person in the locked room. "The professor has put things in motion and now we're all dying, one by one."

"Enough." They turned to Fisk again. Powder ran in streaks down the man's face as he perspired, and his milky eyes roamed the room blindly. He clasped a bony fist around the sunglasses in his lap. "You need to stay together now. To believe in one another. To fall apart and blame each other for what has happened—that will not help anyone."

Alex turned away and looked out the window. Reporters were milling down there, watching the windows of the mansion for movement.

"Crazy, isn't it?"

Keller moved beside her. All the anger she had felt about the missing manuscript suddenly dissipated. If she had an ally here, she knew it was him.

"Maybe we screwed up," he went on. "Back in Iowa."

"We didn't, Keller. You know that as well as I do."

"I know that this looks like something Aldiss would dream up," the man said. "Some kind of human puzzle."

Alex looked at him. "I don't want to talk about this anymore," she said weakly. "I want to get my mind off all of this. Aldiss, Michael, what we saw down there. Let's talk about something else."

"Not books," Keller said.

Alex smiled weakly. "Okay, not books."

"What about history?"

Alex turned back to the pane, saying nothing.

"Me first, then," Keller said. "Her name was Jessica. My ex-wife. She taught math at the high school. We liked the same things, we showed up at the same places—it seemed natural. Right."

She didn't look at him. Couldn't. "What happened?"

"She thought I was too secretive," he said. "She wanted to know too much about Jasper, about the class. Of course that wasn't it. There were other things. Her toenails, for instance."

Alex laughed.

"Since we split up," he said, "I've been living in an old restored farmhouse and coaching football. We've got a good team. You should come down and see us sometime."

Maybe I will, she thought. Then she remembered Peter and—

Someone screamed.

Alex turned quickly and saw Lucy. She was attacking Frank, punching him and scratching at his eyes, her face contorted into a mask of rage.

"Liar!" she screamed. "This man is a fucking *liar!*"

The young cop rushed over and pulled the woman off, and she relented, kicking and thrashing, blond hair wild and teeth bared. Alex watched as Frank sat up, his ears red, a claw mark dotted with blood on his cheek. He smiled the charming smile that must have won him roles in so many auditions and said, "It's nothing. Ms. Wiggins is just having a bad morning. She's far away from home, and with all that's happened in this house—"

"Liar," the woman said again. "Don't believe him. Don't believe anything he says."

When Alex looked back at Frank, the man held her gaze. He was still smiling but his eyes said, *Help me, Alex. I've done something awful.*

Before Frank could say anything aloud, the oak-paneled door opened and someone called Alex's name. Detective Black wanted to see her alone.

"Good luck," Fisk said as she left the room. "And remember: you do not have to protect him now."

Black was waiting for her in the dean's study, the lights on and every volume on the shelf starkly lit. Instinctively, her eyes ran across the books.

"Sit, Dr. Shipley."

She did.

Black cleared his throat and said, "I will ask you what I am going to ask the others. Where were you this morning just before the memorial service?"

"I went out."

The detective cocked an eyebrow.

"Nothing to do with Aldiss," she said. "I just wanted to see my old campus again. I hadn't seen much of it since I came back. I needed to clear my mind. For my eulogy, of course."

"And what do you think of the place?"

"It's changed," she said. "All is evolution."

"And that was it. You just went out."

"Yes."

He looked down at the desk, made a show of shuffling papers. "Lewis Prine . . . had you spoken to him recently?"

She didn't have to think. "I spoke to him briefly a few months ago. The last meaningful conversation we had was four years ago. I remember it well."

"What did the two of you discuss?"

"Lewis thought he'd found a page from an unpublished Fallows and he wanted me to check the writing. To make sure he was correct."

"And was he?"

Alex said nothing at first. She was thinking of the empty space, her hand clutching at the darkness, Keller's innocent smile when she saw him later.

"Dr. Shipley?"

She raised her eyes to the detective. "Yes. I think so."

"And did you talk with Lewis about anything else?"

"We spoke about a lot of things, Detective. We were old friends, after all."

"Did you speak about a game that Lewis Prine had been playing?"

So he was involved in the Procedure. Shit.

"No," she said. "I stayed out of that."

"But you have played the game before."

She held his eyes. "I have. When I was in the night class."

"And were you good at it?"

"Good?"

The man waved his hands. "Games are supposed to have winners and losers, Professor. Did you win?"

She looked at the cluttered desk, at the row of Fisk's pill bottles there. Then she sat up and said, "Not at first. At first I was terrible. But in time, yes, I became very good."

Black scratched a note to himself. "Let's talk about this morning. What time did you leave?"

"Around eight."

"And was anyone else awake?"

She thought of the house, the smoldering fire in the empty great room, the darkness of the kitchen. "Not that I could see," she said. "It's a huge house, Detective."

Black nodded. "I believe Lewis Prine arrived around nine a.m., just as everyone in the house was leaving for the memorial service. He was running late. A witness tells us that his car had broken down, and out here it's common for cell service to be out. So he arrived possibly just as the last people were leaving the house and——"

"We were all at the service," Alex said, a memory stopping her short: *Frank and Keller were late.* She scolded herself for going there, for allowing her mind to turn on itself. Suddenly she was breathless, reaching for something that she knew was just out of her grasp. "We were already gone by the time Lewis got here."

"Someone might have returned," Black explained. "Someone might have stepped back into the house just long enough to commit the murder and still make it to the service. For that reason we must keep you all under surveillance until we exhaust the possibilities and rule out everyone who is inside this house."

Someone in the night class did this, she thought, remembering Aldiss's words. *Someone who was there.*

"But this murder," she managed to say. "Nothing adds up. If the killer is the same man who killed Michael Tanner, then he's changed his methods. Everything is different except the book."

"Sometimes," Black said, "that means nothing."

"I'm afraid I don't understand."

"The killer might not have had enough time. He might have needed to move quickly, and a gun could have been his—or her—only option." The detective paused, breathed in deeply. "Do you know of anyone who might be carrying a firearm in this house, Dr. Shipley?"

"No," she said. "Of course not." Could he tell she was lying?

A second passed, then two. Black finally nodded and said, "Let's talk about Richard Aldiss."

"What about him?"

"You returned to his house last night."

She nodded.

"And?"

"And he offered nothing about Michael Tanner. He claims he is innocent."

"Of course he does," Black said. "Aldiss's problem is that he lives so close to campus. It would have been easy for him to come here, murder Lewis Prine, and then get back to his house before the memorial service broke up."

"He didn't do it."

Again Black arched that eyebrow. "So sure, Professor?"

She shrugged. She wished she could go on, give the detective something that would convince him, but there was nothing. Nothing but her gut.

"You were out there such a long time," he said. "The others in the house say you were gone for almost three hours. What did you talk about, you and Aldiss?"

"The past."

"Aldiss is a smart man. Surely he must have theories as to what is happening on this campus."

She looked past him, at the skirt of the campus in the distance through the window. Wondered if it would ever be the same, if it had ever been the same since the night class. "He thinks it's someone from his class," she said.

Black plucked at an ear. There was a scar she had never noticed on his jaw, red and irritated. She thought of her father. "And do you agree with him, Dr. Shipley?"

"I think it's been proven that Aldiss is usually right."

With that the room fell silent. Black's jaw worked. He clicked down the nib of his pen.

"You can return to the room," he said. "Send Keller in."

Alex rose and left the study. She passed her bedroom on the way down the hall, and since the hallway was empty, she stepped inside and furtively shut the door behind her. Went to the bed and lifted the mattress, careful not to make a sound, and found the Fallows novel there. Quickly she opened the fake book and looked inside and—

The gun was there. It had been undisturbed.

She exhaled and turned to leave. As she did she noticed something on the nightstand. It was the card from before, the one Aldiss had given her at their dinner.

To Alexandra.

She picked up the envelope and tore it open.

It was a simple greeting card. *To Old Friends,* it read. *We do not get together as often as we should, but when we do it is bliss to me.*

Alex shook her head and opened the card. Aldiss had written something inside.

My Sweet Alexandra,

They will be coming for me soon. You have to believe that I had nothing to do with what is happening now in that house. And also know this—

Alex's eyes ran over the rest of the note, and when she saw what Aldiss had written next, her breath caught in her throat.

—the Procedure has begun. Everything they say, everything you hear could be part of the game. Trust no one.

Your teacher,
Richard

Iowa

1994

26

The morning they were to leave for Iowa, she visited her sick father.

The house was heavy with his illness—water ticking in the sink basin, her mother's radio burbling in a back room. The house was cold because his medication made his body scream with heat, and Alex pulled a coat around her as she crossed into the living room. Her father sat in his favorite chair, sweating, his teeth chattering. He wore a shirt that read MY DAUGHTER IS A JASPER COLLEGE TIGER.

"Hi, Daddy. How have you been?"

The man's eyes were rimmed red, and the strands of his thinning hair were pulled away from his forehead. She touched him there, pushed his moist hair up with her palm, blew softly onto his cheeks.

"The same, Allie," he said. "Always the same."

"Mom have you doing chores?"

The man smiled weakly. Even this was a task. "She's good to me. Don't talk about your mother like she isn't here."

"Hey, Mom."

Alex turned and saw her mother. She had been crying, as she usually did in the mornings. A Kleenex was balled in her fist, and her nose glistened. "My girl." The woman came over and wrapped Alex up in a hug, and for a skittish moment she thought, *I won't go. I'll stay here with them and I won't finish the class.*

But then it passed and her mother stepped back to observe her.

"Skinny!" she said. "Have they been feeding you over at that college?"

"Yes, Mom," Alex said. She drifted into the kitchen, opened a cabinet and took out the Ovaltine, and filled her favorite VERMONT: FREEDOM AND UNITY glass with milk. This, all of this: familiar, safe.

"He's declining," her mother said now, her voice at a whisper. Both women were in the kitchen, the morning light bleeding through her mother's grapevine curtains above the sink. Alex turned and stared through the slit at the white foaming trees in her old front yard. "When you go off to Harvard, Alex, I just don't know what we'll do. What I'll do."

"What if I don't go to Harvard?"

She felt her mother close in on her. "What do you mean?"

"I mean . . ." She stopped. She didn't know what she meant, not exactly.

"What's wrong with you, Alex? What's going on?"

"Nothing's going on, Mom. Nothing."

"Something is. I can see it."

"It's . . ." *A boy,* she wanted to say. *A new boy.* But that would have only been part of it. A small part.

"It's that class, isn't it? That evil man. I told you not to get involved with him."

"No," Alex said, maybe too defensively. "It isn't that."

"Then what?"

Alex opened her mouth, wanted to say something, to tell her mother that this morning she would go off to a place she had never been, would board an airplane for only the third time in her life with someone who was still a stranger to her, and together the two of them would try to solve a twenty-year-old mystery. It was comical even to her.

"I just want you to know I love you," she said. "Whatever happens, whatever comes at me, just know that I love you both more than anything."

Her mother's chin quivered, one tear toppling over and sliding down her face. "Well. I'm sure your father will be pleased that you took some time to check on him."

Her father. Alex poured the rest of the chocolate milk out and went back to him.

She leaned down, got close to his ear. "I'll come back to see you in a few days, Daddy. I promise."

The man finally turned and looked at her. Smiled again, his lips cracking in places, the purple skin underneath showing through. It was as if the cancer were tearing him apart.

"It's okay, Allie," he whispered. "Everything's going to be okay."

Then she was gone. She had a plane to catch.

He was waiting for her in front of Culver, his backpack slung across his shoulder and the note cards out. He tapped his foot nervously, mumbling to himself as she approached him from behind. "Don't even know the plays yet, Keller?"

He turned on her. She knew by his eyes that he hadn't slept. "Just ready to get going," he said.

"Do you think the others . . ."

"No," he said. "It's only us. We're the only ones brave enough to finish it."

"Or crazy enough."

They walked toward the east campus, where Keller's pickup waited to take them to the airport. They had pooled all their money together— five hundred and eighty dollars, just enough to last them until Sunday.

"You okay?"

Alex looked up. "Yeah, just thinking."

"You scared?"

She thought about the question. Turned it around in her mind and said, in a voice as pale as a whisper, "Yeah. Yeah, I am."

And with that, Keller took her hand and they went out together into the unknown.

27

Just before two o'clock they stepped out of the airport and found that winter in Iowa was a different animal than it was in Vermont. The cold was sharper, the wind laid bare. They looked around and saw nothing in the distance. No trees, no mountains. It was as if she and Keller had entered a room devoid of furniture, a landscape without context. *Strangers,* Alex thought. *We're strangers here.*

Shivering off the wind, she followed Keller to the rental car. It was a small Mazda, better than the rugged little car of her father's she drove back at Jasper.

"Go on," he said, reading her mind.

"Thanks."

He tossed her the keys and Alex got behind the wheel, gunning it out of the lot. Out of the corner of her eye she saw him grab frantically for the handle above the window.

They found a Ramada five miles from Hamlet. "There it is," Keller said, pointing. "Our war room." Alex pulled off the road, tires screeching. When she stopped, he fell out of the backseat and kissed the ground.

Inside, they lumped their packs on one side of the room, removed the books they thought they would need. Of course there were the two

Fallows titles, *The Coil* and *The Golden Silence,* but there was also an Iowa tourist guide. She had even brought along a book she'd found in the Fisk Library that morning: Richard Aldiss's *Ghost.* Alex turned it over and saw the author photo—the man in prison, his face haggard and his eyes cold and wan. Inside the front cover of one of her volumes she saw a jagged strip of paper, and Alex pulled it out and read.

> *The two mysteries are one. Best of luck to you on your journey, young Alex. What you are involved in is of the greatest importance, and you are almost to the end. Almost there now.*
>
> *Stanley Fisk*

She smiled and slipped the note in her coat pocket before Keller could see.

After they had unpacked, Keller lay down. Looking up at where she stood tentatively beside the bed, he said, "It's okay. I don't bite." She lay beside him. *Normal,* she thought. *It's like this is all normal.*

For a while neither of them spoke. Finally she said, "So. We made it to Iowa."

"We did," he echoed. "Now what?"

Alex stared up at the ceiling. She'd always wanted to get away from Jasper, to assume a new identity somewhere. A new life. Her acceptance letter from Harvard had been a kind of promise: that she would soon be away from there, untethered and fending for herself. But now she couldn't shake the certainty that everything was wrong. That they were walking into one of Aldiss's traps.

"Alex?"

She turned. The last sunlight gashed through the curtains and fell on his face, and she wanted to hold him. To grab on to him and let his strength pull her from the depths of her fear. But there would be time for that later. Now she was weary from the flight and they had work to do.

"Now," she said, "we have two days. Two days until our return flight and the class ends. Two days to find Fallows."

Alex

Present Day

28

Dean Anthony Rice was the sort of man who could not tolerate the flaw of human stupidity. Red-faced and constantly out of breath, he was forty-seven pounds overweight and looked more like a numbers man at a small-town accounting firm than a professor of dead languages.

On Friday afternoon, as the former students of Unraveling a Literary Mystery were sequestered in an upstairs room of the Fisk mansion, he paced his office on the second floor of the Tower. He had taken his heart pill, his blood pressure pill, his antidepressants. There was a half-peeled banana going brown on the walnut desk. Lamplight streamed over the surface, illuminating a copy of Paul Fallows's novel *The Golden Silence.* The book's back was broken, and Rice had littered the text with a hundred pink Post-its that held incomprehensible notes. On the floor was a pillow and blanket where he had slept the night before.

Rice could feel it. The sudden rage of his predicament.

The problem was bringing in Shipley from Harvard. It had been Detective Bradley Black's idea. She might have been a cult hero at the college fifteen years ago, but not all cult heroes were to be celebrated. Some—he thought of old Richard Aldiss in particular—were only remembered by their mistakes. And Shipley had made so many mistakes during the night class. Yes, she had exonerated Aldiss—but to Rice that meant nothing. It was not the victory those who seemed to *worship* Shipley made it out to be. He had met Aldiss once, and there was something about the man. Something almost inhuman. Maybe it was his frozen smile, or maybe the way his black eyes held you, judged you, drew you down. Rice shivered at the memory.

He thought of the professor now. Not surprisingly, the incompetent Shipley had been able to get nothing out of him. What if someone else spoke to him, someone with nothing to gain but the truth? Aldiss would appreciate his honesty; Aldiss would see him as a man with equal, perhaps even greater, intelligence. No more slutty young professors with the motive of making their name at Harvard, no more petty games. He would go to Aldiss and ask him about the murders of Michael Tanner and Lewis Prine, and they would speak to each other like two learned men who were after nothing less than truth.

Yes, that was it exactly. No more digging in a forgotten novel, no more of this nonsense. He would pay a visit to Aldiss that afternoon and end this thing once and for all.

29

Alex returned to the room from her meeting with Black, feeling the heat of the others' eyes on her. She sat down and caught her breath. *This has to end. It just can't continue like this. We can't stay caged in this old house like animals.*

"Frank was telling us about Daniel Hayden and your—Aldiss—while you were gone, Alex." It was Lucy Wiggins. The woman leaned against the wall beside the fireplace, a cool smile on her face. Frank Marsden stood across from her, a hand covering the angry red mark on his cheek where the actress had torn at him earlier.

"Lucy," Frank said weakly. "Please."

"Tell her, Frank. Tell her what you told us."

The man sighed and said, "I spent a little time with Daniel the summer before he . . . you know. I was preparing for a role, just doing a little research on the NYPD. I felt like I was getting to know him. I don't think any of us really got to know him back then."

Alex leaned forward, focused on the man's words. "What did he tell you, Frank?" she asked almost breathlessly.

"He said . . ."

"Say it, Frank," Dean Fisk prompted. "Go on and tell her."

"Daniel told me that Aldiss wanted him to do something for him.

At first I thought it was insane, but the more Daniel talked the more I believed him. We were on the Upper East Side, driving around in his cruiser. It was clear he wanted to just get it out, tell someone his secret."

"What did Aldiss want him to do?" Alex asked.

Frank looked at her and said, "The professor wanted him to investigate us, Alex. He wanted Daniel to check into us, to dig up dirt on us. He was convinced that someone from the night class had gone bad."

Alex looked at the familiar TV actor and old friend, the weight of what he'd just said pressing down on her. Could Frank be believed, or was this an act, a script written to throw her off?

The door opened and Black appeared. He asked to see Sally Tanner, and the widow grudgingly followed him into the hallway. The younger cop closed the door behind Black, locked it with a heavy *thwick*.

Alex looked around the room. *One of these people,* she thought again, *is a killer.*

30

Rice had trouble finding the little house. In all his years at Jasper he had never visited Aldiss out here, even though the house was only a few miles from campus. Too busy, he told himself, too much of a course load. The truth was he'd heard stories about the professor, stories that made his skin crawl.

He got lost in a town called Burnaway and stopped to ask an old man at a gas station. The man was all jowls and lean muscle, and Rice stood back so that he would not have to smell him. This part of Vermont was unknown to him. He would have rather been up the coast, maybe at Harvard—it couldn't have been that difficult to win a professorship there, not if people like Shipley were doing it. The man smeared something over his windshield and then wiped it away, and the glass burned blue.

Rice knew he'd need to ingratiate himself, get on the old man's level. He started dropping his *g*'s, felt the pang of superiority course through his veins.

"You know where the professor lives?" he asked the man. "It's gettin' a little late and I need to be gettin' back to campus soon. Just thought I would come up to see if I could—"

"You mean Aldiss. The smiling one."

"Yeah, him."

The old man wrung water out at his feet, then swept around to the other side of the car. Rice caught the scent—tobacco and sweat and heat. He would have been fine staying at Jasper for the rest of his days and not getting into this. But there were things to do, a task now. There had been a second murder this morning. His time was running out; everyone's time was. He felt his stomach constrict and belch out something hot.

"Try Route 2," the old man said. "Right at the red barn up at Mansfield, then the road dies away. Take the gravel up the hill and you'll see it in the distance. Little house on the hem of the woods up there. But be careful."

"Careful?"

"That Aldiss is a mean one. People tell stories. All the time they do."

Rice thanked the man and left the way he'd come, the old map tumbled and destroyed in the seat beside him, thinking about leading the professor to Black, pushing him through a threshold and calling out to no one in particular, *Got him. I finally got him.*

He was so lost in the reverie that he almost missed the turnoff.

A darkness had fallen over the house, a kind of disrepair. Like everything else, this was symbolic. As Rice approached up the little gravel road, he saw the house as a mind, withered and soft and gone. How simple this would be.

He got out of his car. A basic screen door, its edge flaking with bluegray paint. A lake in the back. The simplicity had shocked him even before. Aldiss seemed more complicated than that. But here he lived, in this nothing place, with the locals. With the stinking and putrid common, with those who had no business even standing in a room with a man with the sort of intellect Aldiss possessed.

Why? Rice asked himself. *Why here?*

Smirking, he knocked on the screen door.

The thing bounced on its hinge. Noise shot out into the house, rattled around inside the place. Darkness thrummed.

"Professor!" Rice called. "Professor Aldiss, it's Dean Anthony Rice from Jasper College. I've come to ask you a few questions about what is happening on our campus."

Nothing. He stepped back, looked around the side of the house. The trees ruffled in the wind. The grass, dead and torn and uprooted here and there, its black underbelly exposed, tickled. Beneath him were the skeletons of flowers in an old trellis.

"Professor Aldiss!" Rice called again, louder this time. "I really need to talk to you. It's urgent. Michael Tanner has been dead for three days now and now Lewis Prine has been—"

Something moved inside. A tiny shift of light, silver against his cheek.

"Professor Aldiss?"

He waited. Five seconds, ten. Fear pricked up in the back of his mind and he swallowed it down. Nothing to be afraid of here, Rice said to himself. Nothing but an old man who has chosen to live with the locals. Nothing but a has-been, a relic. Gathering strength, he knocked again. The screen door bumped, revealing a fraction of space next to the jamb. That was it. That fraction, that slice of interior. He could if he wanted to, Rice told himself. He could. He should.

His heart hammering now, he opened the screen door and went inside.

31

"Why?" someone asked when Detective Black had escorted Sally out of the room. It was Matthew Owen, still standing behind Dean Fisk. The nurse looked stricken. "Why would Aldiss think that one of you—"

"Because he hates us," Christian said. "He always did."

"Christian," Alex said.

"It's true, Alex. You didn't see it, but the rest of us did. He hated it that we were free and he lost most of his life in that prison. He wanted to punish us for that. He wanted to create this, this—*dominion* over us, even when the class was over. And he did just that."

"Crazy," Frank muttered. The others agreed.

"Maybe he's right."

Everyone turned to stare at Lucy Wiggins, the outsider in their group.

"I mean, the detective said that someone in this house must have shot that guy downstairs. Maybe this professor of yours knows something that we don't." Her eyes seemed to sparkle with the mystery, as if this were a TV movie and she the unlikely heroine.

"Or maybe this is his way of manipulating us," Keller said.

"Go on, Mr. Keller." Dean Fisk's voice crept up from the shadows of the room.

"It would be just like Aldiss to turn this into one of his games. He might have been trying to turn us all against one another, to cause exactly what's happened, just so he could sit back and watch from afar. That's the kind of person he is."

Alex felt a pain in her chest as Keller spoke. *No,* she thought. *Please, not you.* She wanted to say to him: *Iowa was not a mistake, what we did there was not part of one of Aldiss's games.* But she could say nothing. She was frozen in fear, the locked room and the people inside churning chaotically around her like the dust that raged down from the high, dark shelves.

"But the question still remains," Lucy went on, gaining confidence in the part of the drama she was playing. Her eyes wide, she pulled herself up to full height and intoned, "Who killed your two friends?"

They all looked at one another. For the longest time no one spoke, and when a voice did come, it belonged to Dean Fisk himself.

"I believe," he said, "that I know the answer to that question."

32

Rice walked among the city of books. There were so many of them here that they had become part of the house, fused themselves into the walls. It was as if, he thought, the little house were made of paper and glue. There was no delineation of where the walls began and the books ended, no crease of space between—

He turned. His senses pricked up. He stared into the dark.

"Hello?" he asked. "Who's there?"

But no. It was his imagination. There was no one here. The house was small enough to see every room from this vantage, and yet there was something deceptive about it. It was like a maze—one could get lost inside here. Rice ran his eyes over the great room and the three rooms off the main hallway. A room like a study with an old ratty chair that looked out on the lake, a tiny nook of a bathroom, and wedged between those rooms was another. A bedroom, he presumed. And how strange, Rice thought, approaching not of his own accord now but moved by something not of his volition, getting close to the room and *smelling it*, smelling the air and knowing, knowing inside him that he had found something based on this and this alone.

It was feminine. He smelled the scent of a woman in the air.

Fuck, he said to himself. *Fuck, fuck, holy fuck.*

He backed out into the hallway, the tiny house pulsing now around him, the air and light and everything else congealing around him and making it difficult to move. To stand. To breathe. He had to get out of here. He had to get back to Jasper.

Rice went for the nearest door, broke out into the daylight.

Gulping for air, he took a few steps. Fell down, his knees digging into the wet earth, then pushed himself up and took another step. He looked up, his vision swimming clear, and realized that he had come out the wrong way. He had gone out the back, had gotten lost inside the maze of books and found himself here, on the opposite side of the house, right in front of the lake. Now he would have to—

The lake. Rice looked at it, watched as it burbled and gulped in the wind. It was black as sludge, the banks having shed over the years and deposited themselves inside the water. He was on the north bank, looking over the water to the opposite edge. Nothing but Vermont over there, fluttering blue in the afternoon sun. And here, where he was, he smelled the rancid water. The disuse of it, the crazy way it curled and flowed like a black quilt being swept off a bed. In the middle was a swimming raft, and Rice watched the thing spin in the water. Overhead, a flock of winter wrens turned upward in the sky, the sound like the pages of a thick book being thumbed.

When he looked down again, he saw something just beneath the surface.

It wasn't far from where he stood. It was there, just beneath the skin of the water, flicking in the light like the signal of a dying television. There, not there; there, not there. The sun refused to stay still.

"No," Rice said, the moisture in his mouth totally gone. "No. No."

Then he was bending. Bending down, his knees in the slickness, his body sliding down into that muck, his hands reaching, his face just inches from the seal that broke his world from the water's, the *taste* of the lake there, the cloying metal sharpness of it, but he was down in the cold, his arm immersed in its glass, and he was reaching, trying to touch the thing he'd seen shimmering, half of him disappearing into the blackness and then finally, finally, he touched it. And the feel of it strangely set him right, set the world on its axis, made everything okay again. The feel—it felt exactly how he thought it would feel. It was exactly what he thought it would be.

It was a hand.

33

"Who did this?" Keller asked. "Who killed our friends, Dean Fisk?"

The dean looked ahead, his eyes pausing for a moment. "Isn't it clear by now, Mr. Keller?"

There was something in that empty gaze. Something insistent. Pleading.

"No," Alex said.

"Isn't it clear?" the man repeated, his dead eyes wandering over them all, moving from face to face. "What's happening to each of you? Isn't it obvious what he's doing?"

34

Rice sat on the bank. The wind had stopped. The water was quiet.

He had his cell out. His hands were shaking, palms smeared with black mud. He squeezed the phone just to feel something. Just to calm himself. His stomach flashed with heat and he turned and spit onto the earth.

Rice dialed a number.

"Yeah?"

"Black," he said. "You've got to get over here. It's Aldiss. Melissa Lee . . . she's dead. She's in the lake behind his house. I found—I found her. I found her and it's all over. Did you hear me, Black, it's all over."

"I heard you," the detective was saying. The man was running. Rice heard the rush of wind on his end, the snap of a car door, the sound being dragged out of the reception like a bag closing up and taking it away. Then he started the engine of his car and the phone jostled with the movement of him fighting the wheel.

"Get over here," Rice was saying, his voice ruined and weak. "She's here, Black. The woman is in the water. The son of a bitch hid her in the water and I've found her. I felt her hand. I . . . my God, I *smelled her* in his house."

"Ten minutes," Black was saying. "Ten minutes and I'll be there. But you have to stay away from that house, Dean. He might still be there."

"No," Rice said. His voice was desperate now, breathless.

Black said nothing. He waited. He seemed even then to know.

"Richard Aldiss is gone," Rice said. "He's running."

Then the call was cut and Dean Rice lay back and looked up at the sky, thinking about that hand. The way it had felt. The way it had seemed to grab on to him when he touched it, tried to pull him back. To pull him closer. To pull him under.

Iowa

1994

35

The two students drove into Hamlet, Iowa, at twilight.

Keller had taken the wheel of the Mazda because he was afraid that Alex would wreck it. But she didn't mind. She wanted to see the landscape. Wanted to experience the place as Richard Aldiss had years ago, to know it as he had.

Hamlet was a two-stoplight town. The boundaries of the place were flat, the frameless geography running away into the pink sky like the top of a table. An ordinary downtown, sections of cubes abutting one another, fissured pavement and a group of old men sitting on a bench outside an abandoned building. Cars edged down Main Street on their way to the end of town, where better things must have been going on.

"Fucking Iowa," Keller said.

"Yeah," she agreed.

They crept on. Their plan was that they didn't have a plan. At least not yet. Keller had agreed with her that Aldiss had indeed sent them here. The clue inside *The Coil,* the strange photograph Keller had been given, and the fact that the two Dumant victims had been here not long before they were murdered—all of it suggested this was the heart of the professor's literary mystery. "Let's go," Keller had said that morning. "Let's go find Fallows."

Now he drove them past the cubes and they were at the fringe of town, dead brown cornfields stretching away into the distance on either side of the rental car. The sky at this hour seemed to be on fire. Alex thought, *That? That was it?* She looked out the car's window to hide her disappointment.

But what had she expected? What had she really hoped to find in this place?

Don't give up, she reminded herself. *They were here. The Dumant killer's two victims drove down this same street.*

This was where the two mysteries had to come together. In Hamlet they would discover Fallows's identity and exonerate Aldiss for the crimes he did not commit. It was what she had been preparing for since finding the book in the Fisk Library. This was the end.

"Turn around," she said to Keller now. "I want to go back through."

"You what?"

"I want to see the town again."

So he spun the car around right in the middle of the barren highway, and again Alex studied the downtown. The buildings, split and cleaved, and the old men, who stared at them a little longer this time. She marveled at the emptiness of the place, the absolute deadness of it.

"Where now?" asked Keller. There was fatigue in his voice.

"Now we go find him," Alex said. "We go to Olive Street."

It didn't take them long to find the Rutherford house.

Olive Street ran parallel to Main. The drive there took them four minutes. It was a picket-fence neighborhood, clumps of melting snow pushed off the road, two cars in each driveway. A pack of boys rode past them on bicycles, staring suspiciously inside the car.

"Where the hell is it?" Keller asked, scanning the addresses on the eaves of the houses.

"Here," Alex answered. She pointed to a woman walking down the street, her head down to stave the wind. Keller pulled over and Alex rolled down the window.

"Excuse me," she called. The woman stopped, warily, her eyes jumping from face to face. "We were wondering if you could tell us where Charles Rutherford lived."

The woman relaxed. Clearly this was a question she was used to being asked. She removed a mittened hand from a pocket. "There," she said, pointing to a redbrick house on the corner. "His widow still lives there. But . . ."

"What is it?" Alex asked.

"You look like students."

"We are."

The woman made a face. "Lydia doesn't care for students."

"Why not?" asked Alex.

"It's the house. They believe . . . the students think something happened in that house a long time ago."

Alex waited.

"But you two look sweet. Maybe she'll talk to you if you don't bring him up."

"Him?"

"The writer. That Paul Fallows. That's why she distrusts students— that's all they want to talk about. They're never interested in her life or how Charlie is doing."

"Charlie," Alex said. "You mean her husband?"

"No, of course not. Mr. Rutherford has been dead for years. I'm talking about her son."

The house was tiny. It was a throwback even on the block, an antique. The brick had faded, the shutters were cracked, and a ragged American flag snapped in the wind. A fence of tall hedges loomed up outside the front door, perhaps to keep the Fallows scholars at a distance. Alex looked at the place and once again felt nothing; no tinge of knowledge, no whine of electricity. For the first time she wondered if this was truly where Aldiss wanted them to be.

"Doesn't look the least bit spooky," Keller said.

"What'd you expect?" she asked. "A haunted house?"

"Obviously."

They watched from the curb. Nothing moved inside, no one passed across the wide front window. The house was the very same one Charles Rutherford had died in, the same one Aldiss and his mentor, Benjamin

Locke, had come to when they'd made this same trip. Thinking of Aldiss, she felt the first spark. *He was here.*

They approached the front door. Alex stopped and let Keller walk up the steps of the porch between the hedges; she felt that he should be the one to greet the widow. He was better at this sort of thing than she was.

Keller knocked and the two waited, listening. Movement from inside, and then the door dragged open and a woman stood before them. She was at least fifty-five, her face wrinkled and sagging. Yet there was something alive about her, something that suggested a former beauty.

"Mrs. Rutherford?" Keller asked.

"Yes?"

"We're . . . we just wanted to, um . . ."

The woman eyed the boy, leaning against the frame of the door.

"We wanted to . . ."

"What my friend is saying," Alex said, stepping forward, "is that we wanted to speak to you about your son."

Something changed in the woman's eyes. "Charlie?"

She and Rutherford had a son, a young boy who was very ill.

"That's right," Alex went on, so perfect with her lie that she surprised even herself. But she knew these lines, this script—Aldiss had given it to her in an early lecture. "We heard about his illness in an article we read in school and we wanted to see how he was doing. He still lives here with you, doesn't he?"

"Yes," the woman said. "He has his own room upstairs. Where did you say you were from?"

"Vermont," Alex said.

"And you've come all this way to . . ."

"We really do think Charlie has an amazing story."

What are you doing, Alex? This is something Aldiss would do. We shouldn't be—

But Lydia Rutherford was moving out of the way, and Keller was pushing inside the small house. Alex had no choice but to follow.

"My husband died in 1974," the woman said when they were all in the kitchen. "Charles Jr. was nine. He grew up without a father. His condition made it that much more difficult. But we made it—somehow we made it."

"Your husband," Keller said. "What did he do?"

"A salesman," Lydia said. "He sold encyclopedias door to door. We think that's what killed him. He exhausted himself. He wanted to work up to the main office one day, get up there with the suits. He just ignored the symptoms. Died right there on the front porch. I never remarried."

The woman's eyes drifted away.

"Sometimes people like you come here," she went on.

"Like us?" Keller asked.

"University students. They call themselves *scholars*. They think . . . this is going to sound crazy."

"Not at all."

"They think my Charles was a famous writer. That he wrote these novels under a different name. That he was this—what is it called? A ghostwriter. It's all this crazy game to them. But some of them are so adamant. They used to take pictures of our house from the street. There was even a couple who got married on our lawn once. We were going to move—my sister lives in Des Moines. But we never did. Charlie loves it here, and the neighborhood has always been so forgiving of his problems."

His problems, Alex thought. *What's wrong with her son? What kept this woman here, alone, all this time?*

"He used to be much worse," Lydia went on. "He used to be so *angry*. Some people in the neighborhood think he still is. But I know the truth. I know how much better Charlie is than before." The woman paused and Alex studied her. *What happened to her? What is she protecting?* "Charlie's father wanted to institutionalize him. He knew there was something . . . different about our son. And, well, I'm not proud of this, but we sent him to a home." The woman blanched. "I was weak, and Charles was very firm about these things. Then, when he died . . ." She trailed off. "It was a miracle. Dr. Morrow changed Charlie into the man he is today. He saved my son."

There was a sound from behind them, the sound like the coo of a small child.

"There's Charlie now," Lydia Rutherford said softly. "I'll tell him he has company."

The woman left the kitchen. The two students sat around a small dinner table, neither of them saying a word. In the next room Alex heard muffled talk, the widow's feminine trill, and then a long silence.

"They're going to find out about us," Alex whispered. "She's going to catch on. It's only a matter of time."

"You lied to her," Keller hissed. "You got us into this."

"I didn't know that she would actually—"

Footsteps approaching. Alex sat up and folded her hands on her lap.

"He's ready to see you now," came the woman's voice at her back.

They went into the living room. It was semidark, just a small lamp spilling light into the room. A man sat in a recliner, rocking gently, his eyes straight ahead.

"Charlie hates the light," Lydia Rutherford whispered. "Always has." Then to her son, in a voice that suggested the man may be hard of hearing: "Charlie, here are your guests. They've come all the way from Vermont. They read about you at their school. About you and Dr. Morrow." She looked expectant.

The son turned to face them, and Alex drew in a sharp breath.

She was looking at the photograph on the back of the Fallows novels. She had finally found the man in the dark suit.

Alex

Present Day

36

Richard Aldiss had disappeared, and they were all in danger.

Word spread through the Fisk mansion like a fire. At first there was shock—at hearing Melissa Lee had been the third victim, at the knowledge that Aldiss was on the run and could be on his way to campus. Then realization set in, and Alex felt the others staring at her. Accusing her. *He tricked you, Alex. He deceived you, and you let him.*

Black locked them inside the house and put his men outside to watch for any sign of the professor. Alex heard the words "armed and dangerous"; she knew that if Aldiss showed his face at Jasper he would be shot on sight.

How? she wondered. *How did it come to this?*

Keller stayed beside her. The others went off to their own rooms but she didn't move. She couldn't. She had been wrong about everything.

"Say it," she said.

"What?" Keller asked. He rubbed a hand exhaustedly over his scalp.

"Say what you're thinking, Keller. That I dropped the ball. That I fucked up."

"You didn't . . ." But there was no use; to go on would only be to patronize her, and Keller knew better than to do that. "This is what he does, Alex. It's what he's always done. These puzzles—he lives for them."

"But everyone told me, Keller. They tried to warn me." *And now three people are dead, and I could have stopped him.*

He shook his head. "You can't blame yourself, Alex."

Anger rushed to the surface. How dare he tell her how to feel! Did he think they were in Iowa again? Did he think they were kids, running around trying to find some crazy writer? She looked at him, her jaw working and red throbbing behind her eyes.

"Where is it?"

His eyes narrowed. "What are you talking about?"

"You stole it last night. You saw the manuscript on the shelf and when I came back from Aldiss's it was gone. What did you do with it?"

A look of pure confusion. He had no idea what she was talking about.

Don't let him do what Aldiss did, Alex. Don't let him fool you.

"Where is it, Keller?" she asked again, leaning closer.

The look remained, that boyish bewilderment, and then slowly he broke. Piece by piece his face returned to the one she knew.

"In my room," he said. "I'll let you see it."

"Then let's go."

"Not now. There are too many people around. Later."

She looked at him. "Is it real, Keller?"

At first he simply looked at her. Then he nodded.

"The only unpublished Fallows," he said. "Come by at ten o'clock and we'll look at it together."

Then he left the room and she was alone with her guilt.

Just before nightfall, with the reporters down on the quad dwindling or retreating to better shelter on the west campus, Alex drifted off. A swatch of a dream: she felt herself walking, following the footsteps of a man down a corridor. The man was Richard Aldiss. She did not know how she knew this, because she could not see his face.

Where are we going, Professor? she asked.

You'll see, said the man. *Do you trust me?*

In the dream she didn't hesitate: *Yes, Professor. I trust you.*

And Alex followed him, realizing that he was a much younger version of himself. His hair was fuller, darker. And he wore the suit she had seen him in years ago, the suit he had worn during his trial.

"Dr. Shipley," someone called. "Dr. Shipley, wake up."

She did. She sat bolt upright and focused on the face of Detective Black.

"It's me," he said. "Relax."

"Is he . . ."

"No," Black said. "Aldiss is still missing. You need to get back to your room."

"But—"

"No," he cut her off firmly. "No objections, Alex. If Richard Aldiss is still out there, then we need everyone in the house protected. This man is incredibly dangerous."

She wanted to protest, but there was nothing to say. Black was right.

She stood up and walked out of the room. His voice came up behind her.

"There will be more questions if Aldiss is found. When he is found. You must understand that if you hear anything from him, anything at all, then we will get it first. If you are protecting him or lying for him in any way—"

"I'm not."

"—then you will be buried along with him. Did you hear me?"

She swallowed. "I understand."

"Good. All-night surveillance tonight. If Aldiss comes anywhere near this campus, we will have him. And my men have been told to shoot to kill."

Alex said nothing. The dream stung her eyes: *Do you trust me?*

"And Dr. Shipley?"

She turned, waiting.

"What you discovered in Iowa?"

"Yes, Detective?"

"You need to think long and hard about it now, because it looks like Richard Aldiss may have been playing his game for a very long time."

Iowa

1994

37

"I got the idea from Lydia Rutherford," Keller explained.

They were in a lonely Main Street diner, a few suspicious regulars bellied up to the bar, waxing poetic about the cold. A waitress whisked by and refilled their drinks, hovered there for a moment. "Studying on a Friday night?" she asked.

Alex looked up at the woman. Said, "If we don't finish this lesson, then a man in prison for murder is going to be really disappointed with us."

The waitress shook her head disapprovingly. Then she was gone and Alex turned back to Keller.

They had come from Lydia Rutherford's to the diner, hunger having been temporarily eclipsed by the shocking image of a Charlie Rutherford who was identical to the photo Keller had received. Someone had been pointing them toward Charlie even then. "It's him, Alex," Keller had said breathlessly as she drove them away from the house. "Holyfuckingcrap it's him."

Now they ate burnt cheeseburgers and sucked at chocolate milkshakes, and Keller reached into his pack and removed a book. It was Fallows's *The Golden Silence*. As Alex finished off her burger, he went through the pages, making tick marks in the margins.

"It was something she said back there," he said. "Something about Charlie."

Then he was flipping through the text. *The Golden Silence* was the second of Fallows's novels, the book that had really begun the search. He gestured for Alex and she scooted into the booth with him. It had been hours since she'd been this close to him, and she wanted to stop, slow the scene down so she could just be with him. Alone, relaxed. But there was no time—in less than two days they would be on their way back to Vermont, and what they'd found in that house had changed everything. The two leaned over the book, looking down into the page as if it were a well.

"*The Golden Silence* is about many things," Keller explained to her. "We never got to it in the night class, but I did."

"You what?"

"I cheated, Alex. I read on."

"Show-off." Alex nudged him with an elbow. "What's it about?"

"Well, it's a story about Iowa, for one. *The Coil* was a New York novel, but this book is about here. Where we're sitting now."

"Page's Diner?" asked Alex playfully.

Keller made a face. "You can tell Fallows loved his home. Even if Rutherford is not Fallows, I still think we're dealing with an Iowan."

"Go on."

"*The Golden Silence* is a story about a man in prison."

Alex broke away from the text and craned her neck to look at Keller. "A what?"

"Yeah, I know. Right up Aldiss's alley. But this guy escapes." He paused, looking down at the book as if its very existence troubled him. "He's in there because of something. Something happened a long time ago. A crime. But it's never explained what this crime is. It's something awful. A murder, maybe—I don't know. Fallows is intentionally trying to throw the reader off. This thing is like *Finnegans Wake* on steroids."

"And the main character is put in prison," Alex said, guiding him back.

"Yes. But, like I said, he escapes. He pretends to be someone else and then—this is strange, Alex. Really damn strange. People start believing him."

"What do you mean?"

"He tells them he's another man. He starts using this alias. First on his cellmate, and then on the guards. And slowly . . . well, it's like he hypnotizes them. They just start believing that he's a different man. Surrealism, of course—but Fallows was after something else with this. *The Golden Silence* has all these trapdoors, these broken passageways. In a lot of ways the book is this house of mirrors. But it's also poetic and, in its own way, sad."

"What happens to him when he gets out?"

"Not much," Keller said. "He lives the rest of his life. He writes and reads poetry. That part is nonessential. What is essential, and what made me think about the book tonight when we were at that house on Olive Street, is this."

And then he moved his arm and showed her the page he had marked. Alex saw his notations at the edges of the text. But she could make sense of none of it—at least not yet.

"What is it?"

"It's the connection," said Keller, as if it were all right there, on that ink-heavy page under his heavy right arm. "In this scene he's talking to someone in the prison. Telling them this false story about his identity, this lie about who he is. A throwaway conversation, you think. But . . ."

"What is it, Keller?" Alex urged.

"See for yourself."

He turned the book around, and Alex scooted out of the booth so that she could get right above the page. She began to read the lines Keller had highlighted.

The prisoner looked into the shadows. The guard stood outside his cell, looking in at him. The guard's eyes glowed. Everything was dark. These, the prisoner thought, these feral beasts who kept him here. He couldn't wait to spring himself, to free himself from this . . .

"Where did you grow up, prisoner?" the guard asked.

"Iowa," he said. "In its very heart."

"And your youth?"

"Troubled."

The guard nodded. He had expected this, was used to being

around torn and broken men. Somewhere deep in the prison a man screamed.

"And your first crime?" the guard said, tapping a finger on the cold steel bar. "Your baptism?"

"Theft," the prisoner said slowly. "I stole books."

The guard smiled, teeth parting slightly. He was interested now. This man, this prisoner—he wasn't like the rest.

"And what did you say your name was?" the guard asked.

The prisoner looked at him. Gauged him. Readied himself for the lie, the tale. As always, his heart grew and the golden silence descended. He was ready. "My name," he said, "is Morrow. Dr. Isaac Morrow."

She read the section twice, then sat back, slumped down beside Keller in the booth, and turned it over in her mind. *What's happening?* she thought. *What's he doing to us?*

"I don't understand it, Keller."

"Lydia Rutherford," he said. "She used that name tonight. Dr. Morrow. She said it plain as day, Alex. We both heard it."

Alex stared forward. The diner had fallen away. "Why would she do that?"

"I have no idea. My only thought is Lydia Rutherford is in on it somehow. She's trying to tell us something without telling us."

The last stragglers were leaving the restaurant, looking at the two college kids as if they were beings from another planet. Alex felt unmoored, rattled loose—again she wanted to move closer to Keller. Take comfort in his warmth, his strength. She moved her arm so that it touched his.

"The timing," she said finally.

Keller looked up. "What about it?"

She reached across and took his pencil, made a notation on a napkin. "Fallows wrote *The Golden Silence* in what year?"

Keller turned hurriedly to the front of the book, found the copyright date. "Seventy-five," he said. She scribbled the year.

"Charlie Rutherford Jr. would have to be how old?"

"Wait, I remember. Lydia said he was nine in '74, when his father died."

"That means he was born in the midsixties. And she told us Dr. Morrow cured him *after* her husband died. If Charles Rutherford is Fallows, how could he have known about Morrow?"

Keller said nothing. He kept his eyes down, staring at the napkin Alex had just written on as if it might tell him a secret. Reveal something. Then he sat up, his eyes opening wide. He closed the book with a heavy *thump*.

"Maybe it doesn't have anything to do with any of that."

Alex blinked. "What are you talking about?"

"Maybe," Keller said, "Lydia Rutherford is Paul Fallows."

Alex

Present Day

38

Where are you, Aldiss?

It was just after eight o'clock now. Alex looked out the window of her room, down at the twinkling Jasper campus. Everything was still, still and silent. Black's men would be waiting and Aldiss—would he come back here? Would he return to the campus to finish off the class? They were all here, after all, all in one place and so easy to find.

Once again she reached beneath her mattress and felt for the false Fallows book. She removed the book and opened it, saw the gun gleaming inside. Had Aldiss given her a way to save herself from him? Did he want Alex to end his life? She thought about Iowa again, about the awful person she'd met there, the true Dumant killer.

Unless that too was a lie.

Unless all they had found there had been put in place by Aldiss.

Jesus, Alex, get ahold of yourself. That's impossible.

She returned to the window, wondered how long until something happened—

There was a knock, and she turned around quickly.

"Who is it?"

"It's me," said a familiar voice. "May I come in?"

"Please do, Dean Fisk."

The door opened and the dean was there. He waved Matthew Owen away, and the nurse—his eyes fearful and quick—disappeared down the hall.

Fisk pushed his chair into the room and Alex sat at the foot of the bed, looking at the frail old man. A spike of regret for what had happened tore through her.

"I'm so sorry, Dean Fisk. I thought Professor Aldiss was—"

"Shhh," the man said. "Now is not the time or the place for apologies."

She nodded.

"I came up here to speak to you in confidence."

She looked at him. "Please, go on."

The dean began, and then stopped himself. This hesitancy was so unusual for Fisk that Alex was taken aback. She waited for the man to continue.

"It seems," he said, "that I have not been completely honest with you, Alex."

"What do you mean?"

"I mean that I have lied," the dean said. He stared blankly at her, his eyes wet and pleading. "What happened to you in Iowa—I feel partly responsible for that. I lied to you on your visits during the night class and I live with those lies every day of my life."

Iowa

1994

39

Alex awoke to find that someone else was in the hotel room with them. It was a man. He leaned back in the shadows, his face distorted by darkness, watching her. She didn't like his gaze. Not at all. It was as if he was *learning* her, studying her and teasing out her secrets. She sat up in bed, feeling Keller's body beside her, and stared deeper into the room. The darkness tingled like static. And sitting there in the room's lone chair, his face bathed in the swath of light that fell through the parted curtain, was Richard Aldiss.

Alex tried to scream. Tried to stand up, to do *something*—but her body was frozen. Her mind locked. She reached for Keller, thinking, *Please, please wake up.*

Then Aldiss wavered, just a slight flicker like the interference in a television image, and stood up. He took a step toward her, his boots (they were so dirty, she saw, and thought, *He's escaped*) sighing on the carpet. A second step, and then—

"Alex. Alex, I'm here."

She opened her eyes. Found that she was clutching Keller, sweat pasting down her hair and the sheet balled in her fists. She sat up, wiping sleep from her eyes. The bedside clock read 3:12 a.m. It was Saturday.

Keller sat up in bed and put his arms around her. She slumped against him.

"Nightmare," she said. "About him."

Smoothing her hair with his massive hand, the boy said, "We should go back. We'll just go back to Jasper and forget this. All of this—this class, Aldiss, Fallows. It isn't worth it."

"No." Her voice was a slight whisper. "Not now."

Keller began to speak, to protest, but then he fell silent. She curled into his chest.

"We've found something huge," she said. "We're too close. With Charlie and Dr. Morrow in *The Golden Silence* . . . we can't stop now. The night class is almost over. We almost have Fallows."

He leaned his head back and closed his eyes. A car whispered past out on the Iowa highway, a grid of light sweeping over the wall.

"Tomorrow," he said. "Where do we start?"

She wiggled closer to him. To be here, alone with him . . . under different circumstances it would have been pure pleasure. But now, given the task they had in front of them—Alex was unsure if this was something true or if it was just a product of the night class. If she and Keller had been brought together not by destiny but by the whims of Aldiss himself. Maybe their pairing, like everything else, was another twist in his plan.

"He was famous," Alex said at last.

Keller sat up. She could feel his gaze on her. "Slow down for us simpletons, Alex. I'm not following you."

"Paul Fallows. He would have to be the most famous thing to ever come out of little old Hamlet." She stared at him, at his dark shape. "In every small town in America, the locals keep up with their prodigal sons."

"So, what," Keller said, "we take a trip to the Hamlet Historical Society?"

"Not at all." She leaned up and kissed him, the sting of the Aldiss dream finally dissolving behind her eyes. "We tap into the town gossip mill."

The next day, just after the noon whistle pealed in the distance and a cold, muted sun finally broke through the clouds, they returned to downtown Hamlet and found a bar called Easy Living. A skin of blue smoke clung to the ceiling. Billiard balls cracked behind them, and now and then laughter echoed out. Keller, clearly out of place here, held everyone's gaze in the room. He took up two stools and drank a Tab with his arms draped across the bar.

"Where's home?" someone asked.

Alex turned. The bartender was a skinny man with yellowed teeth and a rumpled, splotchy apron. She was used to lonely bars; she did her best studying at Rebecca's. "Jasper College," she said. "Vermont."

"A long way from home, honey."

"It's a sordid tale."

"I've got time." The man smiled crookedly. There was a pack of cigarettes and a lighter on the bar, a community gift, and she reached over and took one. A sometimes thing, a thing she did when she was nervous or studying for an exam or thinking about grad school. She lit a cigarette and held it like she knew what she was doing. *Go for it.*

"We're looking for someone," she said.

"Oh yeah?" The bartender leaned closer and put his elbows on the bar. "And who would that be?"

"Paul Fallows."

Something changed in the man's eyes. "The writer."

"That's right. Know him?"

"Honey, there isn't anybody who *knows* him. That guy is a figment of somebody's weird imagination. A ghost."

Alex exhaled toward the ceiling. "Surely you must know somebody who can tell us something. We've come a long way and would hate to leave this beautiful town empty-handed."

The man eyed her. Was he suspicious? Did he see what she was doing? "What is this?" he asked cautiously. "A school project or something?"

"You could call it that."

He hesitated, then said, "I guess I can tell you one thing."

Alex wiggled forward on the stool, her heart kicking into gear. "What's that?"

"It isn't much, like I said. But there is somebody who lives way out on Deacon Road who knows more about this than anyone. He's an older man, but he was still kicking last time I checked. An old professor who claims he knows who Fallows is. He used to come around sometimes, but you don't see him much anymore. That whole Fallows thing—nobody talks about it that much now. It's gone the way of the cuckoo clock and the cross-country drive. It's 1994 now and folks have moved on."

Alex took another drag on the cigarette. The room seemed to have gone quiet, the music and the motion behind her and Keller totally fallen away. "This old man," she said. "What's his name?"

The bartender leaned close. His tongue darted out, crept slowly over cracked lips. She smelled his awful breath. "Benjamin Locke," he said.

They went. Across the flat tarpaulin of the landscape and into more flatness, the fields breaking up and becoming dirt at the edges of town, the afternoon pulling down like a drape over the western edge of the sky. They drove into the sun, following the directions the bartender had given them.

"There," said Keller, pointing with the edge of their napkin map.

A house just ahead, a small clapboard on the corner of Highway 281 and Deacon Road. Alex pulled in the driveway and they sat looking at the simple, black-shuttered house.

Keller parked the car and got out. He climbed the porch, glancing back at her once, and then he knocked. Someone answered, someone she couldn't see, and for a moment Keller slipped inside. She imagined him there, broken and bloodied on the floor. She thought of the two girls, the two Dumant grad students, of their last days—

A knock on her window. Alex jumped.

She rolled it down and stared out at Keller, blinked into the midday sun.

"Dr. Locke wants to speak to us," he said. "He says he's been waiting for us since he heard about the night class."

Benjamin Locke served them nothing. He sat across from the two students and stared with an intense precision, as if he was deciding whether or not he could trust them.

"Lydia Rutherford is one of the world's great liars," he said finally.

He had an academic's voice that had gone sour down the line, deep and thick but affected in the way of a final defense against the geography. His face was windburned and chafed but he was dressed like the famous professor he had been at Dumant. "I knew that the first time I met her. What she has done is simple, yet it is quite remarkable: she has hidden her husband's secret for years and years without telling anyone."

Alex stared at the man. "His secret," she said. "I'm afraid I don't understand."

"Charles Rutherford is Paul Fallows."

Alex didn't move, only nodded slightly. Her hands had begun to tremble. Locke didn't know about Morrow, she thought. Didn't know as much about the timeline and the texts as they did. Yet, he sounded so *sure* of himself. So convinced. "But Richard Aldiss has his own theories about Fallows's identity," she heard Keller say.

"Richard always had a lot of *theories*," said Locke. The room was lit by a simple lamp, and on a table beside the professor Alex saw photographs of what she knew was the Dumant campus. On the wall was a framed photo from *Life* magazine with the heading WORLD-RENOWNED LITERATURE PROFESSOR MAKES WAVES WITH RESEARCH ON RECLUSIVE NOVELIST.

"Do you still speak to him?"

"Not since the murders," said Locke. "Richard changed in a lot of ways after the summer we came to Iowa. When I heard about what had happened up at Dumant . . . well, I have to say I was not surprised."

"How did he change?"

Locke searched for the right words. "Richard," he said finally, "was different than my other pupils. He was brighter, for one thing—but he was also darker. More brooding. He began to obsess over Fallows. When we traveled here together that summer, I began to see this side of him more and more. And I came to be afraid of him."

"What was he like back then?" asked Keller. "What kind of student was he?"

"Richard was always eager to hunt Fallows, but I held back. You know about my phone call, I presume." Locke glared darkly at them. "It was . . . disturbing to say the least. But then *The Golden Silence* appeared in January of '75. A copy was sent to me anonymously at the university. Of course, Richard believed it was Fallows reaching out again, and this time I couldn't deny him—us—the hunt. When we finally made it to Iowa after the term ended, Charles Rutherford had been dead for six months." Locke looked away, something almost grave in his countenance. "We spent many days with his widow—talking to her, learning about Charles's encyclopedia jobs. When we brought up Paul Fallows, she seemed appalled. Almost shocked. She swore her husband had nothing to do with it, that he was not the writer and that the photograph of him on the books was some kind of trick . . ." Locke trailed off, looking out the front window at the fields that stretched away beyond his small house. "Richard believed Lydia. This woman, this widow who was raising her sick son on her own—to Richard it was heroic. He saw something of that in his own history. His fugues, you know, and his own father had died young. He began to protect her."

"Did you hear from him again when you returned to Dumant after that summer?"

Locke said nothing at first. His eyes drifted away again, a blue vein throbbing at his temple. "I banned him from my classes," he said flatly. "I told the dean that I couldn't look him in the eye again, not after I had seen what he was on our trip to Iowa. It became so difficult for me to even be around Richard that I left Dumant to teach at another university. Some years later I would find another protégé, but he was not the same as Richard."

"Is there any way Aldiss is innocent of the Dumant murders, Dr. Locke?"

Locke laughed. "Impossible," he said. "That man killed those two girls." He hesitated, stared out the window. Rain had begun to fall, spitting against the glass. Then he turned his eyes back on the two students as if something had just occurred to him and said, "If he has made you feel sorry for him in this class of his, if you are here to absolve him, stop now. Letting Richard Aldiss free would be the absolute worst thing anyone could ever do."

Alex

Present Day

40

"I don't understand, Dean Fisk. What did you lie about?"

The dean shifted his weight. His eyes searched her, slid across the small bedroom's only window. The Fallows book with the object hidden inside was on the nightstand, but she made no move to hide it now.

"I wanted Fallows," the old man said. "I wanted him so badly . . ."

Colder now: "What did you do?"

"I was never sure about Richard."

Alex sat back on the bed, the dean's words tearing through her.

"I always had reservations about his involvement in the Dumant murders. Always."

"But when I visited you during the class you said—"

"I know what I told you," Fisk said curtly. "But I went along with Richard's scheme because I needed his information. I wanted Fallows found and the mystery solved. I needed it to end." Fisk's eyes closed, as if he was reliving an awful memory. "I went to visit him once at Rock Mountain. He told me about a class he'd been thinking about, and I paid off the board of trustees at Jasper to make it happen. I had so much power at this college that no one challenged me. The next time I returned to the prison Richard told me about a book, about writing a message there . . ."

"Christ."

"The part about his innocence in the book you found, Alex—that was my doing. I wanted to believe it was true, but Richard never flatly denied the murders. Not really. He told me how to do my part, told me that one student would be 'chosen'—that's the word he used—from the class to be our eyes and ears, but he never talked about his innocence. It was all about the search for Fallows. In fact he never mentioned Dumant University or those two dead graduate students. Not ever."

Alex shivered. She looked again to the window, saw the spires of the college in the hazy distance. "Do you think he's coming after us, Dean Fisk?"

The old man looked at her, seemed to focus on her for the first time. Then he said, "I do. I'm sorry, Alex, but I think I may have led you right into his trap."

At 10:00 p.m., Alex's phone rang. She removed it from her bag and looked at the display. *Peter. Damn it.* She looked at it, considering. She didn't answer.

Instead she went out to find Keller.

The house was dark, the only sound the indistinct patter of Black and his men on the bottom level of the mansion. She wondered where Lewis Prine's body had been taken, wondered what he had seen in his last moments. If Aldiss had surprised him or if the two had spoken before Lewis was killed.

Trust me, she thought. *Don't you trust me?*

She shook the thought and went on.

When she got to Keller's door she stopped. Someone moved off to her right.

She looked up and saw Frank Marsden approaching her.

"Frank."

"They can't trap us here, Alex," the man said urgently, a waver in his voice that suggested he might be cracking. "We aren't fucking animals."

"Aldiss will be found soon and—"

"No, to hell with that. I'm leaving as soon as I can. Lucy and I have to get back to a shoot. We don't have time for this bullshit. If I stay in this house much longer I'm going to go insane and . . ." The man shook his head as if to clear a horrible image and continued up the hall. Alex entered Keller's room.

He was perched on a stool on the far side of the room, his wide back to the door. Even here, at this late hour, Alex could sense how awake he was, how *ready.*

"Do you remember when we found Fallows?" she asked. Her eyes were getting heavy and the silence of the house was weighing on her.

"I remember," he said. "We shouldn't have even been in Iowa."

"But we went, and we found what we were looking for. We found out who he really was."

"A lot of good it did us."

She stared at the man, at the night table beside him. No sign of the manuscript there.

"What does it feel like?" she asked.

"It . . ."

"Killing someone?"

He stared at her. "You don't want to know."

"I do, Keller. I want to know if I could do it. If I had to."

"You won't have to."

He sat down at the foot of the bed, box springs groaning beneath him. An image flashed: the boy in the hotel room the night before everything happened in Iowa, she lying beside him, the shape of her body tucked into his.

There was a quick *snap.* Alex's eyes jumped to the window, where one of the beech limbs nicked against the pane. When she refocused, she heard Keller's voice in the closed room.

"I burned it," he said.

"You *what*?"

"I burned the manuscript, Alex. Tossed it in one of the fireplaces and watched it go up in smoke. But I kept one page. I wanted you to see. I wanted you to . . . to know that I was right. That destroying it was the only way. That manuscript would have done nothing but harm. It would have pulled you under."

She glared at him. Again she thought of the boy he had been, of what he had done in Iowa. For her; everything he had done, all those irrational decisions he'd made during at the end of the night class, had been to protect her. But Alex felt as if this act erased all of that. Obliterated it. She hated him now with a precision she had never known. Standing there, in that cold room with him, a thought rushed through her. It came black and complete, like a door slammed shut: *I could kill him.*

"Four years," she growled. "Four years I've searched for that manuscript and you *destroy it*? This is just like you, Keller. Take what we did in Iowa, all we accomplished in the night class, and throw it away. Is this what you did with me? With us? Did you just toss us into some old fireplace too and move on with your life?"

"Maybe I did. And maybe it was best for both of us."

There was a feeling inside her of something coming loose, of the tether unraveling. She moved toward him. Keller reacted fast, catching her by the arms and restraining her. They were inches away from each other; she could taste his breath, could see the flare and hold of his pupils. *You bastard. You coward.*

"I was protecting you," he said, his voice like a lash. "Trust me: you didn't want to read it. Didn't want to know what Fallows was doing with that book."

She looked at him. "And did you?" she asked. "Read it?"

Almost imperceptibly, he nodded.

"Was it a Fallows?"

"Yes."

Rage. She felt it again, tasted it like acid on her tongue. She heard herself scream, the sound somehow not of her but primal, terrible. Again she pushed against him, dug her nails deep into the skin of his palms. When she spoke, her voice was tight, ugly. "What was it about, Keller? Or is that another of your secrets?"

At first he said nothing. The branch scratched against the glass beside them; his heart fluttered in his wrists like a thread being unwound. They stood there, locked together in a kind of frozen dance. When he spoke, his voice was full of pity. She had heard it before: it was the voice Keller used when they were students to talk about Aldiss.

"It was about us," he said.

She blinked. "I don't know what you're saying, Keller."

"It was about what's happening here, Alex. About this house, these murders. The novel was . . . it was a kind of locked-room mystery. It was about a group of old friends who come together, and each of them gets plucked off the wire. One by one by one."

She stared into his face, trying to find the words. To understand what it was he was telling her.

I'm sorry, Alex, but I think I may have led you right into his trap.

"Are you saying Fallows is behind all this?" she asked. "Fallows is dead, Keller. You know that as well as I do."

Keller flinched. Then he said, "Let me show you."

At first she didn't budge. She held him, pulled at him with all the strength she could muster. But then she relented. By degrees she pulled away until he was free, massaging his palms where she had torn into him. *I have to see,* she thought. *If I'm ever going to forgive myself for letting him find the manuscript, then I've got to see what he kept.*

Cautiously, she backed away. Keller turned around and went to a small writing table in the corner of the room. He opened a drawer and removed something. It was a yellowed sheet of paper. When he held it up for her to see, the light shot through, revealing unbroken, heavily struck-through typefont. He held the page at a distance, as if it might infect him.

"One page," he repeated. "It's all that's left."

He placed it on the dresser beside her. In the half-light, Alex read.

There were nine of them. His job now was to bring them all together. But how?

This question had consumed him for the last few months. He waited on some kind of special knowledge—a secret whispered by a passing stranger, a note handed to him at the library where he spent his evenings—that would explain how it could be done. Instead there was nothing but endless days of confusion, impotent nights where he lay in a sweat and turned the plan over in his mind. And then, almost by accident, it came to him. They could all return to mourn. Perhaps he had been going backward, taking his plan from the end and trying to weave it through the needle's eye. Here was the way: give them a reason to come back. And suddenly he knew how; stuck there in his darker nature like a shard of black glass was the first act. One of them would die—a suicide, perhaps, so there could be no questions about him—and then he could truly begin. The eight would inevitably return to the old house and he would be there, waiting for them. Observing.

Alex read the page, and then a second time. She traced the bubbled type with her finger. Even the words, the way they were chipped and broken and hanging apart like a busted hinge—tilted *e*'s, frantic and struck-through lines—held an intensity. A pulse. *It's Fallows.*

"The end," she said then, her voice a hollow croak.

Slowly, Keller looked up.

"How does it end?"

He stared at her as if trying to find the words, to put this awful thing into some kind of context. "They . . ."

"Tell me, Keller."

"They all die. All of them except one."

She waited for him to continue. It was the last thing she wanted to hear, but she couldn't turn away. Not now.

"It was Fallows himself, Alex. The last line of that"—he made a face as if he'd just tasted something awful—"goddamned thing was that Fallows lived. The author himself is the narrator. He killed them all and made it out of the old house. Aldiss must have gotten to the manuscript. Re-created it. Put the game into motion"

It hit her in the gut. She drew back, nearly doubled over. *The game. Aldiss is the one. Aldiss was there all along. Aldiss created the* cyndrot.

But then she looked up at Keller. She saw him dropping the manuscript into the fire, watching it burn, the paper falling into shreds and the flames licking in his eyes. She saw him smile.

"You're lying," she said.

Keller blinked. He looked like he'd been slapped.

"This is all bullshit. I don't believe a word you're saying." He reached out for her, and she yanked her hand away. "Don't you dare or I'll scream. I'll fucking scream for them and tell them that you're the one who did this. That you're the reason we're all trapped in this house."

"Alex . . ."

But she was walking away, leaving the room. Out in the hallway now, her anger disorienting her, she saw the form of a man standing on the other side of the hall, hidden in shadow. It was Frank again.

"You scared the hell out of me," she said.

The man said nothing. He was looking out a porthole window down onto the front lawn. Alex stepped out into the hall and Frank still didn't move. He stood there, leaning against the wall and looking outside—

Alex stopped.

She stared at the man.

Thought, *No.*

She looked closer. Noticed the unnatural way his head was bent, how his chin cocked at a strange angle. Then she saw something glisten in the window, the thing catching the moonlight and running upward like a spider's web. And Alex followed the thing up, up, to the top edge of the porthole that had been pushed inward. Saw a wire anchored there, yanked taut to the windowpane.

She screamed for Keller.

Iowa

1994

41

"What is wrong with Lydia's son, Dr. Locke?"

Keller's question was where they had been moving for the last half hour. Locke was loosening up to the two of them. Perhaps it was being around students again; perhaps he simply wanted to discuss Fallows for the first time in years. Either way, Alex saw a change in the man. He had begun to trust them.

"No one is quite sure," the professor explained. "My guess is paranoid schizophrenia. But I was never around him enough to know. She hid him away in that house on Olive Street. Every time I saw him he was watching cartoons like a child."

"He was in a home for a time, wasn't he?" asked Keller.

"That's right. But Lydia became convinced the experience would damage the boy. That she could raise him on her own. So she brought him home, and that's where he has been ever since."

"And now he's thirty."

"Twenty-nine, I believe. Exactly the age of Charles Rutherford when he died."

Alex looked at the old professor. They were so close, but not quite there yet. She could feel it, feel the pull of Richard Aldiss from his prison cell. He'd learned something new. New. Locke appeared to have stopped looking decades ago, so sure was he that Charles Rutherford was Paul Fallows.

"The doctor," she said now. "Dr. Morrow."

Locke looked at her. "Young lady, I'm afraid I don't—"

"Fallows used that name in *The Golden Silence*, and Lydia Rutherford also said it. Dr. Morrow treated Charlie."

Locke looked startled. "I don't believe," he said slowly, "that you will get anywhere if you follow the 'clues' in those books. People have been searching for years but have yet to come up with anything substantial. Lord knows I spent a great deal of my life doing the same. My theory is correct: Charles Rutherford was Paul Fallows, and his novels were *stories*—nothing more and nothing less. The books only grew in importance when Paul Fallows became a ghost."

"But if we were to follow this route," Keller said, "and find this Morrow, where would we go?"

Locke eased back in his chair. There was something in his eyes: *Don't. Don't do that.*

"I'm sure the man is retired by now," Locke said cautiously. "Charlie would have been under his care in the seventies."

"The home," Alex said. "The place where Charlie stayed for a time. Where was that?"

"That place." Locke's eyes went to the window again, as if he was remembering something horrible. When he spoke next his voice was low, almost strained. "It's about an hour's drive from here in a town called Wonderment, just outside of Des Moines. The home itself is called the Shining City. But I wouldn't go there if I were you."

"Why not?"

"Because all you will see is human misery."

It was another thirty miles, as Hamlet receded into the gray distance behind them, before she understood what it meant.

It was a memory. A recollection that she knew had dawned on Keller at the same moment. As the landscape rattled past and as Alex drove the rental into the fading sun, he looked at her. The expression on his face said, *Finally.*

Shining City.

That was the name of the place, the home where Charlie Rutherford had stayed. And those were the same exact words Richard Aldiss had used in one of his lectures at the beginning of the night class. So innocuous then, so meaningless—but now it was heavy in the cabin of the little rental car.

"But you will go nowhere without the knowledge of who Charles Rutherford was," Aldiss had said, "and of the shining city from where he came . . ."

Charles Rutherford. Charlie. Father and son, puzzle pieces that fit together in the most natural way. Alex smiled. They were almost there. They had almost passed Richard Aldiss's night class.

Alex

Present Day

42

Alex reached out and grabbed Frank Marsden, touched his shoulder and felt him shift, fall toward her, slump like the dead weight he now was. She fought with him, her mind a wreck, the wire around his neck keeping the man upright as if he were some kind of puppet, the blood from his mouth smearing against her shirt and—

"Here. Don't."

Keller behind her now, moving the man back against the wall. The wire sagged, then snapped taut as the actor slumped.

"How?" Alex asked. It was the only word she could manage.

Keller looked. The wire had been dropped in through the window. "The roof," he said. "Aldiss is up there. We need to get Black."

Movement. It was the dead man writhing, twitching. Blood bubbled at his mouth. He groaned and Alex stepped back. For the first time since Iowa, Keller looked afraid.

"Go," he said to her then, reaching out for Marsden. The man's eyes rolled back and he gargled again, his throat ruined. "Get someone."

She screamed for help.

"No," Keller said. "The house—it's too big. We're in an entirely different wing. You'll have to go."

Alex ran. She turned the corner and sprinted for the stairs, her sock feet stinging on the threadbare carpet.

She stopped. The elevator Fisk used to move between floors was to her left. She pushed the down button and waited, heard the thing grind to life three floors below. As it approached she thought about what Keller had said. *The roof.* She imagined Aldiss pushing in the window, dropping the wire, slipping it over Marsden's head and then yanking it taut.

"Help!" she shouted again, her voice echoing.

A door at the far end opened and Christian Kane appeared. The man had been sleeping, and it took him a minute to focus.

"Alex, what's happening?"

"Get someone, Christian. Get Black. Something's happened to Frank." The elevator ground to a stop and its ancient doors parted. She shoved Christian inside. "Go! Go!"

Alex turned then and ran back the way she had come. She had to get back to Keller, see if she could help him (*He's dead, Alex; you saw his eyes*) with Frank. She rounded the corner in a sprint and looked down the hallway.

Nothing.

The wire hung there, limp as a vine.

Keller and the dead man were both gone.

Iowa

1994

43

Aldiss had led them to the end of the world.

Shining City had been an insane asylum in another era: Gothic-fronted, black-shadowed eaves, a turret that jutted anonymously from the side of the building like a portent. It was out of place amid the starkness of the land—and yet weren't the students as well? *Nothing fits here.* Alex thought as they passed the security gate and approached the building. *Especially not us.*

A drab, blackened sign announced the place: SHINING CITY, HOME FOR TROUBLED BOYS, EST. 1957. The two stood outside the entrance, perhaps willing themselves to go inside, maybe waiting for a signal that would explain why they were there.

Because we have to find Fallows. Because Aldiss is innocent. Because the two mysteries are one and the same.

The place held no promises. A few orderlies swept in and out of the great room, but otherwise it was silent. No manic patients, no wandering insane—the home had been left behind in the seventies. Even the wallpaper was stripped, outdated, its rainbow pattern suggesting a sort of happiness that was alien here.

Alex was flying blind. And yet Keller followed her down a long antiseptic corridor and into another just like it. She heard him say, "I don't know about this, Alex," the tentativeness in his voice urging her on to prove him wrong. She didn't know, either—and the thought enraged her. If they had made a mistake, if this was not where Aldiss wanted them to be, then there was nowhere else. Tomorrow they would be on a plane back to Jasper College and the night class would be over.

"Can I help you?"

She turned. The woman who had spoken was standing a few feet from them, clutching a stack of folders. She wore flat shoes and a white coat. A doctor.

"We're looking for someone," Alex said. "A therapist who worked here at one time. Maybe he still does."

"There aren't many docs left now," said the woman. "They're razing this place, and we're in the process of transferring patients to an institution in Des Moines right now. What was his name?"

"Morrow," Alex said. "His name is Dr. Morrow."

"Can't say it's familiar," she said. "But I've only been at Shining City for two months. Let me ask someone who might know. Wait here?" She gestured toward a dim lobby.

Alex sat in the kind of unwieldy chairs you only find in hospitals. She offered Keller the chair beside her but he waved it off as if he was fine with standing. Then she saw: the plastic chair was too small for him. Alex smiled despite herself.

Two minutes later a thin, silver-haired man stood at the door. He looked weary, as if this was his last stop of the day. He eyed the students suspiciously and said, "Terese said you wanted to ask me a few questions."

"Dr. Morrow?" Alex asked.

"No," the man said, a hesitant smile breaking across his lips. "My name is Allen Bern. I interned under Morrow. He died in '91."

Her heart stuttered. They were too late.

"But maybe I can help you?"

"We're here because of a patient Dr. Morrow was in charge of," Keller broke in. "He would've been very young, only a boy. He was at Shining City for a short time. But we believe Morrow had a profound effect on him. His name was Charles Rutherford Jr."

The man's eyes jumped. He knew something.

"I'm . . . I'm sorry," he said. "I think I should be going. I don't want to—"

"Please, Dr. Bern," Alex said. She heard her own desperation and didn't try to check it. "We've come such a long way and we just need a few answers. If you know anything about this patient, anything at all, then—"

"He lied about not being able to speak."

Alex blinked. "Excuse me?"

"I saw Morrow with so many patients over the years," Bern went on. "So many troubled youths came through Shining City, and Morrow was brilliant with them all. Every one he treated as his own son, as if that boy was special. Unique. But Charlie . . ."

"Go on."

"I had just started," Bern explained. "I was young, not long out of med school. I was still learning my way into therapy, and to me Morrow was a sort of deity. I had read his articles at university, had begun to appropriate some of his methods in my own sessions. Everything he did with these patients I wanted to replicate."

"And did you watch him treat Charlie Rutherford?" Keller asked.

Bern nodded. "I want to say I still think of it, but the truth is I don't. I haven't thought of it for a very long time. Almost twenty years now. Maybe I wanted to put it out of my mind. To forget it ever happened."

"What happened?"

"He was performing the Rorschach test," Bern said. "He was showing Charlie the ink blots. I remember Dr. Morrow shuffling through the cards, the sound of them against his fingers. That was the only sound in the room, because Charlie—of course he wasn't speaking. He never spoke. He wrote his responses on a little pad Morrow had given him."

"What did he write?" Alex asked, and glanced at Keller. The Rorschach test—they were both thinking of it. What could it mean?

Bern turned to her slowly, resolutely. His gaze held the past now, the memory heavy and fierce. "Atrocities," the man said. "Every blot, every image was another violent detail. One was fire; the next was pain; another was blood. All of these words scratched onto the pad. Sometimes he would *copy* what Morrow showed him. Draw his own blot and then hold up the card to the therapist as if he were some sort of mirror. Then he would smile as if he had done something grand. When the session was over I looked at Morrow and saw . . . I don't know. I saw this *distance*. He was afraid of the boy."

"But Morrow must have seen violent patients before," Keller said, keeping his voice calm and steady. "It would have been common at Shining City for children to come through who had that kind of temperament."

"No," Bern said quickly. "Not like Charlie. The other boys, even the ones with violent pasts—they were acting. Playing a role. But with Charlie you felt it was real. He had been damaged innately. He had been *turned*, somehow."

"You say he lied about being mute," Alex goaded the doctor. She wanted to get to the bottom now, get out of this place. She was beginning to understand why Aldiss had sent them to this private little hell, but some piece of the puzzle was still out of reach.

"Yes," he said, his gaze drifting away and his voice softening. "This was three months after he came to Shining City. They were having another Rorschach session. They were just to the end, and Charlie looked at Morrow and said something. It was one word—we both heard it. When the boy left the room Morrow came to me, pale and shaking, and said, 'Did you . . . ? ' Of course I did."

"But that must have been a breakthrough," Alex said, remembering Lydia's praise of the doctor the night before. "Morrow's work, it would have been changing Charlie. Healing him."

"No," Bern said quickly. "That wasn't it at all. There was something about that word—something almost *teasing*. It was then that Morrow asked to be removed from the boy's case. Charlie had come a long way but there was no question—for the first time, Morrow had failed one of his patients. But I also saw relief. He had gone inside Charlie Rutherford's mind and had seen something truly ugly. Obscene. He wanted out."

"Did you ever see Charlie again?" asked Keller.

"No. The boy's mother came a few weeks later and removed him from Shining City. I heard she lived alone in Hamlet. A beautiful woman, so different from her son. The husband had died by then. But by then none of it mattered. We just wanted to be free of that child."

Bern walked them out. As she moved down the hall beside the doctor, she turned what he had said over in her mind. She thought of the Rorschach, of the photographs she had seen of the Dumant victims, of the word Bern had used: *violence.* Aldiss had wanted them to know these things about Charlie. He had wanted them to draw a line between the damaged man and the murders at Dumant.

"The word," Bern said now. They were at the exit, and outside the sky was darkening. Close to the end now.

"What's that, Doctor?" asked Keller.

Bern looked at them with such intensity that Alex shivered. He was trying to warn her.

"'Daddy,'" Bern said. "Just that one word, the only one Charlie Rutherford ever said. "He was saying 'daddy.'"

Alex

Present Day

44

Aldiss was here. He had somehow gotten into the mansion; he'd killed Frank Marsden and now Keller was in danger. She felt defenseless standing there alone in the pulsing emptiness, the only thing in the corridor the empty, looping wire. Everything else was dark.

She took a step. Another. And where were the others? Why hadn't Black or Christian Kane come to this wing to check on her, to save her? Why—

There was a sound then, a ticking noise inside the blackness.

Alex froze. It had come from the far end of the hall, beyond Keller's room.

Fear welled up inside her, forcing her to move. One step, and then another—she had to get to the far end of the hall. She had to get off this floor and down. The closest exit was there, not twenty-five feet away, and she had to get there.

Another step. She was beside the window now where Frank had stood. There was blood stippled on the wall, and something else— heavy tracks on the corridor's carpet. A black slither of blood sweeping away from her, as if Frank had been dragged away.

Alex forced her eyes away from the stain. Moved on.

She moved fast toward the steps, thinking, *He could be downstairs right now. He could be on any floor of this house, waiting for me.* She pictured Aldiss's face, the grotesque smile greeting her in the darkness.

Downstairs now. She took the flight of steps in two leaps and then turned, torquing her body with the rail, and pulled herself—

Out. Out into the cold, where the wind sheared away her fear.

There were people on the front lawn, a group of them standing over something on the ground. A clump of something, human-shaped. A thought screamed through Alex's mind: *No. Not Keller. Not Keller.*

Tentatively, she stepped forward into the crowd and looked down.

It was Frank. Someone was doing CPR on him. Others were shouting, pointing toward a bundle of dark trees a hundred yards from the dean's house. She saw Black gesturing wildly, organizing something. The man's eyes fell on her.

"Shipley," he said. "What the hell happened up there?"

"I . . . I don't . . ."

"We saw someone running," Black went on. "Someone came out of the house and dropped Marsden, and then he took off toward campus."

"Keller," Alex said. He must have been going after Aldiss.

Black's eyes flared in the half-dark. Then there was movement on the ground, and the paramedic who had been working on Marsden shouted, "I've got a pulse!"

The detective turned away. The others in the circle all looked down at the man, who was still coughing blood and reaching out. Alex saw Lucy Wiggins there, crouching beside the fallen man. "Tell me what happened, baby," she was saying. "Please tell me."

Black took a step toward the dying man. A wild thought burned in Alex's mind: *Go. Now.*

Another step by Black and Alex took off on a dead sprint toward campus.

Toward Keller.

Iowa

1994

45

Night.

Back in the hotel room they didn't talk. Not about Charlie Rutherford, nor about Shining City or what it might mean. That was for later. Keller turned off the lamp and they lay together in the darkness. Finally, her voice searching for him, she said, "I'm scared."

She felt his gaze. Felt his touch on her. She closed her eyes.

"I'll protect you," Keller whispered.

He kissed her. She had a thought that it was ending. It had already ended, perhaps, on the night she walked into Aldiss's classroom for the first time. Something would happen that would tear them apart. It was like driving a car in the dark, the feeling that something was plunging at them but they just couldn't see what it was. Then Keller was touching her and Alex closed her eyes and gave in. Let go. He was the first man to have done this, to have gotten this far, this deep: here, then, it all flipped inside out. The guilt, the fear that she wasn't doing something with what she had learned, that two girls were dead and she still hadn't figured out why—it turned itself to a sharpness, an electric kind of *pain,* and she held on to him and lost herself completely.

I love you, she said when they were finished. She wasn't sure if she'd said it aloud but Keller pulled her closer nonetheless. He too saw that object in the distance. He knew what was bound to happen when the morning came and the night class ended, and so he held her. He held her but gently, cautiously.

She slept. She did not dream of Aldiss, but when she awoke in the postdawn gray, she felt as if he'd been there in that room. Guiding her. Pushing her. She slipped out of bed, gently enough to not wake Keller, and said to herself, *Okay. Okay, Professor, I hear you.*

Alex started the car and let the heat rush over her face. She wasn't totally awake. Not yet. She'd spent the past few hours thinking, debating whether or not to go back to the house on Olive Street. After they left Shining City she wanted to return there, but it had been late. Keller felt it was too dangerous. There were too many unanswered questions, he thought, too many loose threads.

But no. Alex knew that was wrong. So many questions had been answered now.

She had dressed and showered, returned to the room and stared at Keller. He slept peacefully. It was just before seven in the morning. *When are you going to tell him?* she thought. *When are you going to show him the book you found in the library?*

But she wasn't ready. Alex was learning something about herself that maybe Aldiss had known all along. She wanted to win. She felt like the night class was hers. Hers and hers alone. The only way she could truly finish the class was to exhaust every angle. To go back to where she knew Aldiss was leading her. To return to Olive Street.

Alone.

46

As she walked toward the front door of the Rutherford house, she thought of Shawna Wheatley and Abigail Murray, Richard Aldiss's dead students. They had come this far; they had been this close. And then something had stopped them.

What had they found? What had they uncovered to get themselves—

Don't, she thought. *They made mistakes that you won't. Aldiss has given you too much.*

She knocked.

The door gasped open. Lydia Rutherford stood there with her robe cinched, her eyes suspicious. Something about her had changed. *Does she know why I'm here?*

"Mrs. Rutherford," Alex said, "I'm sorry for coming so early."

"What do you want?"

Everything froze. This moment—Alex had practiced it in the hotel room that morning. Ran over it in her mind, got her lines exactly right. But now, standing before the woman, she could say nothing. She dropped her eyes to the porch.

"Charlie had a bad night," she heard Lydia say. "Got real sick."

Alex looked up. "I'm sorry."

Something in the woman's glare broke. And as it did Alex saw that this woman only wanted an ally. She wanted someone to tell her that everything was going to be okay, that her son was going to make it. Pity shot through Alex and she said, "I know how it is. My father . . . he's dying."

Lydia moved back, her gaze still on Alex. She looked to be battling with herself, debating on the purpose of this student with her bed hair and her sleepy eyes. Finally, the better part of her won out and she opened the screen door wider. Said, "Come in. I'll fix you tea."

Then she was inside the house. There was a flash of light, a mad cartoon soundtrack. Alex turned and saw someone sitting in a corner chair.

"Charlie?" Lydia said to the man's back, and when he didn't answer she said it louder: "Charlie!"

Slowly he turned and looked at his mother. The television light bathed his face in sickly greens and reds. He opened his mouth slowly but said nothing.

Lydia looked down at the carpet. Alex saw it in her eyes: she was afraid of her own son. "Charlie, we'll be in the kitchen," she said weakly. Then, to Alex: "Come on." Alex glanced at Charlie, who had turned away now. She knew that she would have to get alone with him, find out what he knew. The impossibility of the task made her shudder, and she turned and followed Lydia into the kitchen.

Alex sat at the table. Lydia moved around the kitchen, began slamming cabinets, muttering something to herself. Alex stared at the walls. It was 1960s Americana, unchanged probably since before Charles Rutherford's death. Above the sink was a frame, and inside the frame was a needlepoint square: CHARLIE'S AND MOMMA'S KITCHEN.

Alex looked at the woman. She thought of Charlie in the next room. *Now or never.* "Where's your bathroom, Mrs. Rutherford?" she asked.

Lydia pointed and Alex slipped out. Charlie was still sitting in his chair and watching his cartoons. She moved toward him slowly, as if approaching a wild animal, braced herself, and said, "Your dad—I bet you really miss him." *How idiotic, Alex!* But it didn't matter: the man didn't turn, didn't move.

Alex shook her head and continued down the hall. It would have to be done sometime; she would just have to find the right words. Approach him somehow. Get him to tell her more about his father. It was the only way. *The mysteries are one and the same.*

In the hallway she took in her surroundings. There were family photos on the wall, some of them of Charles Sr. Here was the man and a much younger Lydia, and in her arms was the baby. They were smiling, but Alex couldn't help but read something in their gaze. Something of the future pain. She went on.

Into the bathroom, where she stared at herself in a streaked mirror. *What are you doing, Alex? Why did you come back here?* She splashed water on her face and then closed her eyes. She saw Aldiss sitting in that cell, head in his hands, his books arranged before him. His new information there on the cold stone floor as he waited for her to return and—

She opened the door and left the bathroom. She took one step and paused; something had caught her eye.

A room. It was there on her right. A cluttered room, boxes and detritus slung everywhere. Down the hall she heard Charlie's cartoon soundtrack blipping, and behind that was the teapot beginning to churn. Alex turned to look at the room again, wondering, *Could I?*

She stepped inside and closed the door behind her.

The room smelled like must. Motes spooled down from buckled shelves, and Alex pulled the cord on a bare ceiling bulb and looked at the junk. The boxes were old and feathered, a skin of dust lying atop them. Some of them were unlabeled, but others were marked *Charles*. She removed the lid on one of these boxes and looked inside.

Books. Bound manuscripts, photocopied and laid perfectly inside the box.

But there was something about these books. Hands shaking, she removed one of them and flipped through it. As she did, the knowledge dawned on her. The slow, horrible knowledge that she was looking at what Shawna Wheatley and Abigail Murray had found before they died. The last piece of the puzzle, the final clue in Aldiss's literary mystery.

The books were encyclopedias.

Alex

Present Day

47

Alex ran toward the dark campus. There was someone a good distance in front of her—a man. She called, "Keller!" but he did not stop. She moved on into the night.

Then she saw where he was going, and it made her blood go cold.

He was heading toward Culver Hall.

Alex thought, *This is where it ends, this is where it ends, this is where—* her pulse roaring and the wind striking her face full on. She had no choice but to follow the man.

At the front door now, where he had entered. She stopped herself, thinking of Black. But there was no time to call for help from the detective. If Keller was in this building with Aldiss, then she was the only person who could stop what was going to happen.

She pulled the door open and stepped inside Culver.

48

The first thing she noticed was the light.

It was a bleeding light, a slow strain of whiteness on the walls. Otherwise the classroom building was pitch-dark. Alex climbed the three steps in the vestibule and then turned the corner into a long corridor. When she did she saw a man. He was crouching just in front of her inside that pool of security light. *Aldiss,* she thought. But no. It wasn't the professor.

It was Matthew Owen.

"He's hurt," Owen said. "Get someone."

Alex looked down. Owen's hand was on Keller's back. Keller lay on the floor, motionless. Injured. There was nothing in Alex's mind but confusion. Why was the nurse here in this building? What the hell was going on?

"Matthew," she managed to say, her tongue thick and clumsy. She looked at him, tried to place him here. "What are you doing?"

"I saw Aldiss running away from the house," he said breathlessly. "I followed the professor in here and found Keller like this."

"Where is he, Matthew?" she asked. "Where's Aldiss?"

"I don't know. I lost him in the hallway, but he's still here. In the building."

She took a step toward Owen and looked down. There was a gash on Keller's head, and the nurse was applying pressure to the wound. She saw how he looked at Keller, how concerned he seemed about the other man. *It's time to stop,* she told herself. *This is not the night class. This isn't part of Aldiss's game. He's trying to help.*

Seeing her relax, Owen nodded. "Aldiss hurt your friend. I need help. Can you help me, Alex?"

Slowly, carefully, she knelt beside Keller. She listened to the shallow keen of his breath, running her fingers through his hair as Owen inspected the wound. The hall was quiet.

"We're in danger here," Alex said. "The professor—he'll come back for us. For me."

"I don't think that's going to happen," Owen said without looking up. There was something distant about his voice. Something almost detached.

"What are you talking about? He's here, Matthew, in this building. You said so yourself. He's going to come back and—"

"Shhh," he said, pressing harder, dark blood trickling out around his fingers.

Alex stood up. "Well, I'm going. I'm the only one who can convince him to turn himself in. Stay with Keller until I get back, okay?"

She began to move into the darkness. She knew her way through this corridor, even though there was little light. She'd walked here in her dreams many times.

She moved down the hallway, keeping close to the wall. Emergency lighting bled onto the floor, and she followed the grid with her hands on the cold stone. Counting steps, her heart roaring in her ears, she felt the terror replaced by a hopeless inevitably. Three steps, four. Before she could take another something stopped her. A slight hush from behind, a flit of shadowy movement. She stopped, listening. *Go back. Go outside and get Black right now. This isn't your job, Alex.* But it was. It had been hers since the beginning, since she'd found the book and its hidden message. Now she had to finish it.

Another step, and again something made her hesitate. Footsteps? She turned around and—

—everything exploded into whiteness. She stumbled back against the stone wall, an arm blocking her vision. A powerful flashlight had been aimed directly into her eyes. She saw a man's legs approaching, his dark shoes softly vibrating the tile beneath her. The upper half of him was invisible, sheared away by the manic light. Owen? Aldiss? She had no way of knowing. The world had simply winked out. "What are you doing?" Alex shouted, her voice a panicked and warbling screech.

No response. The man drew closer.

Her vision swam, tiny pinwheels spinning behind her lids. She blinked madly, her eyes watering, and felt the man there, in her space. Felt his heat. Smelled him. She still could see nothing but his dark slacks. There was something familiar about the way he stood, about the cant of his posture. But before she could figure out what it was the light pressed forward, blotting everything out again.

"Who are you?" she said.

No sound. He kept the light high. There was a kind of controlled violence in it; that light could have been a knife. An axe.

"Professor, is that you? It's over, Professor. They know all about you, about what you've—"

Closer now. The light was almost pressed against her face. The bulb touched her cheek, stinging her skin. She slapped him away but he restrained her, pushed her back into the wall. And it was then, as he moved his hand toward hers, that the light shifted. Was knocked upward the slightest degree. And beneath it, in her blurred vision, she saw the man's face.

"Matthew."

"I only want to talk to you," the nurse said. "Just stay there."

Things were moving in her mind. Conclusions, connections. "Aldiss . . ." she managed.

The light remained. The figure behind it, silhouetted by the beam, stiffened. "I already told you, Alex," he said. "The professor is somewhere in this building. He's hiding from us." There was a mechanical quality to his voice now.

Could Owen be the one? Alex thought. *But how could that be? Aldiss said to look for someone who was part of the night class.* And yet here she was, trapped in the hallway, the wild light still flooding her vision.

As she backed away from him Alex thought of what she knew about Owen, of all the things she'd seen from him the last two days.

He was a nurse who'd left his old job after a falling-out of some kind. Now he stayed with Dean Fisk, lived in the mansion, learning its secrets.

She remembered the card Aldiss had given her: *The Procedure has begun. Everything they say, everything you hear could be part of the game. Trust no one.*

Another memory: Dean Fisk in his study saying, *But Matthew tells me that he sees them playing it on his walks across the east campus . . .*

"Alex," Owen said now. "Keller needs help. He's bleeding badly. Aldiss hurt him."

A thought. A seed of something. A reason. Everything became clear in that one second; everything was revealed in that fraction of no-time: the reason Owen was here. The reason he'd come to Jasper College to care for Dean Fisk.

She looked at the man. Then she said, her eyes steady and her voice level, "Why are you doing this to us, Matthew?"

Owen's hand wobbled slightly; the light danced. Silence.

"You said you were brought here by the college, but that isn't true, is it? This is a job you coveted for a long time. You've been waiting for this moment."

"I don't know what you're talking about, Alex," Owen said, "but you really need to—"

"You killed them," she went on. "You killed Michael Tanner, and then you put Melissa Lee in the lake to frame Aldiss. It was you all along."

Owen took another step, the light shifting erratically. Alex listened for movement outside Culver Hall. Nothing now but the howl of the wind. She shut her eyes again.

"It's not what you think," he said. "Just listen to me now. Listen, Alex—"

A memory descended, fitfully: Iowa. That morning in Iowa inside the Rutherford house. She realized for the first time how much she wanted to be done with it now, to be free of the night class and Paul Fallows and all the rest of it. To finally have it behind her.

"You killed them," she said again.

"No, you killed them, Alex."

Alex froze. "What are you talking about?"

"When you went to Iowa you set in motion all that would happen," Owen said. "You ruined the game for everyone else." He made that face again: that sour, childlike face that said to her, *This is happening whether you like it or not.* "Now I am going to win it once and for all."

He grabbed her. Grabbed her by the hair and pulled her out of the screaming light. And it was then that Alex saw the nurse's face up close; she saw what was strange and familiar about him. That thing she could not place before. It was the eye, Owen's one blue eye visible while the other remained hidden in shadow. Below the eye was the patchy down of his beard, pale skin reddening in the cold beneath it. She remembered Aldiss during one of his seizures, the camera jostling just enough to reveal a face behind him. Yes—she had seen Owen before.

It ends, she thought as the light fluttered and began to seep away. *It ends like this. Like this. Like this.*

Aldiss had been right all along. The killer was part of the night class.

Matthew Owen had been one of Richard Aldiss's prison guards.

Iowa

1994

49

Alex looked around the small room. The air was thick, musty, dust hanging everywhere. It had begun to choke her, and she used the crook of her arm to cover her mouth. She stepped back into a corner, reached for one of the books, and—

The whole box slid forward, then toppled to the ground. She froze, waiting for someone to come. The hall remained empty. Quietly, her mouth bone-dry and her heart pounding, she knelt down and picked up another book. When she saw what was there she breathed in sharply, the shock of it hitting her like a blow to the chest.

Names.

The encyclopedias contained names, each entry the name of another girl. And they were all girls, Madeleine and Mary and Marybeth and Marissa. Last names too, and . . .

Yes. Addresses.

These were real. As real as she was.

Alex leaned down and flipped through one of the books. Its binding was crude, red string looped through holes, but it was there. Physical. She could pick it up and flip through it in the semidarkness. And this she did, the dust clogging her airways and making her gasp silently, but she kept on turning, flipping through the pages and taking in the names of these girls. There were hundreds here, perhaps thousands, each of them arranged by the name of the town. When she was at the end she flipped back to the title page and saw what the book was called. And this, too, struck a kind of wild fear in her. A blind terror at seeing, at knowing what these books were. What they contained.

The books were called *The Encyclopedia of the Dead.*

Their author was Paul Fallows.

50

Alex reached down again and took up another book. There were perhaps fifty of them on the floor, and the boxes in the cramped room were endless. *Who are these people?*

As she was flipping through the next book, she heard something. A slight sound, just the tiniest scuff of movement. Her blood froze. She looked up.

Charlie Rutherford was standing in the doorway.

At first she could say nothing. Her throat seemed to be destroyed; she was mute, like him. The man looked at her unblinking, his hands perfectly aligned at his sides. In the other room there was a cartoon honk, the jittery beat of children's music.

"Charlie," she whispered. "What are these books? Are these your dad's?"

The man said nothing. He simply stood there in the threshold, watching her.

"Are these people your dad knew, Charlie? Are they women he met when he was—"

"Mom!"

The voice was a child's: loud, rebellious. And as he said it his eyes flashed with mischief: *I know what you're doing. I know why you're here.*

It didn't take Lydia Rutherford long. She turned into the room, a hand clapped over her mouth. Alex tried to step back, but there was nowhere to go. She was trapped.

The woman began to say something but stopped. Then, her voice soft as a whisper, she said, "You aren't supposed to be in here."

"I'm sorry," Alex managed. "I'll leave. I'll just go back to Vermont and—"

"No." Lydia took a step into the room. There was something of a smile on her face now, wide and animalistic. She approached Alex and reached out, and Alex flinched. The woman took a strand of Alex's hair and tucked it behind her ear.

"Please," Alex gasped. "Please, I'll do anything. Anything."

The woman's eyes dropped. She said, "I know you've been asking questions about Charlie. He's a good boy. It's just that something happened to him. Something happened at his beginning." She stopped, gazed at her son with pity.

Alex's knees wobbled. She looked again at the door, at Charlie standing there so resolute. So still. Blocking her escape.

"He got his father's sickness, and what am I supposed to do about that? He's my son. My blood. I must love him. That's what they don't understand about us. That's why they call us *strange*. They don't see, they don't know how a mother loves her son. They don't *know*."

Lydia turned then and smiled at him. It was a motherly smile, and when she looked back at Alex it was gone. Replaced by a wrath that burned hotly in her eyes.

"Charlie," the woman said. "Go and get Daddy's axe."

Alex

Present Day

51

Matthew Owen strained against her. The light wavered. His face was inches from Alex's now.

"I tried to eliminate Aldiss first," Owen said. "If the brain dies, then the body will fall. When he was at Rock Mountain I was in charge of treating him, of controlling the seizures. But I didn't go far enough. I missed my chance and he gave Fallows to you on a silver platter." A shadow passed across his face. "So I worked with what I had. A struggling cop. A few phone calls, the suggestion that Aldiss was searching for him. He put his revolver in his mouth. Easy."

Daniel. Goddamn him.

Owen smiled, and in the coldness of the gesture Alex saw for the first time. She saw how it had happened, the brutal series of events that had led her to this black hallway. Owen had murdered Michael Tanner, had drawn them all back to the campus, and then—

"Lewis," she said, her voice tight. Choked. "How? You were there, at the memorial service."

"No, Alex. You *thought* I was there. I had run back to the house for Stanley's pills and found Lewis all alone." His voice quickened. "Afterward, Melissa and I slipped away."

Alex willed her mind to come back on, her eyes to open. *Where?* she thought. *Wherewherewhere?* Owen read her thoughts. "Do you want to see what I did with him?"

She nodded.

Then he was yanking her by the hair down the hallway. They were descending stairs, the temperature plummeting. A heavy steel door opened and Owen pushed her into a room.

She looked up to see that she was in the place where it had all begun. In the basement classroom of Culver.

There were student desks arranged here in the same pattern they had been in the night class. And at the front was Richard Aldiss. He had been stripped and beaten and lashed to a chair. Owen had carried in his flashlight, and he pointed it at the man. The puzzle tattoo was revealed: Aldiss's entire body was a jigsaw puzzle, his chest and arms and legs. Owen made a sound, disgusted with the sight of the professor, then he swung the light back into Alex's face.

"Alive?" he said. "Not alive? It makes no difference now."

Alex hung there in the man's arms. Her throat was raw, bloody.

"Everything I did," Owen said, "was because of the manuscript. Getting close to him in Rock Mountain, going back to school, getting that job at another prison, poring over Austen, Eliot, Dostoyevsky— I was probably the only guard at Oakwood who could talk to Lewis Prine about the Modernists."

Alex startled. *You set Lewis up, you bastard. You set all of us up. I'll kill you with my bare hands.*

Owen continued, "It was all because of the third Fallows." He saw her confusion, and when he continued his tone was more deliberate. He wanted her to see, to understand exactly. "I mastered the first two novels through the Procedure. Found their open doorways, Alex. Walked around inside them. And when I heard that an unpublished Fallows existed, I knew I had to find it. Whatever it took."

Alex shivered, more alert now. "A game?" she said. "All of this—setting Aldiss up, murdering my friends—was because of a fucking *game*?"

"You don't understand. You can never understand. The Procedure is no more a game than the printing press is a machine. What I was doing, Alex, was understanding Fallows. Reaching inside his mind. You couldn't learn him through books, through your innocent little night class. The only way to plumb those novels was through the Procedure. It was how one became enlightened."

Keep him talking, Alex. Find out how he did this, then turn him on himself. You can do this. She urged her voice to life. "I don't understand, Matthew. When did you find the manuscript? How did you beat us to it?"

He raised an eyebrow. "There were always whispers that a third Fallows existed, and at Rock Mountain I deduced that Aldiss must have found it. But I couldn't find where he hid it, no matter how often I checked his cell. After his release I continued my search. I was desperate, hungry to continue the game, and there seemed only one place to go. You're beginning to catch on, I see."

Alex nodded. *The boxes labeled* ALDISS *in Fisk's study. Fifteen years ago, it was all right there.*

"Yes, I knew that Stanley was a frequent correspondent of Aldiss's. Knew he'd sent boxes and boxes of documents over the years to Rock Mountain. And I suspected that if Aldiss had entrusted the manuscript to anyone it would be Fisk." He paused. "After I was hired by the college it took me only a few months to find the manuscript in his mansion. I read it and saw, immediately, what Aldiss had done. He'd been playing a game as well—nine victims in the manuscript, nine students in the night class. It was his clever way of continuing the Procedure from his prison cell. But I knew a better way. A purer way."

Alex turned her eyes to the wall. She couldn't look at him, couldn't bear to follow his story any longer. But Owen reached out, dipped his hand inside the light, and took her face. He turned her gaze toward him and held her there, her cheeks squeezed painfully, so that she could see him as he spoke. Could see how exactly how it ended.

"You erased Fallows," he said. "Aldiss led you to him and you destroyed the legend to the map. All we had then were the doorways the Procedure opened. When I found the manuscript I searched for those doorways. And when I found them I began to see. I saw how I could bring the Procedure to life."

A line from the manuscript flashed through her mind: *Perhaps he had been going backward, taking his plan from the end.* There was something about those words, something that might allow her to escape from this hell. Yes, it was right there in front of her now, the connection that Owen had failed to make all along. *The end . . .*

"Fallows is dead," she said defiantly, holding her eyes on him. "You've failed."

Owen smiled pityingly. "You still don't understand, Alex. I've gone farther than Fallows. I've outdone him. Through the Procedure I got inside the beating heart of his manuscript. It was like . . . ecstasy. An epiphany." He hesitated, his eyes cast back toward the slumped shape of Aldiss. "I don't need Fallows. I *became* him." Owen closed his eyes briefly at the thought, and a smile passed across his face.

Alex knew what she had to do.

Iowa

1994

52

"My Charlie was turned differently," Lydia Rutherford said. "I knew that from the beginning. At first my husband was afraid of Charlie. He wouldn't hold him. Perhaps he saw himself mirrored in the boy. Perhaps he knew what was bound to happen."

Alex stared at the woman and the man beside her. The cartoon soundtrack rippled down the hallway and into the tiny room. "What happened?" she managed.

"Don't you see?" the woman said, for the first time managing a smile. "Can't you figure it out, college girl? My husband was a ghostwriter."

Alex stared at the woman, at the axe she wielded. "I don't—I don't understand."

"He had been writing about women for so long, about how to destroy them," Lydia continued. "When he fell into the Mood, I left, you see. I took the baby with me and I got out of Hamlet. And when I returned, something had changed. Charles had brightened. I thought it was the encyclopedias, thought his sales numbers had been good. But I was wrong. I found out that he had taken a girl. Murdered her in the woods, dropped books around the body—but not on the face. That came later."

The woman stopped. The wind blew and tickled a wind chime hanging from the eaves of the porch. *Now,* Alex thought. *Now comes the end of the story.*

"Charles needed to be found," she said. "He needed to be found and cured, just as every person with a sickness does. Do you understand? He wanted the investigators to know what he'd done, what he planned to do with other girls. So he tried to tell people, to warn them, to show them who he was with his novels."

"How?" Alex asked, her voice quavering.

"Charles's mind was strange. His sickness was real. And the scholars thought he was a genius; those students who came to my house thought Paul Fallows was a god, a deity." The woman stopped, laughing. "Fallows was a name. Nothing more than a name. A ghost, someone my husband made up to hide himself. Those two novels he wrote, especially *The Golden Silence*—it was a map to him. To find him. To punish him."

"But *The Golden Silence*—there's a reference to Dr. Morrow in that book. Your husband didn't know about Morrow. He couldn't have. Charles was already dead when the doctor . . . sent Charlie home." Alex was careful not to say "cured." Not after what Dr. Bern had told them. "What happened to Charles, Lydia?"

The woman frowned. "Apparently you're not as smart as I thought you were. We sent Charlie to Shining City, where he met the good doctor. It was *our* decision." At this Lydia bristled. "It was Charles's bad luck to die before any progress was made. It was a clot in his brain that dislodged and then exploded. A mind bomb. And I did what Charles told me to do: I sent *The Golden Silence* off and had it published. But by that time Charlie was . . ." She looked back at the door, at the man. She shrugged: *What could I do?* "Like his daddy."

"No," Alex said.

"The two girls from Dumant discovered the truth," Lydia went on. "They came here together because that Aldiss told them to, but only one of them came back a second time. The smart one. She found this room, just like you did. And I think Charlie told her things about his daddy. He told her because she was"—her voice soft, ashamed—"a whore. I think she touched him. She would have done anything to get what she wanted. And Charlie talked. He told on his daddy. He told about all the girls, about the bodies and the encyclopedias. But this girl and her friend left Iowa before I could do anything. It was only a few days before we worked up the courage to go to Dumant. It had to be done. Dr. Morrow had not really worked miracles, you see; no one could change the Mood. No one."

Alex began to see the picture forming in her mind. Shawna and Abigail had been here, but, like her, Shawna had wanted to come back. Alone. To dig deeper. To win. Had she even told Abigail what she'd found?

"I regret my haste, of course," Lydia went on. "I didn't realize until we'd returned home that Shawna had stolen something from us. Something private. For years I've waited for that book to come to light. For someone like you . . . well, it's no matter now."

Another step, the woman drawing closer in the tiny, packed room. Alex thought, *Move now.* She tried to push herself back, away from Lydia. Tried to move, but she was up against a box. She felt the sharp edge cutting into her leg.

Lydia looked down. She frowned as if Alex had ruined things, as if Alex had stepped into the plot and discovered exactly where it was going. As if the end had come upon her too fast and too soon.

"Charlie," she said, her voice clipped and mean. "Come here, please. It's time."

Alex

Present Day

53

Breathe, Alex.

Owen had taken his hands off her, but the phantom pressure of his touch remained like a wound, an incision. He had been growing more and more animated as he spun his tale, regaling her with his dominance of the Procedure. His years of plotting, planning, scheming for his chance at the grand stage. He'd taken the last Fallows and twisted it into his own personal chessboard, brought them together only to kill them off one by one.

"I began to see that I didn't need Fallows," he said. "I didn't need Benjamin Locke and his old-fashioned ideas of literary theory."

Sensing her confusion, Owen smiled.

"You're not the only one to have paid him a visit, Alex. Where do you think I finished my studies after I left Rock Mountain?"

Of course: *Owen* was the failed protégé Locke had mentioned to her and Keller. Alex scolded herself for not seeing it earlier.

"At first Dr. Locke was impressed with my obsession for Fallows. We spent nights discussing those old, tired theories about his identity. But something changed. I began to see that Locke would never go far enough. He refused to see the Procedure as legitimate scholarship, and of course he had no idea where the third manuscript was hidden.

I moved on and came to this campus, and it was here that my plan took full shape."

She shivered at the thought. But he was slipping, Alex knew. Because if he killed her and Keller, there were still others. Christian at the house. Sally. He'd never finish the game, clear the board.

Use it against him, Alex. Convince him to let you go.

"You'll never win," she said. "There are others, others who will know what you—"

Owen dismissed her with a shake of his head. "Good try, Professor. But I've come this far, what's to stop me now? After all, the madman Aldiss is here, right here in this room." Owen's voice rose in pitch, became almost demure as he acted out the role of the victim. "That *evil* man, Detective Black. You should have *seen* what he did to her. You should have seen how ghastly it was. And I tried to stop him. I tried so hard . . ."

He shook his head, his shoulders slumping just slightly. And as they did, when he dropped the light a fraction of an inch, Alex glanced over the nurse's shoulder at Aldiss and saw two things.

First, the professor's eyes were open.

And he had freed his right hand.

Iowa

1994

54

Charlie came toward her. Alex knew there was nowhere to move in the small room. She was at the end.

Then he was standing over her, twisting the axe.

"Not here, boy," said Lydia Rutherford. "In back."

Charlie picked Alex up by the shoulders and began to carry her. He muscled her out of the storage room and to a bedroom door and shoved her inside, where she fell to the floor. Then she scrambled backward to the wall, pressed herself there, shivering uncontrollably. Waiting to die.

"Those two girls could be erased," Lydia Rutherford was saying. "That's the way I explained it to Charlie. We couldn't take the chance that little whore Shawna hadn't bragged to her girlfriend after all. It would be so easy to pass it off on one of the scholars. Everything his father and I had done could be protected."

"How?" Alex gasped, hugging herself against the shaking. "How did you frame Aldiss?"

"When you are studious," she said, "you learn things. I remembered him. He came here years ago with his mentor. He'd had the girls in class, he was distrusted by many in the faculty. One call. One call was all it took for the seed of doubt about him to start to grow and our tracks to be erased. I put a book over those girls' faces just like Charles did, just to make it perfect. And then we returned to Iowa."

Alex pulled her knees up. Fear ricocheted through her. Her mind spun madly.

The woman's face changed. She regarded Alex now with a look of motherly concern. A look of compassion. "I'm sorry," she said. "I'm sorry it had to be this way."

Then she stepped out of the way. Charlie came forward, his laceless boots approaching her. Alex saw the axe go up. She flinched at the way it hummed in the light, at the sight of it above her. Her body shut down.

The axe came.

Alex closed her eyes.

The next thing she saw was the body of Lydia Rutherford being ripped open like a seam.

The woman was there and then she was not. She was destroyed in one arcing blow, removed from the world, flayed and bloodied on the floor as the man stood above her and twisted the axe from his mother's flesh.

Then Charlie brought the weapon up again and then down. The sound was like a melon being cut, wet and thick and viscous. Alex tried to close her mind against it but couldn't, could do nothing but turn away and feel the warm blood fleck against her face.

When she looked back at Charlie, he was as composed as ever. He looked at her and shrugged. Then he came forward.

"No," she said. "No, Charlie. No."

For a moment he stopped. He stared down at the girl before him. And then he said, "The end."

55

A blur of movement in Alex's periphery.

The door burst open and Keller stood there, panting and frantic. He saw the torn body on the floor; he saw Alex. Alex reached for him, her mind still moving slowly, weakly. She tried to touch him but he was too far, too distant. He said one word: "No."

Charlie turned on him, tried to bring the axe up. But Keller was too fast. He charged against the man and drove him back. The axe spun away, clattered on the bedroom floor. Alex watched it all unfold.

"End!" Charlie said again, and there was another crash.

"Alex," Keller said. "Get. The. Axe."

She stood and picked up the weapon. Took a step toward the men, who struggled on the floor. Keller turned and saw her, reaching out with his hand.

The end, she thought. *The end.*

She saw Keller lock eyes with Charlie and then bend him backward, as if they were fighting on the line of scrimmage, the other man stumbling for just a moment. Enough. Keller took the axe from her and stood with it above his head.

Charlie could only watch. He was wild-eyed, breathing hard. He did not reach out. He did not try to stop Keller. In fact he did nothing at all.

"Yes," he said, smiling. "Please."

And Keller brought the axe down.

Alex

Present Day

56

Now.

It was a matter of getting Owen closer to Aldiss and his chair. But how? Owen was just inside the door, at least ten feet from the professor. Alex squinted into the darkness, looking for something, anything she could use as a weapon. As she was doing this a memory descended. Another dark room, another desperate situation. She knew how to beat him.

"I understand, Matthew," Alex rasped, her throat searing with pain.

He looked at her. He was so close she could taste his breath.

"Do you?"

"Yes, I do," she said, trying to move him, to gently steer him toward Aldiss. "I know how it is, to be great at something. To be dominant. I know how good you are at the Procedure. How expert. And I also know what you want."

This confused him. His shoulders dropped, the beam swinging wildly onto the concrete wall. "And what do I want?"

"To win."

His eyes flashed. She'd been right.

"You want to be the best to ever play the Procedure. Better than any of Benjamin Locke's Iowans, better than Aldiss or any of us who took the night class." She paused, tried another step. Another inch toward Aldiss. "Everything that's happened on this campus—it's all about the game. Ending it. Finishing it forever."

"You know nothing," he said. But she knew this wasn't true. Knew she had struck something, found a hidden part of him. Just a little farther now.

She strained against him. Pushed him so that he tripped over her feet, grabbed at her and yanked her back against him. "Bad girl," he said, smiling—but then he saw where he was in the room. Saw how close he was to Aldiss. He froze. The light tipped up on her, washed over her face. Blinded her.

Owen was unmovable now. He had her in his grasp, was pulling her to him as if they were in a cruel and brutal dance. Again he began to squeeze the life out of her.

How long? How long until everything went black?

She opened her mouth but the pressure was too much, the air winding out of her, the light bouncing in her periphery like a bad reception.

"And I liked you, Alex," Owen was saying, his voice muffled, fuzzy. "I liked your company in the house. You were different from the others. Sharper." She closed her eyes.

No. It doesn't end like this. It can't.

She screamed. She wrenched her body to the left, and Owen released some pressure. Enough for her to put in one quick, short breath. And her eyes opened. When they did she saw the classroom door. She saw the man walking through it.

Keller.

Owen tried to turn, but he was too late. Keller planted and drove, and just as he did Alex jumped out of the way. Keller hit Owen full-on, a lineman's block square in the chest, knocking him back. Just a foot or two, just enough.

Just enough for Alex to remove the gun. She had tucked it in the waistband of her pants earlier, before leaving the room. Before Frank Marsden and any of this.

"You bitch," Owen shouted. "You fucking whore."

She fired. One shot. The sound of it surprised her: it wasn't loud, wasn't deafening, more of a small *pop* that elicited only a simple reaction. Owen's eyes widened. He looked down, saw the bloom of black blood on his shirt. His eyes were angry now, his jaw fierce and set, and he stepped forward—

But he was stuck. Trapped.

Aldiss had him.

Owen tried to pull himself free but it was no use. The professor had a clump of his shirt, and when he pulled, Owen came down on the chair, toppling it. Both Owen and Aldiss went to the floor, then, but Aldiss was on top, his free hand grabbing at Owen's face. Alex looked away as Owen screamed.

Then Keller was leading her away, into the hallway and up the stairs.

57

Later, after the badly injured Matthew Owen was removed from the building and Aldiss was taken for questioning, she and Keller sat together in a hospital room and held each other.

They did not speak at first. There was no need. Everything they might have said had been spoken.

Keller's head was bandaged and his eyes were black, but otherwise he would be fine. For Alex there would be no lasting injuries. Frank Marsden had lost his battle in the last couple of hours, and a group of entertainment reporters scrambled up and down the hallway. Everything that had happened in the last two days at Jasper College would heal—but it would not go away. It would never go away.

She said, "I've always wanted to tell you something."

Keller turned to her. He was leaning over her hospital bed, and a deep memory came to her: Iowa, morning light falling through the curtains, both of them so uncertain of what was outside those hotel walls.

"What?" he said.

"I found something. It was a message in an old book. It said that Aldiss was—"

"I know," Keller said. "I mean I figured it out. It took me a few years, but I got there." He smiled. "Dean Fisk—he was working with me as well."

Alex sat back, stunned.

"Don't look so surprised, Alex. You're not the only hero in this room."

She laughed, reaching out for his hand. Their easy silence descended again.

"I'm sorry," Keller said finally. "For the manuscript. For not reaching out to you after Iowa. For—"

"Shhh. It doesn't matter now." She leaned against him.

"I think," he said, "I should probably plan a road trip to Cambridge now."

Alex nodded. "I think you should."

Then someone knocked on the hospital door, and she turned. It was a nurse; the woman was holding an envelope.

"Professor Alex Shipley?" she asked.

"That's me."

The nurse gave Alex the envelope and left.

"You going to open it?" Keller asked.

Alex shrugged and tore out the note inside.

It was from Richard Aldiss. As Keller breathed softly beside her, she read.

Dearest Alexandra,

That blank space, the last piece of the puzzle, was what she did when she returned to Dumant.

I punished myself for not going to her that morning. There had been a snow, a whiteout—the roads were impassable. She and Abigail Murray returned to campus, and I waited. I had sent her, you see; had given her the information she needed. Everything—all that I had discovered on my own trip to Iowa with Benjamin Locke, all that I had learned as a scholar. Shawna Wheatley's mind was afire. Like you, I knew that she would go.

And when she returned to Vermont she spent the night finishing her thesis. The last chapter, the identity of Paul Fallows, was so easy now. She'd discovered everything. She finished and brought the manuscript she had stolen from the house on Olive Street and dropped it off at the campus copy center. This would be her last act as a Dumant student.

The next time I saw her was in a photograph. Her face had been masked with a book. On the wall above her was a Rorschach stain. One hand grasped at nothing.

I always feared that Fallows was never really dead. It's a fear you live with when you have come that close to evil.

Eleven years. Eleven years I waited, biding my time in that animal's cell. I had nearly given up. Then one day a visitor arrived. A man I knew then only as a fellow scholar. Stanley Fisk brought with him a box inscribed with my name. It had been brought to Fisk by a graduate student who'd gone through my things at Dumant. The box must have arrived at my office the day I was arrested. Inside were documents, sheaves of dusty paper, detritus—and at the bottom, wrapped in brown paper, was Shawna Wheatley's thesis. Two copies, neatly bound, with a prepaid invoice. A model of efficiency, the copy center shipped them off to the address on Shawna's cover letter: mine.

I destroyed one copy immediately. It was exquisite, scattering pieces of Fallows over the prison yard, sending his words up in smoke, plotting my next move. The other I kept very close.

For it contained Charlie Rutherford's confession.

And a lost Fallows.

This was my new information. My reason for teaching the night class.

Now we are here again, past and present having collided, and yet you are alive. If you don't mind, I have a simple request for you: I would like to see you, Alex, one last time. I have something important to show you before you leave. Please.

Richard

58

Instead she returned to Harvard and picked up the pieces of her life. Peter was gone, and the rumors were that he was seeing one of his grad students now. Alex wished him the best. She too had moved on.

Keller called on a Friday. "Summer break," he said.

"When are you taking your road trip?"

"The last day of your term. I'll be there then. Promise."

She almost screamed with joy. She had missed him terribly.

The package arrived that Monday. It came in a simple manila envelope. Her name had been written on the front in Aldiss's tight, careful hand.

The note inside read, simply, *You should have come, Alexandra.*

There was something else. A page from a book. Thin, grayed—it was a simple paperback page. Aldiss had X-Acto'd it out, and she stood in her bedroom holding it, her fingers visible on the other side. A name in the top right corner—Christian Kane. It was from *Barker in the Storm.*

There was nothing else.

"Not this time, Professor," she said aloud. "I'm not going to play along." She dropped the page on her bedside table.

*   *   *

Two days later she graded the last of her semester exams in her office and then rushed home, feeling as if she were walking on air. Just a few hours until Keller arrived.

Back home, she showered and toweled off. Afterward she walked through her cool apartment, trying to decide what to wear. Today was a fresh start, a new life. After what had happened at Jasper, after all the horrors of Matthew Owen—

No. She wouldn't think of that madman. She sat down on the bed, let her hair down, and began to dry her roots. As she did she glanced over at the bedside table. At the page Aldiss had sent her. That mysterious page . . .

Despite herself she picked it up. Scanned it. It was nothing. Just another one of Aldiss's games.

Barker in the Storm.

Alex read the title and as she did a memory came to her. There was something about it. Something she remembered from the Fisk mansion.

She scanned the words. Read the paragraphs, then traced her eye back and reread them. As she did a sickening feeling swept through her.

"No," she said.

She knew what Aldiss wanted her to see. The reason he'd asked her to visit him before she left Vermont. It was a paragraph in the middle of the page:

> *She called the man she had once loved. He was a simple man now. He lived in an old farmhouse. Divorced, he was able to cultivate his disguise. It was the night when he prowled. He was best in the dark, when nobody could see him for who he was. A large man, hulking and strong, he had always protected her. Had almost died for her. But what she did not know was that he was part of the game just like the rest of them. He had always been part of the game, and that night he planned to show her who he really was. "When can we see each other?" she asked him. "Soon," he said. "Promise."*

Letting the towel drop, Alex stood. She backed into the corner, fear roiling through her. She tried to remember what Christian had said to her that night at the Fisk mansion. What he'd said about his work, his latest book.

I plagiarized from Fallows. In my last novel, Barker in the Storm. *Not word for word, nothing like that. I simply stole his style, his rhythm. Maybe I had this crazy notion that people would be playing the Procedure to my novels, I don't know.*

She took a step toward the door but stopped. Something moved outside, shifted against her bedroom window. She thought of Aldiss, of her first meeting with him. Of how adamant he had been that someone from the night class had turned. That one of her friends was responsible for what had happened.

Playing the Procedure to my novels . . .

The page trembled in her hand. Alex stepped back. She was against the wall now. Her blood ran cold.

The doorbell rang.

ACKNOWLEDGMENTS

Thank you again to my wonderful agent, Laney Katz Becker, who stayed with me through the tough times as this idea was taking shape. Thanks to my editor, Sarah Knight. Sarah saw this book through and helped me when I needed her most, and for that I will always be grateful. A true professional. Thank you to all the folks at Simon & Schuster, especially Jessica Abell, Molly Lindley, and Kelly Welsh. Thanks to my family in Louisville, Burnside, and Whitley City—Granny, Mom, Dad, Emily, Riley and Isabella, Donna, Jason and Mindy C., Bill and Jennifer S., Pap, Stephanie, Beth and John, Karen, Ann, Jo Ann, Carolyn, Randy, Cherie, Gary, Cindy, Bruce, Jill, and (Super)Joe. Thanks to the folks at LRC—Robert, Katie, Laura, Andrew, Charles. Thanks to Drew Trimble, who listened as I talked about early drafts, and gave some wonderful feedback. Major thanks to the folks who operate Joseph-Beth Booksellers in Lexington, Kentucky. I can honestly say that without Joseph-Beth, you would not be holding this book. A good part of my education happened inside that wonderful store. Thanks to all those who worked the Louisville coffee shops and bookstores where this novel was almost entirely written—the Borders on Hurstbourne, the Barnes & Noble on Hurstbourne, the Carmichael's on Bardstown, and the free public library in Fern Creek. And thanks above all to my family—my children, Jonathan and Jenna, and the love of my life, Sharon Faye. I couldn't even begin to count the suns . . .

ABOUT THE AUTHOR

Will Lavender is the *New York Times* bestselling author of *Obedience*. A former literature professor, he is a graduate of the MFA program at Bard College and lives with his wife and two children in Louisville, Kentucky. He is currently at work on his next novel, *The Descartes Circle*.

Keep reading for an excerpt from Will Lavender's
heart-pounding puzzle thriller

The Descartes Circle

coming soon from Simon & Schuster

1

I hear on the eleven o'clock news that my twin brother is not a murderer. A battery of psychological tests has been run, an expert on torture has given his own verdict on national television, and finally they are letting him come home. I watch it all unfold through a news feed, stay glued to my television at night, waiting for the truth about Henry Malcolm.

It should be too horrible to watch. I should turn it off, get on with my life. When I see myself in one of the stock photos on *48 Hours,* smiling goofily on a ski slope, my arm draped around Henry's shoulders, I don't feel shame or regret or sadness. Maybe I should. Maybe I should seclude myself inside my house, take on some kind of monastic presence, run off the few reporters who show up at my front door looking for a sound bite.

But I do none of these things. I watch, just like you do.

Today there's a telephone message waiting for me when I get home.

I've been out, walking with my notebook and thinking about my brother's homecoming. What it could mean—what it *must* mean. I have ink on my left hand, one of the most annoying side effects of the disease. A word snaking across, disappearing over the wrist and then appearing again on the delta of a vein: *Who?*

What's crazy is I don't even remember writing it. This isn't uncommon with the disease. Sometimes a stray word will appear from nowhere, written across a newspaper page or in the margin of a book. I've even been known to write on other people's bodies as they sleep. Creepy, I know. I wish I could do something about it.

Now I approach the blinking answering machine light. The tabloids still call, promising me everything under the sun if I agree to talk about Henry and his lost week. Just a few days ago someone from TMZ called, offering me six figures for an interview about my brother. It would have been a chance to start over, to move somewhere else. Reinvent my life. I told them to go to hell. When I tell Henry's story, it will be on my own terms.

The red light throbs, and I stand in the dark kitchen and let it hypnotize me. A collage of Post-its hangs over the phone, bubbled black with heavy ink, the missives incomprehensible, as they almost always are. Nothing but a reaction, an impulse to WRITE, to move my hand in a way that forms a word, a sentence, a thought. I curl my fingers around an imaginary pen, scribble air on the wall beside the telephone. My mouth waters.

Finally I reach up, hit Play.

"Jonathan Malcolm, this is Anthony Schroeder." The voice is tight, serious. Not a reporter. I let the message run. "I'm a homicide detective with the Oldham Town Police Department. We spoke once before, after your sister-in-law . . . after the incident. I wondered if you might give me a call back. I want you to know that this has nothing to do with the fact that your brother is getting out of the hospital tomorrow. This is about Laura Malcolm. I know you had a history with her, that you were one of her closest friends, and I called to ask you—"

I erase the message.

It's her name, just the sound of her name, that cuts me the deepest.

And anyway, I know what the detective wants. He's been here before, sat right there in my living room, and told me about his grand plan. It will never work, I want to tell him. Not ever. It won't work because my brother is smarter than us all.

2

Henry was a professor of philosophy at Oldham College in upstate New York. His vitals were revealed to the public slowly, incrementally, like a photograph taken through Vaseline: his age (thirty-four and already a rising star in academia), his famous academic father (Thomas Malcolm, professor emeritus at Oldham), his identical twin (Jonathan Malcolm, the disgraced author), even his dissertation from Yale ("True Deception: A Philosophical Inquiry of René Descartes"). He was accused of killing his wife, Laura Malcolm, bludgeoning her on the stairs of the home they shared at 22 Woodlawn Lane on the Oldham campus. The murder weapon was never found, and for days one question, so horrible in its simplicity, screamed across the ticker at the bottom of my TV screen: MURDER OR ACCIDENT? Even now, I'm certain I know the answer.

Laura was the perfect victim. A famous professor's wife, five years Henry's junior, and strikingly beautiful, she was a fixture at Oldham charity galas and campus functions. Henry claimed to have returned home from a faculty meeting one night to find her at the bottom of the spiral staircase, crumpled and broken like a rag doll. She'd been waiting up for him; they were supposed to watch a movie together, the empty DVD box casually placed on the television, a foreign film Henry had rented from the college video store that afternoon. Henry's frantic 911 call was replayed a thousand times by the celebrity dish shows— scripted, they said, playing it back again and again, focusing on every stutter, every pause and nuance.

There was much talk about how Laura had once been a philosophy major at Oldham. She had met Henry in her senior seminar, had fallen in love with her suave professor, been swept away by him. I knew a different story, and here is the way I would tell it: Laura got pregnant, she and Henry were forced to marry because of Oldham's morality clause, the child was stillborn, and Henry spent a semester drinking and calling me at night and rambling, "John, Jonathan, listen to me—I can hear our son crying. He's just downstairs . . ."

But the media's narrative was different. In fact it was an outright lie.

A constellation of blood undid him. The way her blood streaked and slashed, how it had dried in odd places near the eighteen-foot-high ceiling of the couple's campus mansion. Places where no blood should have been. There was a question about her fall, the plausibility of the killing wounds. The fatal crack in her skull was inconsistent with the shape of the steps. Before this discovery, my brother was merely a person of interest; now he became the prime suspect. Piers Morgan interviewed a colleague who said that Henry had never shown any emotion about Laura's death, Anderson Cooper ominously suggested that Henry had been a member of a secret society ("Yes," I remember shouting at my television screen, "yes, there, focus on *that*!"), and my brother became a villain almost overnight. Ivy League educated, too handsome, too elusive—he embodied everything the rest of us distrusted.

And yet there was no forensic evidence to link Henry to the murder. No physical clues. No sign of a struggle, no bloody clothes, and of course no murder weapon. (On *60 Minutes* I watched blue-jacketed, goggled investigators test objects in a lab: a fire poker, a pool cue, the claw of one of our father's old hammers that was found in the basement of the murder house. But in the end nothing fit, that scribble-like fissure in Laura's skull being too wide or too narrow, and the missing weapon became Henry's greatest coup.) There was even an eyewitness from the college who saw Laura with *another man* on the evening she was murdered. A different man.

Henry remained free. He staged a press conference, stood before a makeshift podium, our father and stepmother flanking him. He pleaded with the media to leave him alone so that he could get back to his students. My father spoke, choking back tears, his beefy hand clenched into a fist. He pointed at his son, his favorite son, and said, "Henry Malcolm loved Laura, and she loved him. Why would he want to ruin something so perfect?"—and at that he lifted the photo of them, the famous one, the stunning shot of the couple standing on a cliff overlooking the sea on their honeymoon, Laura's sunglasses pushed up into unruly hair, freckles sprayed across her bare and peeling shoulders, Henry smiling wickedly, the Mediterranean black as glass behind them.

We waited, then, for the other shoe to drop. For Henry to be charged with the murder of his wife, for the puzzle of the evidence to reveal something new, or for the shadowy man with whom she had been seen on her last day to come forward.

Instead, something else happened.

My brother disappeared.

3

I am often asked if I felt anything. If I could somehow have seen my brother in my mind, could have used the sixth sense that twins sometimes have to find Henry out in the ether during the time he was missing. I always lie, say that I felt a current of pain, that at night a cold sweat overtook me and I awoke saying his name. But really I felt nothing. I never have. Henry and I are absolutely identical on the outside. Inside, we might as well be strangers.

He was gone for seven days—what the media began to call his "lost week." During those endless days, two schools of thought emerged. There were those who believed Henry had slipped away to elude his inevitable arrest. During the investigation he had remained a fixture at the grieving college, even though his course load had been lightened. And it was at Oldham that he disappeared. Henry was seen walking across campus one moment by a literature professor and then, just like that, he vanished into thin air.

There were also those few allies of my brother, most of them pernicious academics who appeared shocked and disheveled on MSNBC asking, "Where are the forensics? If Professor Malcolm is a murderer, where is the evidence to prove it?"

The search for Henry Malcolm began. It was unlike anything New

York State had ever seen. An unmarked car sat outside my front door that week; they thought I had harbored him, I suppose. But I had only seen Henry a few times since Laura died. In the media I was the Identical Twin, the brother who was a constant in Henry's life, but the reality was that I didn't care about Henry. I couldn't. He had done too much, burned too many bridges, for me to come to his defense now. If I thought of him I thought of poor, sweet Laura, who didn't deserve any of this, who once told me she loved Henry despite his problems, and when I pushed her, asking, "Laura, what problems? What do you—" she slipped away into a crowded party.

I grieved for her, not Henry. Henry would come out of this unscathed. He always did.

A hiker found him four miles from campus. He was lashed to an oak tree, drenched in his own blood, beaten and bruised. Henry was alive, barely, and mumbling incoherently when they brought him back to St. Mark's Hospital in Oldham Town.

Police urged him to tell them what happened, but he gave them nothing. He was in shock, and for a month he has remained in the trauma ward, silently recovering, unable to remember—or, perhaps, *unwilling* to remember—what happened to him in those woods.

When he finally gave his statement, he talked about being taken to a cabin. Being held in a drab, empty room with only a stained mattress and a slot for food. He spoke of a solitary man holding him prisoner. Did he see this man's face? No, he did not. Did he hear a voice? No. Henry had been drugged; toxicology proved this. He had been out of it. Nearly comatose. The only thing that woke him was the man torturing him, the hot prick of a knife digging into his arms, his chest. The copper smell of welling blood.

That was all. Everything else was lost in the fog.

Only one thing about Henry's ordeal was indisputable: his wounds were real. On NBC, he lifted his shirt for Brian Williams to see the twisted, serrated mouth of a gash running from his clavicle to his ribs. His face was bruise-black, his arms dotted with cigarette burns, his ankles and wrists red as flame where he had writhed against the ropes.

Even his eyes were different, somehow not-Henry: dimmed, hollow, lacking their previous fury.

Just like that, my brother went from suspect to victim. The suggestion of foul play, the missing murder weapon, the faceless man Laura was seen with on her last day—all of it suggested something too horrible to contemplate. The headlines changed, morphed almost overnight: IS THERE A KILLER LOOSE AT OLDHAM COLLEGE?

Henry Malcolm, it seemed, had been exonerated.

4

The day after the phone message from the detective, I drive the forty miles to Oldham Town and sit outside my brother's estate. I keep my car idling and watch the morbid tourists who have come here on Henry's homecoming day—a few students, a townie or two dressed in rumpled orange slickers, passersby who stare at the windows for any sign of the man. Since he was cleared, Henry hasn't said anything new about the lost week or the man in the cabin, nor will he; I know this as well as I know my own face in the mirror. He will tease them, play with them, punish them for their suspicion of him after Laura's death. And in the end he will reveal something, something only he knows, and the puzzle will fall wickedly into place.

I've seen it all before.

It's raining, one of those cold, bending squalls that central New York is famous for. My windshield is fogged, and I smear a space away with my palm and stare into the distance, where a photographer stands beside a tree, camera slung around his neck, screwing a kerchief across the lenses of his eyeglasses. Just up the street from me is a long dark sedan, two cops inside craning their necks to see if anyone suspicious is watching from a safe distance. Anyone like me.

I have my notebook with me, as I always do, and I sit in the cramped front seat making notes. I've been working on the New Book for months now, and it still isn't clear to me. Just fragments, disparate shards, meaningless pieces of a narrative that has thus far escaped me.

To write is like a hit of morphine, and a relaxing feeling settles over me as soon as I hear the pen's nibble against the paper. I write, *Are you a good person, Jonathan Malcolm?*

I think about that, turn it over in my mind, finally responding, my hand shaking a little, *I am a good person most of the time.*

Is your twin brother a good person?

I look out the windshield again. The onlookers are leaving, ducking into the scrub behind the garden Laura once kept, which is now choked with black snaking weeds.

No, I write, my hand quavering more, the ink smearing on the soft padding of my palm. *Henry Malcolm is not a good person.*

Why do you say that?

His moods.

What do you mean, "his moods"?

I mean

Something catches my attention, and I look up. There is someone at a second-floor window. A man, fuzzy at first and then coming into focus between the slats of rain—Henry. My twin. My heart quickens, my palms begin to sweat, to shake. I watch him, and from this distance it appears that he turns his head toward me. Looks right at me. Impossible. My car is parked too far away for him to see. And yet he appears to be looking in my direction, waiting for me to make up my mind, to explain why I've come to spy on him this morning.

Something moves at my lap, and I look down. I have written: *What happened to her? What happened to Laura?*

But when I look back up, search that window for some kind of an answer, Henry has vanished.

5

I loved her before he did.

Laura was the daughter of my father's publisher. Eighteen years old, shy and quiet, she had come with him on an afternoon visit one spring day before the end of the semester. I was home from Yale, without Henry. I left due to a disciplinary action that never went away, a misunderstanding at an off-campus party, and even though I promised my parents it was just a short-term thing, I never went back.

Henry remained, eroded slowly out of my life, went on to grad school in New Haven and earned a full professorship at Oldham at twenty-six. I wanted to tell them what had really happened at Yale, but they would never believe me. And besides, I liked the absence of him, the way my father looked me in the eye when he spoke, Henry's presence nothing but a muffled voice on the telephone. I slept in his bed, the bottom bunk, his heavy metal posters from high school still adorning the dusty walls. I read his philosophy books—Hume, Locke, and of course Descartes—and purged his closet. I never wanted it to end.

On the afternoon I met Laura, we ate dinner together on a picnic table overlooking the Hudson. It was my father and hers, a mutton-chopped man who smelled of cigar smoke and old paper, and Laura and I, stragglers brought along on a hesitant date. The talk was of books, specifically my father's next project. Thomas Malcolm had already achieved tenure, had written a bestselling book on Derrida, was always gone off to this campus or that, demanding steep lecture fees that allowed the Malcolm family to travel the world. He was the William H. and Martha Barer Professor of Philosophy at Oldham College, a tiny insulated fortress of a school on the banks of the Hudson near Albany. It had always been our home, Henry and I playing hide-and-seek in the campus buildings, getting lost in the basement of the old administration wing one winter and found shivering, clutching one another beside the dead boiler. And later, as high schoolers, auditing classes in obscure topics at our father's discretion—Literature of Modern Israel, Water and War, the Old Testament. I remember Henry in a class once raising his hand, scrawny Tom Malcolm's son, standing up and challenging the adjunct professor. "And why is it that when LeClaire writes about solipsism in the twentieth century, he fails to mention anything after 1970? What about Stoddard? What about Ellis, for fuck's sake?" And the young professor, mortified, staring at the kid and his black eyes, noticing the aggression that always—always—wafted off Henry, at the way his fists were clenched at his sides as if this academic conversation in the Gray Brick Building were some kind of pitched battle.

It was the only thing Henry and I shared: our love of that college.

At first I was annoyed by Laura, this teenager, this intruder. On the day we met she carried a dog-eared paperback copy of Eco's *Foucault's Pendulum,* a pretentious book, I thought, although it (of course) impressed the hell out of my father. But as the afternoon went on the more I found myself staring at her: at the feminine manner in which she sat, the way she read the book during every spare minute, the way she picked carefully at her food, and how she laughed, her head tossed back, a purple-nailed finger to her lips.

She was at Burnbridge Prep now, bound for Sarah Lawrence in the fall. My father told me this, probably as a way to entice me into going back to Yale; I only nodded and yawned. Her own father was oblivious; there was money in his eyes. When she excused herself after dessert, I followed.

We walked down the little footpath behind our house to the river, the one Henry and I had worn flat as boys. The river was quick, darting and restless. The wind roiled and buffeted us against one another as we walked. My stepmother had planted rhododendron and holly along the path, and the air was thick and full and sweet. For the longest time we stood together, the fading sun warming our necks, Laura saying nothing, me making frantic notes in the notebook I'd brought along.

"Inspiration hit you or something?" she asked, still not looking at me. Looking down at the river, where a tug slipped lazily out of view.

"No," I said. "I do this. Take notes. On everything. The river. The trees. You."

Finally she glanced up. "Like graphomania?"

"It's called different things. Scribomania, graphorrhea. It all refers to the same disease—the obsession to write, to just put words on the page. Always."

"Disease," she said. "So you're sick? Is that why you dropped out of Yale?"

I stopped in the middle of a twisted, snaking sentence. "Sort of."

There were a few seconds of silence. I took my pen to the end of the line, wrote her name in the margin, then started back again. *Calm calm calm calm be calm Laura—*

She said, "Daddy says you have a twin."

"Identical."

"What's it like? I imagine it would be . . . exciting."

Again I stopped writing, looked at her. "How do you mean?"

"To always know that someone who's just like you is out there somewhere. To have somebody who's so close, a copy, living a different life. What's he like?"

"Different," I said. "Moody."

"I sense a sibling rivalry."

"You don't know Henry."

"Henry Malcolm." She said the name as if it had a taste, a texture. "Are you a philosopher too, Jonathan?" she asked, her eyes flicking toward my notebook, and at the sound of my own name something happened inside me, an electric tingle. I glanced back down at the ink-slick page, at the quickening water.

"A writer."

"You've published?"

I shrugged. "I will. Soon."

She smiled, freckles stretching tight. "Maybe I'll read your books one day. Maybe my father will publish them."

But as she said this she was walking away, and for the longest time I stood, my heart pounding, the river loud and fast below me, until I realized I was standing in the rain.

It stormed that night, and Laura and her father stayed with us. My stepmother fixed up the guest bedroom, flurried around the house clutching towels and sheets. As much as I would like to speak of a romance, it didn't come. Not then. We were too young, too wrapped up in ourselves. Our time would come five years later.

I was doing a signing in a bookstore in Manhattan. My first book had just been published by Ashbrook, her father's imprint, and there were a few people milling about. They were more curious than anything—*Leibniz and Kant: A Philosophy of Rivalry* would, alas, not change the world.

Signing books, speaking with my eyes down ("Who should I make it out to? Sarabeth? Ah, that's a beautiful name—is she your daughter?"), I heard a familiar voice and looked up. She stood at my table, smiling. She had changed ever so slightly, like a vase turned so that it strikes a different light. There was a hardness in her blue eyes, a weariness.

"Laura," I said, looking up, pen poised above paper, fingers tensing gray-knuckled against one of Henry's fountain pens.

"Daddy says the book is selling well," she said, a lie that I appreciated nonetheless. "He says you're a natural, like your father."

I waved a hand. "And what about your own father? He's a great editor, Laura. Tell him I said so."

"I will."

A comfortable few seconds passed. There was no one behind her.

"So what brings you here?" I asked. "A run on Umberto Eco?"

The smile touched her eyes. "You remembered."

"I wrote it down."

I went back to the page, scratched *To Laura, I will always remem-*

ber our storm, staved off the urge to go on, to tell her everything I was thinking, and slid the book toward her across the table.

"Sarah Lawrence," I said. "You must have graduated by now."

"Life's weird" was all she said, tucking my book beneath her arm and glancing beyond me, at the wide front window, the people streaming up Eighth Avenue.

I said, "Would you like to get some coffee?"

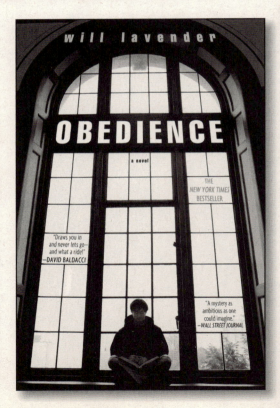